The Lady Mephistopheles
Dean Patrick

2021, TWB Press
www.twbpress.com

The Lady Mephistopheles
Copyright © 2021 by Dean Patrick

Edited by Terry Wright

Cover art by Terry Wright
Cover image by askatao.deviantart.com

ISBN: 978-1-944045-86-9

DEDICATED TO:

LISA MONTOYA

AND

JOSHUA NIELSEN JR.

FORWARD

The creation of a character who represented the horrors of alcoholism and drug addiction came to me one night while I was awake late, in jail of all places. A prison rehab center known as SAFP-Jester One. Awful place designed to break the spirits and rehabilitate those who were charged with felonies due to alcohol or drug-related crimes.

I drafted the horror short story, "She," with pencil and paper. The first story of Terra Drake, who, in that story, comes in the form of sexual addiction and ends up murdering her victim while he pleads for sexual release. It was published 15 years later in the winter edition 2019, *Infernal Ink*. Even though I'm a recovering alcoholic, creating Terra in that story as a sexual predator seemed natural, for whatever reason.

Fast forward to today, the tale provided in these pages is Terra Drake's full story as a horror who lives in delight to destroy the very fabric of small-town America through the wreckage of addiction. During the past many years of sobriety, my wife encouraged me to write a book about the many demons that every alcoholic and addict must face while being wrapped around addiction's death grip, must face with only two choices to make: to overcome, or to die. While this novel is not a memoir in anyway, it is a story laced with various demonic characters who have a contract on every addict's life.

I wish to dedicate this novel, my first, to my dear wife, Lisa Montoya, for her endless love and support, and for believing in my abilities as a writer who can help those just like me, and to my loving nephew, Joshua Nielsen, Jr., for creating a sculpture he called The Hooded Darkness that becomes Terra Drake's grand abettor, Adramelech who claims to have walked the earth since The Garden of Eden as Cain himself.

.

PART ONE

Opening – Stan Smitts – These Boots are Made for Walking –
Relapse – The Hickory Stack

I t's hard to say when it all started, when the bottom fell out of every facet of normal life in the empty jar called earth, in a small mountain town called Duncan. When the demon woman Terra Drake raced through nice and wicked like, when she tore out the hearts and souls of anyone coming near. When she told me she wanted to live in the real-time rage she called anger management. When neighbors turned into monsters, priests into warlocks, and ghosts rummaged through the night like rat savages in search of something sick to fill their hollow guts. When ghouls roamed the streets with nowhere to go but into the frozen underground to feed on the dead voles and the worms that fed on their carcasses. When carolers sang in chants so vile and filthy all the Christmas lights in town burned bright red until each bulb split apart like a mad boil. When the frightful chill of night seemed to never end, when the vastness of endless ink blasted out across the mountains, faces like spewed flashes of tortured, dying flames...all a blur of furious black gushing through every surrounding like dead tornadoes filled with dead tornado things, all of them swirling in messy, bloody, glorious dead gore that pummeled the deep Winter frosts of an eternity in the making. Only laughing gods did more than howl like wolves that anguished under the moons that splashed its reflection across the void of space to illuminate everything below. I wondered if there was any real meaning to any of it.

But I get ahead of myself.

A few years ago, I'd heard about Terra Drake on the

news, before the pandemic, a strange and terrifying woman who had allegedly killed some rich tech writer out of Houston. Death by sexual insanity. Literally. I resonated with this because I'd done plenty of technical writing myself, and now, as an editor, I could appreciate what the guy did for a living. I also went back and forth to Houston myself on a regular basis. Work, family. Whatever. Nothing was ever proven about the murder; it was her word against the dead man's. Didn't matter how gruesome the scene. Another rumor claimed she'd taken the place of another man's wife who transformed into Terra Drake herself, fighting to the death in a bloodbath where the husband faced her in his living room, shotgun in hand, and she fought back with only talons and teeth. So the story went. When police and EMS found him, they'd said his body looked like some hideous hybrid of a giant metal insect fused together in what was once his human side. Not a soul knew what the hell had caused such a Kafkaesque freakshow, other than a colonoscopy that had gone terribly awry. Drake herself had survived the man's twelve-gauge blast, and she'd healed to a point where not even a scar's trace remained.

Like I said, just a rumor. Tabloid trash at best.

Then again, maybe the tabloid trash was anything but.

After a few weeks researching all I could find about this fascinating murderess, allegedly so, I found myself in a Covid moment. One of those we were all feeling as 2020 kicked our teeth down our throats, one healthy tooth at a time. I was walking up and down my driveway, shoveling snow, wondering when the virus would actually effect my life. When would it murder someone I knew and loved? Anna, my estranged wife...it had been over a year since I'd heard a word from her. Maybe she was already dead. Wouldn't have surprised me. Mother or dad? Sibling or friend? My brother, Marion...was he dead or alive? I didn't know because I hadn't called him in years. How would Covid slip its way into my career, which was nearly resurrected from all the decades of ruin I'd put it through with the ole drink and drug combo?

Covid continued its joyous menace as a political weapon, or medical tragedy; I could take my pick. Folks had begun to care not one shit's whisper, but I wanted to know where it'd been in my life. Why hadn't it reached out to give me a nice warm, "Hello, Steven. I'm here. Are you ready to blow out the candles?"

I'd just landed from another long Houston trip, sitting inches from people wearing masks on a sardine-packed jet with signs everywhere telling us all to stay six feet apart. If this was the worst Covid had for me, then I'd take it.

Now, being back home at the ranch, in the small town of Duncan, Utah, sacked back in the mountains, made things seem even more the curious as to the hows of Covid's eventual intimacy.

I'd sent a text message to my next-door neighbor, Stan Smitts. Let him know I was back. Thanked him for watching after the place. Blah, blah. But, it was Covid that answered back; I just didn't expect it.

"I'm in the hospital. Emergency room. Covid positive, but glad you're back."

Stan was 65 years old, overweight some hundred-plus pounds, maybe six-one, and an alcoholic as fierce as I'd ever been. In fact, that was the first thing that concerned me.

He'll certainly go through alcohol withdrawal that'll surely kill him before the virus does.

Over the next few weeks I'd texted with him daily, checked on how he'd been holding up, sent him positive messages of hope and cheer.

Holiday season's approaching, and Stan can't even suck down a brandy, so he may as well have some digital joy.

Several days before Halloween, maybe it was more like a week, it was already feeling like we were deep into Winter's hollow eyes, but Fall had just begun, when I'd come back from Houston, an over-nighter, and hadn't even gone inside to unpack and freshen up, because I immediately started throwing down rock salt to keep the walkways clear and shoveling the snow that had already fallen. That's when Stan's beastly white 4 x 4 creeped down his massive black-top driveway.

I didn't think he should be driving, *but who cares what I think?* I set down my shovel, raised my hand in welcome, and watched his truck inch so close to my wood fence that I wondered if he'd ram right through it. Mufflers growled at me. The electric window whirred slowly down. I stepped over the fence to the passenger door to greet him.

When I saw him, I heard Covid ask if I was ready to blow out the candles. Asked me if I was ready for the horrid tale of a Hooded Darkness, his dreadful dance with Terra Drake and their worshipping *gang of thieves*. I heard the warning of the not-so-distant future, the terror of the demon woman's rape of my town, all of small-town America, my friends, and my own mind that would surely give my tormented halls of loneliness and anguish a good ole horror show, for sure.

***

I saw that all in Stan Smitts' face. His eyes were hollowed out, as if some phantom had bored into his sockets and placed his eyeballs into the center of a tar pool to see if they'd float. His bottom eyelids drooped with such heavy weight they looked more like two small rolls of melted wax.

The sun ducked behind the mountains, and deep cold air was settling in like a velvety barroom whore who wanted one last slow dance before she earned her real money. The air was a biting fifteen degrees, yet Stan's face looked flush and sweaty. I could see the redness of his cheeks glow like one large cigar butt, a grotesque light in front of the inky mountain faces behind him.

He slammed the truck into Park, leaned a little closer toward me, and grimaced. That simple movement was enough of a struggle for him that I could see he was in some kind of crippling pain, probably chronic now that Covid had had its way with him. When he spoke, his air came from broken lungs that sounded more like broken charcoal lumps doing whatever possible to air out the final embers of the sickness, and made his voice sound gravelly and tortured.

"That was a sack a shit, Steve. Let me tell you. Anyone out there who smokes or is sick in anyway will not survive this bitch. Believe it. I thought I'd fucking die, I shit you not. I stopped to say how much I appreciated you checking in on me. Each day like that. Meant a lot."

I didn't know what to say, and I was sure, even in the growing darkness and cold, that my uncertainty and utter shock was impossible to hide. This couldn't have been my neighbor and friend speaking. This creature was something else entirely, like something decrepit had replaced Stan. He was more than just a Covid wreck; I felt it in my bones as much as my bones felt the ice-hardened air, but I had to say something.

"You know, Stan. I'm just glad you're alive. I mean, I

think I am."

Did I actually say that?

I hoped he'd missed the slip, but Stan looked at me with more than just puzzlement. He was sharp that way, didn't miss a beat. He was probably offended. Or was he wounded? Hard to say.

"What I mean, Stan, is I'd never imagined you being so vulnerable, and I didn't even see you. Just texting and so on. I was worried."

He continued to lean in with that grimace of pain then cocked his head to the left a bit too much, as if cracking his neck. The crack resounded so loudly that his head fell onto the steering wheel. When he smiled, I saw his teeth had turned to rot. More than rot, and not just the teeth. There were malevolent protrusions surfacing where his healthy teeth had once been rooted, now rusted and ruined metal chinks. I could see his gums had not only gone into decay but had metastasized into something entirely foreign and rubbery, tough enough to house the metal gore.

I felt jolted and needed to scream, but Stan cut me off.

"I appreciate you, Steve. I'm heading out into the...hmmmm. Seems I forgot. Guess I'm just heading out. Fuck if I know where. And that's God's honesty, if there is such a thing."

With that, the window slowly climbed up to shut me out. The powerful truck was slammed into Drive, but Stan took off slowly, inching away as I stood there unable to move as I watched him drive off into the deepening twilight.

All around me I heard the haunting strains from an opera I'd once seen in New York but couldn't remember its title. The whole of the melody morphed into sounds that echoed and collided across the distant Rockies. Melancholy and powerful. It was music that turned more and more frightening as if trapped in a tunnel and morphed into an angry solo from Jimmy Page on stage long ago when concerts were the reigning thunder of freedom.

All of that seemed gone, including hope, as Stan's truck then stopped as if he'd thrown it into Park then rammed it in Reverse, and headed back at me again. This time a little faster.

Christ. What the hell is he doing?

I thought to run into the house to tell Anna about Stan's sickness when his reversing reminded me she wasn't even home, and hadn't been home for so long I couldn't remember what had happened to cause our love's demise.

The alcohol...oh yes.

I stayed put. What else could I do? I leaned both hands on the fence for a stronger brace as his truck backed into the same position it was in before. His window whined down at the same manically slow pace. Again, Stan leaned forward, showing what couldn't have been more pain, but somehow looked it, all the same.

"Forgot to mention...looked like your wife went inside a few hours ago. Didn't know if you two were back to bein' an item or whatnot, so I didn't ask or say nothin'. Anyway, for someone's been gone as long as her, I thought it'd be neighborly to give you a heads-up. None of my tootin' business, but women have a way of popping in and ruining shit all to pieces. Am I right?" He smiled so grotesquely it was tough to not look away. Deep gashes had formed around his mouth.

I hadn't talked to Anna in more than a year, but no matter how bad things had gotten between us, she wasn't the type to come back without calling or texting, especially after being gone that long.

"Haven't been in touch with her, Stan. Feels like forever. You sure it was her?" I knew how stupid I sounded not knowing the whos or whats of someone walking into my house. Especially my wife. Even stranger was Stan saying anything at all. Even though we'd been next-door neighbors for over a decade, not once had he ever asked me anything about my private life.

Not once.

"Dang craggedy. That's a good one back. She could have been someone else, but hellfire if I know. Anyhow, gotta scoot, my fine fellow. Lotta emptiness to find." He sounded and behaved more and more like someone I'd never met. Someone who had no idea what he was talking about as his mind was completely eating itself to slush.

There were only a few places he'd go, just a few bars nestled into the Wasatch Front that were in the vicinity of Duncan. I thought about following Stan, as if alcohol was the exact medicine I needed to put Stan's horrific condition behind me. However, if by some miracle of the universe Anna *had* come back and let herself in, life would become a lot more intriguing, even though my friend and neighbor was rotting from the outside in. Maybe Anna and I could jump in my Ram truck and do some snooping around and bar hopping just like we'd loved to do back when things were filled with joy and promise, back in a time that had disappeared from the earth.

But that's not what happened at all.

***

Just as soon as Stan pulled off and into the night, I saw a glimpse of something at the edge of his massive driveway. It began walking across his snowy yard between the few dying trees Stan had planted the summer before. The creature looked like something ancient and rickety, moving slowly with a meticulous purpose, tapping a stubbed leg around each area just before stepping forward. However, I couldn't make out any feet, and its legs were more like scarred and knuckled sticks, probably four inches in diameter. Arms looked the same with no hands, but hard to tell if that were true in the deepening night. The body, if it could be called that, was shriveled and charcoaled, and just as frighteningly starved as its limbs. The whole freakish emaciated being somehow held up, with effortless strength, a massive cloaked head, the hood, more like a battered helmet, seemed made of the same knuckled scars as its legs and arms. It appeared to be wearing a cape and a gun belt hung around its gaunt waist. I instantly wanted my own gun with me, because suddenly I felt like a gunfight was a distinct possibility.

I watched this horror of a shape move across the snow as if hovering above each footless step. I could see its head vibrate in contorted movements that would certainly snap the neck of any human, yet maybe it was someone possessed in ways that only Covid could inflict, like *Jacob's Ladder*, when Tim Robbins watched demons in his dreams with heads and faces that were impossibly contorting and shifting in speeds only a demon could sustain. At least I think that's what I saw...hard to tell when I felt the chaos of insanity notch my heartbeat up a few ticks. I wanted to follow *it* rather than go back inside and see if Anna had let herself in, but I was too terrified to move. What if the image was just that, some ghoulish hallucination based only in the paranoid fear I'd felt when Stan showed me his destroyed mouth?

And why didn't the creature cast a shadow across the moonlit snow?

If that wasn't enough to make a drunk drink, what was?

I tried to look away, but the twisted being turned toward me. Even though hooded enough to be shrouded in pure blackness, its face revealed a fiercely gnawed set of teeth that looked more like shattered fragments of razor stone, a nose just as jagged, and deep slashes where eyes once rested. It possessed the blocked and powerful face and forehead of a man as alien as everything else about its appearance. I was spellbound and wanted to run away, but the Hooded Darkness had the power to not only prevent me from screaming by locking my jaw, but the power to lock up my knees, as if I were struck down deaf and mute and crippled in Biblical rebuke.

I slapped my face hard with an open hand to snap myself out of the trance, and jerked my eyes back to my house to make sure I was still at home, then glanced back to Stan's yard where the Hooded Darkness had vanished.

Of course, it did. Over and over again I kept asking: Did it enter Stan's house or amble across the street and down the block in Stan's direction, was it even real, how long had I been standing here in the frozen night, and who had Stan seen entering my house?

It couldn't have been Anna. I knew this the moment I went inside.

***

The chill inside the house bit right through my skin. I could see my breath. The front room lights were off, but the lights down the hallway, through the kitchen, and into the back-bedroom area, the master bedroom, were on. More strangely, Nancy Sinatra's *These Boots Were Made For Walkin* started playing throughout the entire house, coming from the walls as if they were one giant wrap-around speaker system, corner to corner. The song was echoed and distant, as if playing at a concert hundreds of feet from where I stood, but so loud it created a feeling of panic and doom. Maybe that Hooded Darkness that scared me shitless had found its way into my bedroom and was dancing on my bed, obscenely, with the same gnarled violence of its charred body.

As I stalked through my frozen home, Sinatra's voice changed to a deeper tone. I walked carefully down the hallway as if funneling my way around an Escape Room maze.

"Are you ready, boots? Start walkin'." The saxophones and drums raced toward a furious finale.

I was wrong. The master bedroom lights weren't on. It was lit with blood-red candles that created phantom shadows dancing all around the walls and ceiling in demonic rhythms. The Hooded Darkness wasn't there dancing on my king-size bed, but a woman lay in the middle of it, one knee up, the other leg outstretched, and both arms above her head. She was as unfamiliar to me as the hooded figure in Stan's yard. Sinatra's song did a quick, hollow fade when Rob Zombie's *Dragula* blasted from the walls. It created a moment where *speechless* was perfectly defined in real time.

Throughout my career, there were times when I worked as professional speaker, and no matter the audience, I'd never felt speechless. Yet over the course of my life, there were a few times that oddly popped into my head, like once, in jail, housed with a cellmate called Smoke, who, when asked by another inmate if he could borrow a sheet of paper, turned around and drove a shank into the guy's windpipe. I was speechless then, and another time when my mother slapped me across the face and tore my skin open with her nails when she caught me in the middle of downing a ninth or tenth beer. Probably more.

So, I was speechless looking upon a woman I'd never seen nor dreamt of ever seeing, who lay on my bed surrounded by music that filled every space within my home, doing its own form of shapeshifting, an audio hallucination awry that caressed her every curve.

I wasn't surprised she'd gotten in, as anyone could have, especially in a town like Duncan, population a whopping forty-one hundred. The surprise was in every other goddamn question: the how did she, the why did she, the who was she? Why was she here? What business was she up to? And how stupid was *that* question? How did any of this happen: the music, the candles, the woman so real she even radiated a tantalizing scent?

Shadows kept dancing and moving and throbbing on the walls and ceiling, which made my bedroom look like some lust chamber of an ancient civilization designed to produce entertainment for evil kings and priests and their harlots, maybe of Babylon, to dance right along with them during lascivious nights of opium and brandy.

When I thought the speechlessness could never be broken, looking at this woman probably with a jaw so down slobbered I must have looked souped-up on Ativan, Rage Against the Machine's *The Ghost of Tom Joad* twisted in and out of Rob Zombie's screams about digging through the ditches and burning through the witches. Zack de la Rocha spewed on about a New World Order when the woman suddenly propped herself up. Her movement was lithe and effortless, as if her entire body were the bones and muscles of a boa constrictor. She moved from propping herself on her elbows to seductively maneuvering to her stomach. She arched her back, dragged her pelvis across the king mattress toward me, and winked. "You must be Steven Paul," she said, then lip synced Springsteen's lyrics about never being able to turn back, how the world had lost its hope long ago.

Speechlessness prevailed.

She looked at me with admiration, as if I were famous. "Why don't you come over here and sit down with me?" She sat up on the edge of the bed and patted the mattress at her side, indicating exactly where she wanted me. Rage's music, the music overall, simmered sans remote and system of any kind other than the massive seventy-five-inch television I'd recently had installed on the wall that faced the bed.

"Who are you?"

"Call me Lezabel. That work for you?"

"Trespasser works better."

With a pop of her hips, she hopped off the bed and landed in front of me. Her hair was deeper black than the pitches I paid to see on the massive TV on the wall. She was probably in her late thirties, five-nine, and her skin glowed a bluish white in the glow of the dancing candle flames that had somehow appeared on the nightstands to each side of the bed. Her entire body looked as hard as stone, and her eyes were as deep a lavender as the finest candle wax I'd ever seen.

"Your neighbor seemed to think you needed some company, so here I am. Signed, sealed, delivered."

"Stan? Stan sent you over here?"

"He didn't send me, per se. Just arranged it, that's a better way to think of it."

"Bullshit," flew out of my mouth far louder and more aggressive than I'd expected, but I was so stunned at her words, I should have shouted a lot louder. Stan would never have ordered an escort for me. Never. And everything inside me that remained sane refused to believe she was an escort in the first place. "This isn't a Stan Smitts gig."

"Are you certain of that, Stevie?"

"Yeah. I am."

"How do I know about your neighbor? How do I know he's falling to pieces? Needs a good killing, in fact, if it hasn't happened already. But I doubt it. Stan's a tough old bird, I'll give him that. He's one that will most certainly go down with the ship in a sea of alcohol." She walked around the bed to the other side of the room and opened the curtains to reveal the deepness of the aging night, and then turned back to me. The ethereal music changed to the low simmer of Nirvana's *All Apologies*. Kurt Cobain's tortured razing of nests of salt, taking all blame of some weird shame and sunburn freezer burns. All this music and drama was beginning to make me thirst for my own sea of alcohol as the the insanity inside my bedroom increased my psychosis.

"What do you want, Lezabel?"

She cackled at this, a perfect witch's response, or at least the best imitation money could buy on any sound effects CD during the haunted season. "I guess we're not going to do anything here, and it's obvious we're not, certainly not for my lack of allure, right, Stevie?" She quickly changed her voice to a velvety purr. "Why don't we go into the front room and have us a drink?" She walked right past me, down the hallway, and on to the living room. I noticed she was wearing a fitted dress that I didn't remember her wearing a few moments ago while writhing around on my bed. The material was far too thin for the cold air that had invaded my house. In fact, I couldn't even remember what she was wearing on the bed, but the dress looked like it had been poured onto her body then set to dry. As I tried to recall what she was wearing on the bed, I followed her.

***

The chill throughout the house hadn't warmed a single degree, a temperature, I noticed, that matched her icy talons, which seemed recently soaked in the same royal ink that had dried to her phantasm dress, nails that looked prepared for the grandest witching hour of seduction.

She sat on one of three large denim sofas that were positioned in the center of the living room, angled around an oak coffee table. I'd spared no change for the piece, as it was something Anna had fallen in love with the moment she'd seen it.

I sat across from the woman. Though her lavender eyes were spectacular in color alone, tiny pinpricks of light danced around her corneas, as bewitching as they were frightening, a sexual fantasy served up straight from the bowels of hell. Yet my focus wasn't on her sexuality, it was far more on the trance that was overcoming me, a trance that I had no idea how to slow, let alone stop.

The music, in its never-ending changing as if spun up by an invisible disc jockey, switched to a house pulse sound one could find at any heavy techno dance club in LA or New York. Not as blaring as it had been when Nancy Sinatra was yammering on about her walkin' boots, but still, it was resounding enough to where I could feel it as much as hear it.

I'm sure I started seeing it, too.

The mysterious vixen pinned me with an amorous stare. "Before we do anything else, I want to tell you a story, Stevie.

It's important, a get-to-know-each-other tale so we can move on to other things." She sat back into the sofa, legs crossed so perfectly it was difficult to tell if they were made of real flesh or ivory. My attraction to her began to feel more than just hungry, but ravenous, and I knew it was the last thing I needed if I wanted to stay focused and get through whatever else the night had to offer.

"As long as you stop calling me Stevie, I'm all ears. And what do you mean *before we do anything else?*"

"Well that's grand, Stevie. It really is. Most men just want to fuck, and when that's all they get, the relationship always ends badly for them. You're quite different that way. Rather soothing, to be honest. Levels the playing field, and I admire you for that. Most men don't have the discipline, not that you're going to keep yours perpetually."

"Of course I want to fuck you, but I've got no idea what you want, so if you want to tell stories, I'll listen. But if you're not gonna tell me what this drama is all about, let's cut the Stevie bullshit. Can you take note of that?"

She cackled again; it was uncomfortably long. "No one wants to listen to stories anymore." She looked at me even longer, more uncomfortably. "So...how about that drink?"

My willpower broke as cleanly as a rock hammer striking a perfect sheet of newly cut glass. I had no idea if Stan had planned this, no idea why he'd ever do such a thing. He wouldn't, of course, but still, my mind wandered around these thoughts: did Stan miss his old drinking buddy; what was she wearing under that dress, if anything; what the hell had she been wearing in the bedroom, or not; why did it seem like that had happened years ago, not just a few moments ago; what kind of nutcase story was she about to spill; what single knotted and twisted vein in my brain was about to hemorrhage into relapse?

"What do you want to drink?" I asked to put an end to my musing. Actually, I wanted a shot of Crown Royal more than I wanted to get her anything. I also knew what I'd just decided would lead me back to an endless enhancement of everything dangerous, *the* cycle of addiction. Whatever had happened tonight that led me to make this decision to drink again wasn't even considered. The decision was made, but I remained seated.

To say that I didn't realize I was about to get aboard the insane ride of a raging alcoholic binge was a lie every alcoholic told themselves. I was about to begin a relapse that I knew would become something far worse than even this pandemic, though I wasn't so sure about this woman's influence on me in that direction.

Over the past nine years I'd walked through cauldrons where I'd never found relief from my addiction, no matter how desperate my prayers wailed to my God, and not one goddamn drop. Jails. Rehabs. Poverty. Betrayal. Dead siblings. Soulmate and kindred spirit, gone. Bloodied messes created out of pure nonsense. Not a drop. Maybe all of it...maybe every lie I'd spewed over the course of endless months of pity and loneliness that had blanketed my life of sadness and sickness and vivid addiction...every last nerve that had been pinched dry from every goddamn bottle and wine glass had just come to such a buildup that this woman was the final camel's hair that threw me off the edge for a real cliff dive.

"You're not going to relapse on me, are you?" She uncrossed her legs and licked her lipstick.

I felt the lines in my forehead squinch together so hard it caused an instant headache. How the fuck did *she* know *that?* Was *relapse* that boldly written across my face? I had to put up the good fight though I knew I'd lose, as I'd lost so many times before. I scoffed. "*You* wanted a drink, doesn't mean I was going to have one, but how'd you know I used to drink? Stan tell you that?"

"Just an educated guess, you might say. And if you believe that, you're fucking stupid, and you're not stupid, Steven Paul. You think I can't see you running all the options of the game around in your twirly cues upstairs?"

"I don't buy it."

This time she scoffed. "Think I'm asking you to? Think someone like *me* can't see exactly what time it is? Fact, I'm not asking you to do anything. I'm here. With you. Doesn't really matter how I got here. Or what I know, or what I see, or that maybe I fucked your neighbor to cause the disaster he is becoming that you saw. That will all become clear in time. Truth is, you're far too wound up to *not* have a drink. I can see you're just barely keeping your shit together."

"Wait a minute. Just stop. I've been willing to go along with all this...this...this whatever *this* is, but you're getting personal about things you've no clue about."

"How do you know I have no clue?" Her voice raised several notches. "How do you know what I know or don't know? Because I can assure you, Stevie Boy, that what I know, many people would give their lives to know."

I blinked. *Just go with it, Steve. She could be the most fascinating time I've had in ages, for God sake, I've got everything to lose, but let her game play through.*

Or was it more than a thought? Had I heard those words coming from somewhere else besides my own brain? Some whisper echoing through all the chaos that seemed to be gaining momentum with each passing tick of the clock.

"Okay. You're right. Look. I've got some wine...even whiskey I've had up in the cabinets for years. A lot of vodka, too. I'm sure of it. I'm gonna pour me a shot. You can have one with me or not, but I'm having one. After all this shit that's happening, I can't go one more minute sober."

She said nothing, just looked deep into me as if she could read every thought I'd ever had since birth. If there ever was a time in the short moments I'd spent with her that I did not want a pause for effect, it had arrived.

"Okay?" I pressed.

"Since you're gonna relapse...since you're about to freefall from the wagon, I'll have what you're having. Doesn't really matter now, does it?"

I sighed deeply the moment she'd said relapse. After all these years sober, here I was going into the kitchen to dig for my stashed bottles of alcohol and pour a drink for myself and this demon woman whose presence now seemed perfectly reasonable.

At least for that moment.

She slowly moved around on the couch in that same slithery way she'd moved in my bed. "You're just more proof that the world gives not a single shit about the hazards in life that ruin and wreck the soul and the mind. Heard it in a movie once, where the villain is about to kidnap and rape a young girl, then cut her body to pieces, and he's looking at an article in the paper about everyone being upset over the latest political stunt. Villain looks to his partner in crime and says, 'people always worry about the wrong thing.' Ever think about it that way, Steven Paul? Here you are about to take a drink after...what? After how many months and years? You've been in the ring with this one for a good long time, and just like that," she snapped her fingers, "you're steppin' right out of the ring and into the bottomless den of insects. What sense does that make, Stevie Boy? Turn on the news, and what do you hear? A fucked media everyone thinks is the voice of God demanding we wear masks, get vaccinated, when *drunks* like you and *whores* like me are ruining shit nice and ugly like. We can't even tidy up our own shit," she shouted then laughed as maniacally and ferociously as any laugh I'd ever heard.

When she stopped, she slipped her body down low across the sofa, low enough that her ass slithered onto the carpeted floor, her arms then spread, one knee up to her breast, the other leg stretched out until her foot touched the coffee table. She could have been a stunning marionette whose master worked each string in just the right way to position a body that was much too perfect to be human.

My heartbeat jackhammered. "I'll get the drinks, then I'll listen to your story." My voice was just barely below a shout.

***

I found a bottle of Crown Royal with such immediacy it was as if I'd bought it just a few days ago. After pouring two drinks in tumblers meant for orange juice, I rushed back to the living room where I found her walking around and looking at the paintings on the wall. She moved as if dancing in a trance. I handed her the drink and she knocked it back as if it were nothing more than water. As I put my glass to my lips, she stopped me, leaned into me, and kissed my neck, actually sucked it. I was sure she'd had left a hickey, of all things. She may have even drawn blood.

"Pour me another before you drink yours."

I actually wanted to slap the shit out of her, so I did as she'd commanded before I lost my temper. When I got back to the living room, she was again posed seductively on the couch, that damned puppeteer working his erotic magic. The background music was still playing on its ethereal plain.

"Let me ask you something, Steven Paul. Do you have anger issues?"

"Why do you ask?" I handed her the drink.

"Maybe how I kissed you set you off."

"I don't think that was a kiss." I wasn't as angry as I wanted to sound.

"Tell me about them, your anger issues. Because I see them oh so clearly."

"I thought you were going to tell me a story, maybe even tell me about that freaky hooded creature I saw creeping across Stan's yard. At least I thought that's what I saw."

"Later, Steve. He can wait, and there's always time for stories."

I glanced at the drink in my hand, still untouched. *He can wait? Who can wait? She knew the abomination that appeared in Stan's yard?*

"I wanna switch things up a bit." She slammed her second drink. "Right now we need to talk about anger management. But before we do that, go ahead." She indicated the tumbler in my hand. "If you're gonna do it, then do it. God knows alcohol will settle you the fuck down. However, if you want more time to think it over, pour me another drink."

I'd almost blocked out everything else she'd said, but then snapped back to my imminent relapse. "You don't want me to drink this, do you?" I raised my untouched glass.

"Quite the contrary, Stevie." She handed me her empty

glass. "I just need a few shots ahead, drinking with a pro like you."

I poured her another and delivered it to her.

She downed it as quickly as the first two. "Now it's your turn. I can clearly see the rage that's boiling inside you, so get to it."

So, I did.

The instant the hot whiskey touched my lips and raced over my tongue, I knew one drink would never be enough. The bathing glow of warmth that soothed my inner tract soon gave my entire frame relief from every goddamn problem I'd ever slugged through; they all vanished into some easily manageable memory that almost seemed enjoyable. Liquor's lie seemed more clear, more simple, more necessary. I didn't want another, but I had to have another. I nearly ran back into the kitchen, poured a double into my tumbler without even asking what she wanted, nor did I care what she wanted.

"Now, Let's talk about those anger issues, Stevie."

"How did we get to this conversation, Leza...I don't even remember your name."

"Call me Terra so you can stop worrying about my name."

"Terra?" I whispered. "You lied about your name?"

"That's what I do, Steve. Get used to it."

I thought about the stories I'd read about Terra Drake, the mythical killer. Could she be the same woman, the one and only? Not really wanting to know, I threw down the double and sighed in heavenly relief. "How 'bout another drink, Terra? Then we can talk about anger 'til the cows come home. Deal?"

"Can't wait, Steven, since we're about to head out and

live it all again, in real time. Sound wicked?"

"I don't know what you're talking about."

We shot down another round.

"I mean live out anger management in real time. Do it by the numbers."

"The numbers?" My head wasn't clear enough to comprehend numbers.

"That truck you got out there. Bet that gets up and really screams. Am I right? Souped up Dodge Ram looks badass. I tell you what. Let's not sit around here and hash out your anger issues. Let's take this shit on the road, live it in real time. Since you're not making any moves on me, you'd rather relapse into oblivion, so what do you say, Stevie Boy? I'll drive. God knows you shouldn't get behind the wheel. Get the keys and give 'em to me."

"Why should I let you drive? You've slugged down more than me."

"You haven't been drinking for a long time. You're catching up. We're going out. I'm driving. Hurry on and get me those keys, Stevie. Hurry-scurry now."

In fact, I did hurry. I found the key-fob and grabbed my leather coat. I didn't bother to ask Terra if she needed anything to wear over that skimpy dress, and she didn't ask. It was freezing cold outside. I figured she could clearly handle anything mother nature threw at her.

***

She was right. The Ram was sweet. Dual exhausts. Meaty V8. Sport suspension. Four-wheel drive that was fearless. The cab was plush and spacious. It was good she wanted to drive, because all I wanted to do the moment we were in the truck was drink more. Had the whiskey bottle in hand. May as well make it one for the ages, is what I thought.

She pushed the start button and fired up the Ram, found the SiriusXM 41 Turbo station, then blasted the speaker system to a furious power workout as Metallica's *I Disappear* roared to a fury I'd never heard back when I owned the CD.

Thundering bass and drums. Searing, angry guitar riffs sounded more like screaming growls that perfectly matched the throaty bass.

James Hetfield and Lars Ulrich turned the night into rage as Terra rammed the truck into Reverse and shot backward onto the open road where she slammed on the brakes, then shifted into Drive, and away we raced into something only fuck knows what, as Hetfield continued to wail at us like some sun-torched prophet in the Sahara.

Terra hit 60 or more when the deep icy night became ferocious flashes and flames and bursts and auras of lasers and incinerators of glowing charcoal where the limbs of lions and beasts and chopped off bird necks and ruined bloody gore feasts flew across and over us in sprays of unholy mists and chunks of another I knew not what in hellish gashes of under-knuckles and gnarled hairy bumps that should have smashed through the front windshield but did nothing but shoot out more gobs of shit and crusty maggots over and under and everywhere that was not normal, nothing was normal, nothing but oh how did the majesty of hell open her gates even deeper and wider in colors and hues and vibrancy of demons howling and screaming their chants of endless torment, the vastness of the bludgeoned night came apart even faster and deeper as if we were driving into not only oblivion or Dante's Inferno itself locked and loaded in real time where time and the Time Keeper of us all was turned off by some mad toothless god taking control.

I remembered a scene from McCarthy's *Blood Meridian*, and now lived it, when the savages raced and ravaged and raped and razed without mercy, but with absolute glee, the Southerners, the scalps and bloodied hairpieces flying across the acid sky like a field of pregnant flies whose million eyeballs bubbled in micro cauldrons of the surely doomed.

I looked at Terra and had to shout for her to hear me. "Where are we going?"

"Let's go hang out with Stan," she shouted back. "Let's go find him. Give him some good pre-holiday cheer. God knows he needs it after what I'd done to him." She kept complete focus on the chaos beyond the windshield, which seemed to be metastasizing into an open gateway to another realm.

Godsmack's *Whiskey Hanger* burst from the stereo in such a sudden track change it sounded more like the station jockey screwed up the playlist. Sully Erna screamed that he never wanted to be sober in the first place, much more preferred wasting time in his own dreaded hangover that would surely murder him one day, as it did every alcoholic who thought he could run with such a beast.

The stop sign at the intersection with the road leading to the canyon passage didn't phase Terra as she hit the right turn, causing the Ram to tilt on two wheels. I thought I'd be thrown to my death, no questions asked, but she had complete control, some way or another. It was the canyon road that would take us to The Hickory Stack, the first bar I imagined where Stan would be fondling longneck Coors Lights, sucking beer down like kiddies with straws, giving it all they got for that last Slurpy brain freeze. All the air was violently pummeled from me as I realized I was terrified, and there was nothing I could do but just hang on as my life cascaded into a madness I'd never believed possible, even when I was crawling around the jailhouse floor where doom was a daily reminder of reality I vividly remembered as if I'd just been released.

Normally, the winding canyon road lined with mountain rocks that could easily rip the side of a vehicle to shreds if driven recklessly enough, was a gorgeous slash in the earth with postcard visuals that never grew stale or routine. But the faster Terra raced along its treacherous narrow lanes, the more I saw a widening tunnel laid out before us, a tunnel that morphed into an endless tube-like gut with walls that billowed and flashed and raced and blasted rope into veins that acted as lane markers hurling past us in those same insane colors that had burst forth before us when we'd left my driveway. I felt the Ram must have been going near a hundred as lights and flares and lasers shot past us in pinpoint tracers that danced around the tubular stomach tract we'd somehow entered, where all the mountains had vanished in the icy darkness, resurfacing here and there as wildly splashed oil paints thrown all about by a madman's paint brushes, never to dry, never to stick, just flailed about psychotically with no end or purpose in sight. Much like, it seemed, Terra's driving.

Yet none of that mattered as much as my own terror that she'd slipped something into my drink, which caused such intense hallucinations that had developed more quickly than any acid I'd ever taken back in the day. But she never made the drinks. Never poured them. Was never even near the bottle in the kitchen. More sudden and shocking still was all of that worry seemed pointless as Terra pulled into the parking lot of the bar, just when I believed the ride Terra took us on would never end, nor would the surreal visuals.

The Hickory Stack was perhaps the final standing and defining concept of an Old West Saloon anywhere to be found in the entire state of Utah. It most resembled bars back when Sundance and Billy and Doc Holiday and Wyatt were all shootin' the shit out of everything, guns always blazing, violence never ending, whiskey always the go-to. Gun fights and battles were so common they seemed more like sport than anything else.

We both jumped out of the truck, and as soon as Terra walked around the grill to join me, I wondered just how much I'd actually drank since we left. She was wearing jeans now, more tightly fitted than the minidress she'd worn after whatever it was she was wearing while she was writhing around on my bed. But I had no idea when she had changed clothes, and more oddly, how. Her top looked the same as the dress, but how could that be? And now her jeans looked like rubbery material I'd never seen before. Her top neck-line plunged deep, almost to her navel, and around her neck hung a thick silver necklace with a pendant that looked familiar. It was either charcoaled pewter, or black ceramic, maybe even Tungsten, but its shape was a jagged and harsh figure slightly smaller than a dime. I couldn't focus on it long enough to make it out, because she'd laced her arms around my neck and pulled me in for a deep, yet quick kiss, as even her black velvet boots made the whole picture more surreal than the drive up here, like Claud Monet's *Vanilla Sky*, but nothing had made sense since the moment Nancy Sinatra's voice about her own boots rang out as painful echoes all through my invaded home.

"Whiskey must be really hitting me because I don't even

remember you changing clothes."

"Shush, shush, Stevie. Too much thinking for so much drinking. Whatever it is you need, then that's what I'll be. And that's what it will be. Let's go find Stan and keep this scene moving, shall we?"

Whatever it is I need?

We entered through double-paneled mahogany doors, chipped and sun-aged for what looked like centuries. Inside, the bar was built as an instant defining highlight that begged immediate seating. Designed as two endlessly long, single pieces of waxed oak wood planks seamlessly fit and cut at a centerpiece that was etched and manicured in boot spurs, cowboy hats, Bowie knives, Civil War swords and bullet casings. Above the bar hung long and elegant wood shelving that sported a variety of long guns: fancy relics of lever-actions, bolt-actions, even a heavy nickeled .10 gauge scatter gun. The bar itself was fitted with twenty or so bar stools on each side, set upon unfinished pine wood floors where intimate tables were lined up and down the barroom for patrons to eat steaks and polish off shots and local beers. As for patrons, the place looked empty. Maybe six at the most, spread out here and there, few at the bar, few at the tables. Walls were covered in cheap wood-framed posters of state lore heroes like Brigham Young slobbering all over dozens of young floozies, Porter Rockwell killing whatever moved, and various pioneer journeys splashed all over the place as messy and cruel as the journeys themselves. To the far-left corner was a decent stage, the set-up dressed with drum kit, a few guitars, and Marshal half-stacks. Ready for the next gig to hit loud and heavy, but in the meantime music blasted throughout the entire bar, aggressive and fierce. Couldn't make it out though, anything that *was* playing melted into flashy harmonies that all seemed familiar, but completely sinister and foreign, all the same.

I could tell Terra was ready to manage the entire scene as soon as she took a fine long look around the place from top to bottom, her head doing all the moving as she stood cold still just a few feet from a bar stool, taking enough time to finally look up at the chalk-board menu. I thought she'd fixed herself into another strange trance I'd seen her do in my living room while I was beginning my relapse.

Which, at that point, was more than full swing boogie.

When she looked at me, I thought she'd give me her order, but said, "That's Stan over there alone at the table by the stage."

I looked in the direction she hinted, and sure enough, there was Stan sitting alone, long neck in hand, face red and swollen with what looked like boils now forming around his neck. He was looking into nowhere, eyes lost as black saucers on some distant moon landing.

"Yeah, that's him. What's left of him."

"Order me a shot while I grab us some seats next to ole Stan. Crown. Okay?" She was looking at Stan the entire time.

"Sure thing."

She walked right up to Stan's table, pulled out one of the solid wood chairs, turned the chair back end toward her pelvis and sat down, her parted legs straddling the chair seat as if it were a saddle, and then placed her arms, one on top the other, on the top slat of the chairback.

I ordered her drink, and the same for me, then walked over to Stan and Terra, trying to look as relaxed as possible when everything inside me felt like a strand of twine stretched to the last fiber. I took a seat next to Terra, keeping my chair standard layout, then looked to Stan as I handed Terra her shot. I couldn't recognize him anymore, other than the last flicker of sky blue left in his dying eyes, eyes that had once looked bright and vivid no matter how much he'd had to drink. They were fading into oblivion and there was clearly nothing he could do about it. Terra had already been talking to him, but no one was home on the other end.

"I was talking to Stanly over here, Steve, asking him how he was feeling because he's not looking his best, didn't you just say that? Christ, you're right. I mean, look at him. You'd think some kind of super-agent gonorrhea had shot up his pecker like a fire hose of acid that went right to his brain canals." She'd looked straight at him as she said it, then snapped her head to me. "But that's what he gets, don't you think?" She downed her shot. "That's what happens when you play around with women's feelings and emotions one too many times. Am I right? A few nights back, this guy...this guy right here, hits on me out of the blue at the other local water hole, flashes around a stack of cash, has a group of roadies and whatnot hanging on his every word, so I go ahead and play along. Right Stanly?" She shouts at him as her head snapped back in his direct view.

"Go get me another shot, Stevie. We're just getting started here." She didn't bother to look my direction.

Still, there was nothing from Stan. In fact, it wouldn't have surprised me if he'd gone brain dead at that point.

As I stood to walk back to the bar, I could tell she was screaming, yet I couldn't yet hear a word because a newfound light from the ceiling suddenly gleamed down on her as if spotlights were hitting her from every angle in the joint, framing her in a light beam that looked more like a pillar of a golden aura designed to highlight her every inhuman movement. I didn't know what I was seeing other than some awful majesty of the witching hour. She was farther away, or was I moving farther away from her? Farther away from Stan, as I was his last hope he'd ever have on earth again? On a hidden conveyor belt under the wooden floor slats where God only knew what was really cooking in the bar's ugly belly. Pan out. Zoom out. Whatever it was, I certainly didn't understand. I'd just been through one of the most frightening journeys of the short canyon run I'd ever known, so whatever trance-like show that was now being unveiled seemed to make perfect sense.

Just as suddenly as I was zooming out, the light beam enveloping Terra was shut off like someone had flipped a switch, and I could now hear her every syllable.

"Waddfucks like this always think there are no consequences. That women don't matter, they have no meaning. Just notches under the belt or even less. Then what happened, Stanly?! Then what happened, huh?" The Brothers Osbourne's *It Ain't My Fault* burst from the bar's stereo system, so alive and instant I thought the band had just hit the stage right behind the dying Stan Smitts.

I wanted to go back to the table and try to help my neighbor, but I knew it best to get Terra's drink and let it all play out. When it did, as I eased back to the table, this time sitting across from Terra and Stan instead of right next to her, and handed Terra her next drink, she was asking Stan if he'd happen to have seen Joaquin Phoenix's Lecture of the Pigs to The Church of the Elite at The Oscars when he won Best Actor for *Joker*.

"He's up there on stage, Stanley. He's talking about the very sad and frightening disconnect we all have for the natural world. How guilty we all are about having an egocentric view of the world. The natural world. How we rape and pillage it by giving cow's milk to each other as highlights to our cereal and coffee. How we slaughter pigs and the rights that pigs have. The very goddamn rights of a pig that are just as easily as important as our own rights. Fucking Best Actor standing on a golden stage telling people like you, Stan, what a piece of human shit you truly are. And look at you this evening. Just *look* at you. Was he wrong? You've become such a bloodlust of gore and sickness that Phoenix must have been having some prophetic vision when he spoke of the pigs and your own meaningless existence. Wouldn't you say so, Stanley FuckSmitts?"

It was another one of those moments when speechless was defined in real time. Another one of those times when I was sure I must have looked as if someone had struck me hard across the face and left me there to deal with the sting when I was looking at Terra, trying to figure out what to say about it all. I looked over at Stan, and he had the same look of disbelief even though the features of his face had turned to pure carnage. He was already bleeding from every pore when Terra stood up, looked down on him, then raised her right hand high above her head and followed it straight down and across, striking him so hard he was knocked out of his chair and onto the wooden-slatted floor, sprawled out as if hit by a locomotive.

The music intensified to such a level it was hard to hear my thoughts, though not even sure if I had any left. I looked up at Terra. She was grinning and buffing her nails on the fiercely black fabric of her top. The charm, or figure, or whatever it was hanging around her neck, shifted and twisted and dangled about the deep silver necklace as if it were dancing on its own to each rhythmic pulse that pummeled the walls and floor of the barroom. She looked down at me with such a glaring ferocity of authority and rage I was certain such a stare couldn't be human, but if not, then what. She walked over to me and now stood directly above me as I remained seated looking up to her neck, her overly erotic cleavage taking over even in another way that was more frightening than it was sexual. I tried to hold her stare as the dancing necklace figure became quite clear to me that it was somehow, some way, a miniature replica of the hooded creature I had seen shuffle across Stan's yard before I entered my own home and found Terra writhing on my bed. I was stricken with such fascination juxtaposed with horror that Terra herself took notice, so much so her attention from what she'd done to Stan instantly shifted.

"You like it, Stevie? You like what you see? All of what you see? Do you want to be part of it all now? Do you need to be part of it now? You're going to have to make a choice. Right here, right now. It won't take long before the local police force will be here, breathing down our necks like the big bad wolf did to the three little pigs. You're either continuing on with me to live out your anger issues, or you'll stick around to see what happens after I give ole Stan down there one last good fucking before he heads out to never-never land." With that, she uplifted the table with such force it was actually air tossed to land violently some three or four feet from my own chair.

I was more than wrong when I had thought things had played out as they were clearly just beginning.

Dean Patrick

PART TWO

Stan Meets Terra – Terra and Stan Meet the Goldmans – Ron Goldman's Demise – Alice Goldman's Dream – Terra Takes Stan Home

---

Dean Patrick

Steven Paul had no idea that Terra Drake had taken his next-door neighbor, Stanley Smitts, on a hellish joyride of his own, into a mayhem even Smitts never expected, one that rivaled Steve's with the Woman Mephistopheles. It was just after Stan had returned from his hospital stay, taking it up the ass courtesy of Covid. He was peaked and measly feeling, had lost some 40 pounds in the few weeks Covid ravaged him.

Yet Stan's alcoholism, while put in check during his hospital stay, was raging full throttle when he met Terra at one of the local Duncan bars. In the middle of the day of all things. Late morning, at that, cold...little too cold. Place was called The Oak Post. Not nearly as classic Western as The Hickory Stack, but still a saloon, nonetheless. Small. Wooded walls and floors. Low ceilings. Darkness filled every corner. Music low playing. Not loud and obscene as The Hickory. A single pool table sat in the middle of the bar room, so far from level anyone could see without even testing the gleaming solids and stripes and even the cue as most of them nestled around the left corner pocket from the rack's strike mark.

Stan was almost certainly there each weekend night, a lot of week-nights as well, doing his thing as the Big Shot of the town. But that particular morning when he awakened, he got himself into alcoholic shape and slammed a few vodka shots to keep the shakes from knocking him to the floor. He could hear The Oak Post screaming for his attendance, loud and clear.

So, when Terra walked in, sauntered right up to Stan who was, of course, sitting at the bar, sucking on longneck Coors Lights to wash down the burn from the hot vodka he'd drunk at home, she demanded he order her a drink, and Stan was taken aback to be sure. Not at all Stan's style, but he looked her up and down, a fine woman dressed in a black rubber (best description he could think of at the time) slinky dress, and admired a figure sculpted by the hands of God. Hard. Unforgiving. Lacquered. His mind conjured up every filthy thought it could imagine, every depraved act he could do to such a woman, in every lascivious position an old Toolpusher like Stan could muster in a sloshed noodle as wet as fresh spaghetti. Stan had worked his way up through decades of drilling. He'd been a Floorhand and a Derrickman, literally worked himself to death to make Toolpusher, and all those years chumming with his fellow oilmen had created in his libido the most perverted of fantasies, and he had a library of them. The woman in front of him would fit in quite nicely compared to anything he'd seen or met prior.

"Hmm. Well, let me think for a sec... what kinda drink you drinkin', pretty lady?" He was far more curious about her agenda than anything she drank, but still, he would play her game and find out soon enough.

"Double Crown Royal. Neat."

"Neat? Haven't heard that one."

"I don't want ice in it, you Hill Billy halfwit." Terra spoke with such ferocity he actually jerked back as if she'd struck him. First, he was enamored, now this. He looked at her cockeyed. No one had ever spoken to him that way. Ever.

"Hill Billy halfwit?"

"You heard me just fine, Punchy," she replied in her best John Travolta impression from the *Pulp Fiction* scene where he told Bruce Willis, the pro fighter, something damn near similar. She flicked Stan's nose with a red-polished nail. "I'll be waiting by the slanted billiard table. After drinks...if you're game...I'd like to take you out for a drive that's designed purely for the reckless and decadent. I'm just in that kind of mood and this seemed the place to find that kind of man. You in, Hill Billy?" Her voice was so hoarse it sounded burnt.

Stan took a moment to reply, as he was still recovering from the sting of this woman's brashness, which seemed on the edge of something demonic. She had that kind of feel to her. Thought he even smelled burnt flesh as he took a deep breath, and even held it a second before he replied. "Sure. I've got my bike outside in the lot there."

"Never mind the bike. I've got a car. Much rather drive that. Your bike will be fine here, I'm sure.

"And my name's Stan. Not Hill Billy. Not Halfwit. It's Stan."

"Whatever you say, Stanley. Hill Billy Stan. Until then...please, scoot on and get my drink."

Patiently, Stan did just that, then hobbled over to the nearest seating area to the faulty pool table where Terra was waiting. Smoking a cigarette, no less.

"Listen, lady, you can't do that in here. Management will go bat shit. Trust me on this one, okay? I've let things slide so far, but you've gotta put that out."

Terra looked up to Stan and blew smoke into his face as if he hadn't said a peep.

"I don't care for this town. The entire state, just to be clear. Not even sure I like you, yet. Which means...if I want to smoke in here, that's what I'll do. If I want to spit on the floor, I'll do that, too. If I want to go to the lady's room and piss all over the walls, I care not about consequences."

"Piss on the *walls*? Look, that's fine. Whatever. But smokin' in this place will get us both tossed out, and this is *my* place. So to speak. So, please. Do me this one. Can you *please* put it out, lady?"

Terra looked at Stan with genuine puzzlement, then put the cigarette out in her drink, and slammed the drink back swallowing the butt and all. "Better, Stan?"

He looked at her, more than bemused. "Sure. Thanks."

"Think nothing of it, Stanley. Now grab me another shot and come on back so we can talk stories. You like stories?"

"I'm not really one for small talk."

"My stories are anything but small. My stories are those that...well...make the world go round, you could say. Really shake things up are what my stories are all about. Hurry on now."

Again, Stan followed her direction, this time ordering another Coors Light longneck for himself. He'd lost count how many he'd slugged down since his arrival, nor did he care to recall the number. He went back to the table and sat in the chair next to hers, finally having a chance to see what this lady was all about.

He'd paid attention to what she was wearing the moment she slinked into the bar. Everyone had noticed. Looked like she had dressed up as Catwoman in the Batman film with Michelle Pfeiffer playing the part. She even had on black pumps with short heels, maybe a few inches or so, but still every bit the sexual prowess he'd never seen, who could sure as hell knock back shots as if they were water to wash down a peanut snack. He wondered if the booze was all that was keeping her warm in the cold Duncan air.

The music shifted. That's what Stanley Smitts felt. Everything seemed to shift. He thought for sure he heard Mick Jagger singing about Lucifer when Terra accepted the shot glass filled to the brim with amber hell. "Stan, I had this dream recently. Strange one, even for me. Thought I'd start by telling you all about it."

"Wait. Please. Just hold on. I don't want to hear about your dream. That's a bit personal, don't you think?"

"Don't interrupt me. It's rude. Does it really *matter* what I want to talk about? When's the last time you've sat with anyone who looks like me? Why would you complain about what I have to say? Seriously?"

"Actually, I do fine around here with the ladies, believe it or not."

"Yeah Stan Stan. Hilly Billy Stan Stan. I'm sure you do, but here I am, and just look at me. Look me over nice and long. I'm the kind of woman men stare at for hours and come without being stroked. So...if it's just fine all around, Stanley, mind if we get back to my dream? I'm starting to *feel* kinda dreamy, so this one just seems natural to talk about to a perfect stranger. Then again, we're no longer strangers, are we?"

Stan took a deep pull on his beer and nodded in agreement. Why not? She was right. It really didn't matter what she wanted to say. The music intensified. Not so much increasing in volume but increasing in intensity, creating more and more of the shift that was being delivered all around the bar. He felt uneasy at best. Uncertain of his footing, and it wasn't just the alcohol.

Terra was absolutely comfortable, she even sighed in a curious playfulness. "I was with someone, have no idea whom. Not even sure if I knew the person, but for some reason it looked like Karl Marx, or what Marx looks like in all the illustrations. You know Marx?" She looked him up and down, scornful, as if he knew absolutely nothing, let alone Marx.

Stan tipped his longneck to her. "Yeah, I know who he is."

"Sure you do, Stan," she said in mockery. "You're clearly the academic type. Anyway, we...by *we* I mean the person who was with me in my dream.... I don't know who it was, doesn't matter. We were in some odd warehouse setting of a Home Depot, or some other kind of all-included warehouse tool shop. Place was vividly enormous. Of course, there were tools all over the place in that dreamlike sort of blurred look and feel where most everything you think you see is fused together with something else you can't quite make out. But there were these slabs of meat hanging from the rafters on large hooks. Those hooks seem not only used for hanging meat but also large chains for heavy mechanical shit. Most the slabs of meat were still oozing blood. Don't know why I could see that, but I could. Could even smell the iron from the blood on the hooks. We were being followed. I told the person with me...let's just call him Marx for the fun of it...told him such, but he didn't seem to notice or care, and was certainly not aware of what I could feel, which was more than just a feeling of being watched or followed. More like they were right with us in our every step as if part of what we were doing there. Hard to tell sometimes in dreams what's actually happening, or who is actually following or watching. Or even if they're people, right? But I knew something else, something that Marx didn't know. I knew how *bad* they were, how *awful* they were, how *horrible*. Knew that the people with us were brutal in their wickedness, and I know all about that, let me assure you.

"Suddenly, we were in some basement part of the warehouse where I could *see* their evil come to reality. It was like the evil appeared from some wax apparition that was reverse-poured from the floor, if that makes sense. One of them made itself known physically. He was hunched over, and I knew it was a he, like a large witch, or a witch-man. Or warlock. Something fucked up. But as I knelt down to speak to the evil before me...and I knelt down because it just seemed what needed to happen...even more suddenly, and quite dreadfully, a bloodied dog's head appeared from the lap of this witch-thing. I was too stunned to speak, too frightened to even consider any kind of defense. But it got worse. Things can always get worse, Stan, let me testify to you. Always. As the head continued to protrude, one of the witch's companions pulled out a large kitchen knife and shoved it deeply into the dog's face. Its nose actually. And then I screamed, waking up in a smelly sweat.

"Now tell me, Stan, was that not a wild one? Was that not something to go back and tell your drinking pals over there about?"

Stan had no idea what to think, much less say. He could have found a quicker reply had she thrown ice water in his face. A thoughtful man, soft-spoken, and a man of great size and strength who would normally not seem so soft at first appearance, this time Stan went into deeper thought than he'd ever planned to, for all he ever wanted at The Oak Post in broad daylight was to get on a good old fashioned drunk, go back to his massive home and estate, drive around his property on his tractor and drink more longnecks, get more drunk, if possible.

But this was something all together so puzzling in its

oddity that he felt his entire frame shift with what he'd been feeling in the bar itself.

What was she talking about? How did she just come inside and begin such a story? He was wrapping his head around what to say, because he knew he really wanted to say something, when she rambled on.

"Speaking of Marx. Did you know he was also quite the horror show in his physical presence? Did you know that, Stan?"

This time Stan forced himself to speak, but his force felt more like a spent whisper. "Never really considered it, to be honest. Never really considered anything you've said."

"Stop it, Stan. No reason to go into anything that you've *considered*. I know you don't get it. Yet. And I don't care. Your purpose in life isn't to get everything, like you think you do. But since you've got no clue, let me tell you, Marx was a sickly beast. Had sores and boils all up and down his ass, inside his asshole. Never bathed. And drank much like you, a fuckin' fish for sure. He had this friend once, went to visit him late one night—"

"Just stop it, please. Just wait. Hold on, lady. Sorry, what's your name? Haven't even got your name and you want to go on now about another story out of the blue yonder that makes no sense without even telling me your goddamn name?"

"That is rude of me, isn't it. I'm Terra Drake. Kinda passing through this area to give it a nice raping, if you will. And you interrupted me *again*, Stan Fuckley Smitts. Have you really a better place to be than with me right now? Because if so, please, by all means, don't let the door do its thing. I told you from the get go that I wanted to tell stories, and here you are at this time of day with someone like me, whining about it. My stories will all make sense if you just follow along. Can't you just *play*?" Her hoarse voice now held a more velvety tone.

Of course, Stan had no place to be, no place to go. He was retired, had a cool million in the bank, and had always lived his life not giving a shit less about what anyone thought about him or said about him. Again, he was one of the kings in that small mountain town known as Duncan. Everyone who came to drink at The Oak Post knew Stan and loved having him buy their rounds. Round after round, night after night.

"N-no." This word came out a bit slurred, as all the alcohol he'd been consuming since early morning was beginning to settle. "I'm sure...you'll reach a point sometime. Keep goin'...I'll play along." He said this impatiently, but also curiously, then drained his beer.

"Very nice. Another story you'll dig. A Karl Marx Boogieman tale, no less. So, check it out. Marx had a visit from one of his philosophy brothers...can't remember his name. Heinzen, I think. Something. Anyway, this Heinz fellow was up in Marx's flat, late into one creepy sinister night. They're drinkin' much like we are. Slammin' 'em home. Marx begins to drink harder and harder, faster and faster, and as the night aged on, he was getting more and more belligerent and obstinate. Angry. To Heinz, Karl began to take on the look of a devil or something. And he wouldn't stop bantering Heinz. Kept going on and on and on about some bullshit ideology that every fucking kid today thinks is hip and wise and will save the world, when all it will do is send the world the way of Stalin's Ghost. Am I right?"

Stan shrugged.

"Wouldn't shut his hole. Marx then started quoting

from the classics. Specially Faust, 'bout how souls are sold to the devil, how deals are made to the devil that turn the value of the soul into inflated fraud.' Heinz ended up having to get mean spirited to get Marx to shut the hell up, ended up leaving Marx's upstairs flat. Said he almost ran out of the place, that Marx had cast some kind of a wicked spell all over the walls, and even spoke in spells. Or tongues, either one. Like some Joel Osteen wolf prophet. Then Heinz said, and I remember this last part verbatim, Heinz said, 'Dumb with amazement that I had escaped from his spell, he leaned out of the window and ogled at me with his eyes like a wet goblin.'"

Terra leaned back in her chair after finishing the tale, all the way back, tilting the chair on its hind legs so much so Stan thought the chair would fall over, Terra and all, while she roared out a cackling howl, ragged and fierce. Made Stan's heart skip.

The shift affected everything in the bar, including Smitt's mind, which began to spiral.

"Now tell me about that one, Stanley Smitts. Tell me that's not yet one more for the ages *and* the bar stool boys."

Once again, Stanley knew not a whisper to reply, and even though he found no words, what he did find was the memory that he'd never told the woman his last name. But he had to say something. He was indeed Stanley Smitts, and he was fond of his goddamn town, no matter how small it was.

By this time, everyone in the bar had taken notice of her oration, so he certainly needed to voice some kind of retort to keep his credibility at least halfway intact.

"Listen, Terra, is it? Listen, Terra. I don't know one fuckin' thing about anything you've been saying here, or any reason why you've said it. I'm trying to play along. You come in and want a drink then sit around and spew out all kinds of hellfire I've never heard. And that's what it feels like. Hellfire. Like you're breathing the bullshit. Hell, like you're living it. You tell me you're here to rape *my* town? Guess that means fuck it. These demonic stories. What is this all about? God almighty. Who *are* you, lady? For real. Who—"

She stood from her chair, cutting him off, then looked down to him with an insane and instant rage, he was most certain she was about to strike him down with hellfire itself.

"Shush up, Stan. Right now. I see we're done here. Go pay for the drinks. We're going for that drive I promised you, then I'll show you exactly who I am and all our storytime together will make so much greater sense."

Stan and Terra tore out of The Oak Post's parking lot in her car, a 1969 Mustang convertible, DUI red, 302 V-8, stick shift. The exhaust sounded like an angry dragon. What Stan liked about it most: Terra requested that he drive. Demanded it, actually, even drunk as he was behind the wheel.

Townsfolks knew him, of course. Any kind of stops, local law enforcement would likely cut him a break and get him home safely rather than spend countless time filling out all the paperwork on a DUI charge.

"So, tell me, Terra, who are you, exactly? Where are you from?"

"Never mind that now. Drive down the main street of this town. There's a place I need to visit."

"Thought you're new around here. What place could you possibly want to visit?"

"*New* doesn't mean I don't *know* what I'm doing or where I'm going. I've done my homework, as they say."

"You're liquored up is what you are and making no sense." Stan was irritated and losing patience.

"Please, don't argue with me, Stanley Hill Billy." Terra hissed like an angry Cobra. "Drive down the main street and then up to the breaking Y in the mountain. Isn't that what it's called around here?"

Stan looked over at her long enough for her to hiss again.

"Keep your eyes on the road."

He was more than puzzled in his own drunkenness since that road was exactly the way back to his estate. At least they would pass by it. Then again, for all he knew, she could have been lying to him all along, that's what she does, but at that point, he was too drunk to figure out any of it.

Nothing was right about her, not in any way. He'd been around a good lot, being a Toolpusher, and all. He'd known towns all over the country, had seen as much raw ugliness as anyone had a right to. But he'd never seen anything like this woman. Never heard anything like this woman had spewed on about. Endlessly it seemed. He was deeply unnerved. Even with all this alcohol oozing out his pores, he felt far more disturbed than what he normally felt in such a state: liquid courage. It was fear of certain knowledge that he'd never wanted to know, never wanted to dream, as if the woman had somehow invaded the privacy of his own mind, and he was a private man, to say the least.

"Here's the whole bit, Stanny. Listen up, and but good. You wanna know about the *raping of this town* comment? It's not all that hard if you think about it, but men like you don't do a whole lotta thinking except if the thinking makes your dicks get hard. Rape is a lot like infiltration. Infiltrating doesn't take a lot of know-how in the world today, right? Social media and all make things quite simple to learn and do just about anything. In fact, I've seen YouTube videos that claim to teach you how to perform brain surgery without needing a medical degree or license. Can you dig that, Stan? So, if you can watch videos at that level, imagine what the imagination can do in the wrong brain if a person wants to ruin a town or two. And if the person doing the ruining is a little beyond human, let your wet noodle slobber over that for a bit."

Stan kept looking back and forth at Terra and the road, still wondering what she was saying and why, trying to stay focused with his drunkenness heavier and heavier like a drill bit finding each root of his entire nervous system.

"I did some research on this town, Stan. Looked into it quite a bit. Fact is there's some strange shit that's been around here for ages and ages. Strange people in holed up shacks where things go more than bump in the night. Sick shit. Child porn and trafficking all hidden behind religion and God. Drunks who beat their wives bloodless, shoot dogs and cats for no apparent reason. Not really different than a hundred thousand other small towns across this great divide of ours, but this one just tickled me personally. My fancy, that is. Because this town goes a few steps deeper when it comes to things going awry...things going far far past kiddie porn and broken wives. That's really why I'm here, Mister Smitts. I fit in with the monsters, the demons, and the warlocks who howl at the moon with witches and witchcraft and all other dens of fuckery.

"Been doing this for some time, you see. Don't know if you're a news buff. Don't seem the type, actually. You're all booze and bullshit. But I've had my way around the lives of the innocents who need awakening. Slithered in and out like an erotic snake seeking the perfect opening, that perfect vulva in the shadowy velvet nights when all is lost and hope is nothing but a fantasy. You with me so far, Stanny?"

He shifted down to third and spurred the Mustang around a righthand bend. She was full of shit but he loved her car.

A bit later, after driving and driving for what seemed longer than it should have, passing up his next-door neighbor's house, Steven Paul's place, finally Terra told Stan to pull into the driveway of a small ranch house that stood just past the creek, just before The Y as she had exactly said.

Her business there was to attend to something quite nefarious, a word Stan didn't even know but nothing worse than what she'd been ranting about for the past hours in The Oak Post Saloon, and on the drive.

As with anything she'd been saying to him, her request was more a demand, and he was getting used it, figuring out in his smashed stupor that this place was some kind of twist to her tale of infiltration and absolute madness he was certain the woman possessed. Some kind of business in Duncan that she quite possibly had arranged. *She'd certainly not have met anyone past the creek, or into the county, did she?* But he did as he was told, still going along with it all, pulling into a nicely groomed, yet still graveled driveway area just outside the house. A wooden gate opened into a walkway that led to the front door. Two Bruins lights that looked more like lanterns hung on each side of a small patio-type cabin in which the door was nestled. At least that's how Stan had always seen the place as he'd driven past it thousands of times in the fifteen years he'd lived in Duncan. Place belonged to a couple he'd ran into from time to time over the years, but people he didn't really know because he didn't give a shit to know them, as he loved his tranquil secrecy. Also, the couple's property was only a mile or so from his own.

The moment Stan pulled into the driveway area, the stereo from Terra's Mustang blasted alive so suddenly that he slammed on the brakes, as he was that shocked out of his stupor. Black Sabbath's *Nativity in Black* wailed on with Ozzy telling troubled souls that Lucifer simply wanted to take us by the hand, then the music metastasized into REM's *What's the Frequency, Kenneth?* as Michael Stipe's acid voice and lyrics rattled the entire landscape in a new blast of madness.

It all seemed too much for Stan when things did indeed get worse, as he saw a man come bursting out the front door with a jug in his hand. He was probably five-nine, hundred sixty pounds or so, thick curled hair and a nose too big for his face. He made a quick cut to the left from where Stan and Terra still sat in the Mustang. To Stan's immediate left, he saw a woman tending to flowers in a well-designed miniature rock island. She was tall, dark skinned, dark haired, and when she quickly turned toward the man, her eyes were also dark with fear. An instant fear is what Stan saw. Terror actually, a terror that displayed all over her wrenched face, the fact that terrible violence was most likely the common ground in her home. Then he knew why as the man jolted the jug toward her, drenching her in water. To Stan's amazement, the man then doubled over in a belly laugh as if his prank produced the funniest moment he'd ever witnessed on earth. His laughter was obscene. Calculated. Severely cruel. And though shocking to Stan, what seemed even more puzzling, even disturbing, was his notice of Terra's glee about the whole stunt. Instant in its flash of sadism that was all at once a single centerpiece of what the whole world had come to idolize.

Stunned as the drenched and humiliated woman, Stan turned to look at Terra, who by that moment was already out of the car, leaving the car door open. She looked back to him with eyes that looked hollow and filled with rage. A rage within her that had clearly bubbled over the edge of the cauldron they'd both landed in. Clearly Stan was wrong about seeing her with any glee just a moment ago. He'd completely missed what he thought was her initial response. The fiendish move by this piece of shit triggered Terra to what Stan saw now as murderous. That's all he could think when she said, "Follow me. We're going to be here awhile," as she stormed down the sidewalk in a feverish pace that was as frightening as it was graceful, more like a panther than a human, so fast she was upon him that Stan had difficulty focusing on just how she'd done it.

The man who'd drenched the woman didn't have a second to blink when Terra pulled a knife out of thin air and had the serrated blade pressed to his throat, a knife that looked like a Spyderco Police model, stainless steel. A fabulous light bounced off the frightening serrated blade and seemed to race across the entire yard, scattering all around Terra's panther frame.

It was now the man who was suddenly filled with terror instead of his broken woman.

"Get inside, you fuck, or I will gut you right here like a filthy fish." Terra said it with a throaty, smoke-burned hiss.

"You," she shouted to the woman. "Follow us in and tell me where I can fix this for you. Because I'm gonna fix it nice and righteous like. Stan, make sure we're all in with the door shut, safe and sound, locked while we all get loaded. I told you I had some business here, and you're now in it. I told you this'd be wicked. You can leave now, if you'd like. I'd understand. But you're in this as you can see, so make your choice, Stanley boy. And make it quick." She then focused pure and absolute attention on the man she held the knife to. "We're going in. You got alcohol inside, so just lead me to it."

The man didn't really know how to speak, or even if he could, for that matter. He wondered if speaking would move his throat close enough into the blade where he'd be cut deep, bleed out before the hell that was about to happen could even begin.

Still, in the background, coming from the Mustang, *What's the Frequency, Kenneth?* continued lashing the entire front yard as if the car was spitting out the song itself.

"Speak up, you rat fuck," Terra hissed. "If the plan was to kill you here, it'd been done. Bring us to the liquor and all the other delights inside." The man managed to mutter something that sounded like *okay, okay, come on in then*, or something similarly stupid. Stan heard a quiver in the man's voice that sounded like the last effort to hide the depth of a fear this man had certainly never known, as if the fear had so suddenly and brutally come upon him there was no possible way out of it.

The moment the party of four entered the home, Stabbing Westward was pulsing from the stereo inside with its sexual rhythmic anthem of *What Do I have To Do?*, turning and fusing Stan's day at the bar into one mosh pit of cascading rock music and witchcraft in such a rush that he thought he'd just been assaulted, yet again, with one more twisted fate of a day he now knew would never end, and God knew that ole Stan wanted it to end.

Nobody else seemed to notice the fury of music and devilry.

The home was cleanly designed with vaulted ceilings, an open kitchen area, heavy stucco walls, plush carpet, and vast windows that made the place seem far bigger than it was.

The centerpiece on the far-left wall demanded instant attention. It was a painting, or portrait, or some cryptic representation of nothing Stan had ever seen that looked like a hunched over creature made of ancient wood, or torched rock, a figure clearly straight out of hell, a figure that demanded worship in all the wrong and most obscene ways. It was a painting that was so out of place for the character of the woman of the house that Stan thought it had to be a mistake. Maybe he was hallucinating. Was he seeing things? Was all of this really playing out? Just a few inches above the massive painting was a pin light fixture that beamed hairline lasers down and across the painting like a wild black-lit spider web. Stan was instantly hooked into a trance. Terra looked over the painting with awe and wonder, that was clear. And her expression was clearly just as disturbing as the painting itself.

"I see you've not been living up to His wishes," she whisper-shouted, still holding the knife to the man's throat. Evidently, she was talking directly to him, which made everything all the more confusing.

Truly, Stan tried to comprehend all of it the best way his inebriated mind could muster. As the Toolpusher, he mostly thought in segments of instruction that seemed to make the most sense to the people he managed. And that's what seemed to work here as Terra put the knife back into thin air, grabbed the man by his shirt collar and lifted him off the ground. Just as effortlessly, she threw him a few feet into the kitchen area where he landed on the floor square on his ass, probably snapping a wrist to blanket the fall.

She then pulled out a kitchen chair with one hand, the other hand pointing to the man in a gesture to not move, then picked him up and slammed him on the chair, commanding the woman for some ties or rope (ended up being ties) then tied the man's hands behind him and to the chairback, and then commanded the woman to pour them all drinks, except for the man, then began her lecture.

"Have you ever wondered why horror's the only thing left that's got any purity? Any guts? I'm telling you. I'm telling *all* of you this. It's the only thing that's not so convoluted as to always have some cockeyed angle fitting an agenda. Like what's happening right now." Terra stared at everyone in the kitchen as if they were there for some kind of ceremony. "Can you feel the purity of it? Just out of the clear sky, *snap*. I have this cocksucker in a place he'd never imagined just moments ago. That's horror. You see everything else going on around you, right? The politics. The theater. The religions of the world. The hundred thousand different gods worshipped in sacrilege. The schools. The news. Television. Movies. Even the fucking music. There's nothing pure in *any* of it. 'Specially in a town like this. Town that probably got its rocks off with a stint like Game of Thrones, which was so agenda driven, it was hard to concentrate on its soft porn, which was always everyone's welcome relief from the shit that's dumped on us day in, day out, with minute-by-minute playback. Jesus. What do you say, Stan? You agree with me? What about you, miss?" Terra looked to both Stan and the lady.

All Stan could do was look at the helpless victim who'd just humiliated his wife, but now was the center of humiliation as the main event for this demon woman's pleasure. Stan was also far too drunk to do anything but slobber and watch. As for the woman, she just leaned back against the fridge and looked on with absolute fascination.

What else was there at this point? She was convinced that she was living in a movie. At least that's how she *looked* to Stan.

But looks were deceiving...

"What are you talking about?" the tied-up man said in disbelief, legs straddling the chair he'd been forced onto.

Terra looked down at him as if he were an insect that just crossed her path. "I'm talking about horror, you beast. Being scared. Getting scared. Surely you follow me in the shit you're in. Monsters that *really* bite. I mean, you can take vampires for example. Vampires don't really have an agenda, other than to kill. Or to hunt, but that's not an agenda, that's just their survival mandate. Or ghosts. No agenda there but to haunt you. Witches don't even have an agenda, 'cept to cast spells and fuck with you. Werewolves the same as a vampire. Lives to kill. Straight up murder. Then there's *real* monsters, like psychos released from prison because their time's up. Psychotic sociopaths who simply kill because it's interesting, or maybe just out of boredom. Lot like me, actually."

"I see." The man looked up at Terra with a sudden reality resting on his shoulders that the woman who now had him in such a plight was truly the most insane and terrifying person he'd ever seen, and he knew he was in real trouble.

"Oh, you do? Is that right?" Terra now faced the man down, towering over him.

The man just nodded.

Terra seemed to accept his acknowledgement. "Horror's pure. That's what this is all about...ah...what's your name? And your wife's. What is it?"

"Ronald," he choked out.

"Ronald what? Gotta have a last name to make all this horror work."

"Goldman."

"Ronald Goldman? Fuck me silly. You're Jewish, of all things out here in the middle of nowhere. Ronny Goldman, breaking his wife's spirit for all to see in broad daylight. Got anything to say about that one, Stan?" Terra jolted her head toward Stan in a violent movement so malevolent he knew he would never forget it.

Of course, Stan had nothing to say as the miniature carnival from The Whack Show down the hall at the end of the universe just continued to play on.

"I didn't think so." Terra jolted her attention to the woman. "And what's your name, doll?"

"I'm Alice," the woman said as water dripped from her hair to the tile floor.

Stan couldn't stop his drunken mind from latching onto the lyrics from Jefferson Airplane's *White Rabbit: Go ask Alice*. He wasn't ten feet tall, but logic was certainly dead.

"Well...Alice, I don't want any of this horror tainted. What I was saying to your husband here, in case you weren't paying attention, is that horror is the only goddamn piece of purity that's left on earth. Even horror films, for Christ sake, too often miss the mark, and *everything* else is either shit, or so watered down and restrained, it's worse than shit. Notice that? Good horror films are just about extinct. Make no mistake. PC culture's just about ruined everything. Progressives who have no progress want to wreck *everything* that ever was pure. But that's not so with horror. No, no, no. No PC twit warrior can ever ruin it when it's done good and bow-tied. And this is exactly why it has the purity that it is. *Exorcist*, for example. Pea soup vomit and masturbation with a metal crucifix. By a child, mind you. Or *Hereditary*. Remember that one just a few years back? Satanic bitch who went bat-shit nuts on her family? Wow. That one hit a nerve. But that's just film. What we have right here, right now, is the purity of everything I've been saying, and everything I want your husband to never forget, that he's clearly needed a wake-up call for quite some time."

"I'm not sure about the ending of *Hereditary*, though," Ronald said in a pitiful retort. It was almost sad.

Terra, Stan, and Alice were all stunned that Ronald said anything at all. Of course, Terra composed herself so quickly the others didn't really notice she'd been taken off guard.

"Well, well, well, Mister Critic. Let me respectfully disagree to your misplaced debate attempt, you man whore. You need to really watch it a couple of times to truly appreciate how tormented Toni Collette's performance was. Or how truly scary that 'cluck' 'cluck' sound was coming out of the psycho daughter who seems like a twit, but then breaks a bird's neck just because she thinks it's the thing to do. For no apparent reason. Like the sociopaths I was just mentioning. Then her head gets smashed clean off her neck, hitting a pole when she leans her head out her brother's car? Didn't that bother you, Ronny? And then Collette *really* losing it, crawling on the ceiling like a giant cockroach. Christ. No wonder you still remain clueless to it all. That was a good one. That's good horror. Just goes for the throat, then rips it out. Like I want to do to yours, Ronald. But I have to give you a tad of credit for sitting there and having the balls for once in your life to actually speak up."

She looked down and shook her head from side to side as if thinking the topic should make sense, because none of this was in any way sensible. Remarkably, Ronald actually continued the dialog with Terra. Her astonishment this time was almost comical.

Almost.

"I'm trying to get what you're saying," he meekly replied.

Stan realized Ronald was indeed trying to continue speaking to Terra perhaps in order to save his own life.

"I like a good slasher or devil movie as much as the next guy. But I've no idea what to say otherwise, or what you *want* me to say. I mean, you want me to apologize to Alice? Is that what this is all about? You somehow find out things going on here and want to punish me? Well, goddamn it, I am sorry, Alice." He was now looking at his wife who was still leaning against the fridge, making every sane effort to understand what was taking place in her home...in her kitchen, of all places.

As soon as Terra let Ronald speak, she looked around the kitchen with eyes switching into some strange MDMA rush. Like they were rolling, but without the euphoria. Rolling rage was more accurate, far more than what she'd shown in the yard when she'd put the knife to Ronald's neck, then she blasted him across the face with an open palm so hard it tore open his skin. Ronald made an attempt to move with the chair tied to him, pathetic and useless thump movements. Terra hit him again. And again. And again.

Stan had the bizarre thought that the whole scene looked like a tomahawk beating a steak as she then drove her closed fists into Ronald's temples and cheek bones, relentless as it was furious. With each blow, Ronald, with stunning resilience, tried to adjust his body on the chair to avoid falling completely over.

Alice and Stan watched in bathed somberness, lost in a haze of confusion and dulled chaos. Eventually Stan lost track of the number of times she struck Ronald. Alice grew even more confused as Ronald lost consciousness a few times, then suddenly found himself startlingly awake, but barely able to see anything due to the severe swelling above his eyes, the impossible bleeding that poured from them as if in the shower, trying to focus on where he last placed the soap or shampoo.

"Well, well, Ronny Boy. Looks like you have some pieces of flesh hanging where they shouldn't," she said, this time in her best Jack Torrance imitation when Jack was chasing his son, the little Danny, in the haunted kitchen of the Shining's Overlook Hotel, ax in hand, a gleeful murderous rage.

Whereas Stan and Alice were both looking exhausted, Terra seemed refreshed. "Here we sit. Well, it's you who's actually still sitting. But here we are. Like old pals just having a chat about horror movies. I don't think you understood what I was saying before, so I had to rap your knuckles a bit. Had to take out the ole ruler and rap those knuckles a good one. Think I have your attention now? Think I *like* doing this? But you *weren't listening*."

Terra paused after her manic rant, then looked at Ronald Goldman, her glare covering every square micrometer of him, as if he were some curious new entity she'd just discovered. Like a fossil, but moving. Bleeding. Breathing.

God, was he dying? Stan's mind was slobbering.

But this wasn't the time for Ronald's death. There wasn't even time for bleeding, because whatever it was that was happening, the one thing he did seem to know, or think he knew, was that surviving this fuck show was even more important, even though his own importance meant nothing. Still, in his eyes lingered some fragment of resistance. Just as he tried to speak again, Terra hit him once more. So, he shut his mouth.

As for Stan, he started to realize why Terra had told him the uniquely bizarre tales she'd told him at The Oak Post. Started to realize how insane she sounded telling him the stories of Marx and demon dreams of dog heads, were not insane at all to Terra, but completely purpose driven. Like Rick Warren's book on why we are all here in the first place, as if Warren had any clue what he was talking about.

"Jesus, Ronald. Can't you see your situation here isn't one that warrants debate right now? That you're here to shut your mouth and listen? You can see that, right?"

Ronald nodded in agreement, blood oozing from both nostrils, his lips, both eyelids, and of course the opened side of his face.

Terra hit him again for good measure, put her hands on her hips with that same irritation a mother would have with her son who'd just chugged the milk out of the milk carton in the middle of the night.

"You know, Ronny, I'm not sure we're getting anywhere, to be honest. Look, go ahead and nod when I speak to you. Scratch that, you can even talk, okay? I just want to have a discussion with your full attention. Not gonna hit you anymore, Ronnie Boy. Looks like that part's over. Thank God, right?" Terra smiled at Goldman like it was a genuine inside joke between two best friends sharing an inside secret about their most intimate moments as true best friends do. Terra sighed again, took in a deep breath. Exhaled.

"Once again, we were talking about horror and its purity. But let me give you another example about just how pure. Let's talk about dreams. Wicked ones. Sound like a plan?"

That question caused Stan to jerk as the bloody dog's head popped inside his wet noodle even more vividly than back at The Oak Post. Her eyes were shifting back and forth, side to side, clearly rolling on something like MDMA, but Stan sure as hell couldn't remember her taking any drugs. Ronald nodded pathetically while Alice began to actually feel sorry for her tortured husband. Or at least she looked like she did.

"No. No, scratch that. No time for dreams. Now I want you to hear me out completely this time, Ronny. I know all that's happened here is probably beyond your comprehension. I'd be just as baffled in your shoes. You burst out the door to drench your wife with water because you've abused her for years and shit like that to you has become less than fun and games. Yet this time, just as you're about to get really going, all of a sudden you end up in your kitchen tied down and beaten bloody. By me of all people. Maybe you're thinking this is some wicked dream. I assure you, it's not. Let me try and get back to what I was saying when this whole thing went down. You've not been doing what you're supposed to do, Ronald. Not in any way. What do you think, Stan?" Terra turned to Stan once again with that disturbing jolt she'd done so often when looking back and forth between different people. Stan looked more and more confused but was quite certain that her agenda was anything but confusing in her sick, sick, sick mind. Still, he paused to really think about it. Terra let him but continued before he could actually get a word in, walking around the kitchen table, pacing as if to concentrate, as if to prepare for a critical presentation.

"Alice," Terra said, suddenly looking at the woman who had looked as clearly lost as anyone to anything. "Alice, before I ask you to tell us anything here, you're not some fucking fraud like your husband, are you? Or an abuser?"

"No, I'm not." Alice walked away from the fridge, transitioning into an entirely different person. A confidence appeared over her that was like a distant friend who came over to remind her that she never should have allowed the abuse Ron had given her over the years.

That's what Stan noticed most. As if Alice suddenly remembered her purpose.

Terra stopped walking around the kitchen table, pulled out one of the kitchen chairs like Ronald was strapped to, looked over to Stan then to Alice, completely ignoring her tortured victim. "Tell me, Alice. Actually...tell us all. Tell us about the time you found Adramelech, our dear Cain. And how you came about the painting in your living room. And what's been going on since everything has brought *me* here. Why your husband lost his way, and subsequently, why you lost your way even farther along Robert Frost's lonely path."

Both Stan Smitts and Ronald Goldman looked at each other. To say in shock would be far under any understatement. No matter the predicament of Ronald's beating and tie-up to the chair, or the depth of Stan's inebriation, after what Terra had just said, the two men could do nothing else *but* look at each other for some kind of common ground that perhaps only they were feeling. For no matter the absurdity, for what she said to Alice was far more disturbing than anything absurdity could ever mean.

Did the women *know* each other?

At least *heard* of each other?

"Go ahead now, Alice, we're all waiting. The stage is now yours." Terra crossed her legs in that same seductive way that Stan couldn't stop thinking about the moment he first saw her in the bar less than an hour ago, but now any seduction had died.

The music in the home changed over from the blasting Stan first heard to a lower rumble of the deep base and throaty acid of Type O Negative's *Christian Woman*. Peter Steele's dooming voice set the tone, but Stan could have sworn over his dead son's grave that the tide Terra had turned by asking Alice to speak had created a silence that had so deeply fallen into the void of madness that he believed no sanity would ever bless him again. When Alice began speaking with a long willowy sigh out of complete relief that she must have needed to sound like and looked to have been feeling for years, Stan thought he would scream, but found his voice scared mute.

She began in a voice of caution yet committed assertion. "It was one of those nights when it was so dark the crescent moon looked more like a white slash across a black billboard. Much like it's been lately. It was late and I couldn't sleep. Don't know how late, probably the Witching Hour. Sure felt it. I got up to walk around the house to make sure everything was locked and turned off. No matter how many times I checked, I always feel the need to keep checking. One of my tics. I had my robe on and house shoes, walking around each room, then looking out the windows to see what could have been going on. Always seems to be something going on around here. A small town always has its secrets, which seem to come out at the strangest times.

"As I was looking out the front window...just out there," Alice nodded toward the living room area. "I felt I saw something move across the street just past the driveway area. *Felt* I say because I wasn't sure what I saw, if anything. Still...I was more curious about it for whatever reason than

I'd been in a long time, so I went back to the bedroom and put on some jeans under my robe and decided to venture out to see what it could have been.

"As soon as I went out to the front yard, I remember feeling instantly scared. Deeper than scared. Ronald wasn't home, so going back inside didn't matter. Not that he'd ever been much of a protector anyway." Alice scowled at her defeated and bloodied husband. She then looked at Terra as if seeking silent permission to continue. At least that's what Stan thought it looked like, and when Terra gave a slight nod as if to approve, this time Stan looked over to Ronald once more to see if he'd perhaps noticed the exchange. But Ronald's head had lowered in what must have been pure exhaustion. Maybe he'd passed out. Maybe he had died, but Alice continued. "I think I felt scared about how dark it was. Couldn't get used to it. The lights around the homes in the area looked...I don't know, hidden or something. Like Halloween lights look sometimes on Halloween night itself when it becomes very very late and only a few places are lit up, and those lights are scarce. Some *were* Halloween lights even though it was six weeks away or so. Anyway, I looked down the street toward the bridge that covers the creek. Half mile down or so in case you missed it when you drove up.

"I don't know why, but I walked down to the creek, under the bridge. Walked down to the bank using my phone light to see where I was going. The water was far more quiet than normal. Running as always, but almost in silence. I could see the light from the crescent moon flicker all up and down the running creek water. It even cast strange and creepy shadows over the hanging trees and tree stumps. The owls were hooting as they always do down by the creek, and I looked around to see them but couldn't find them.

"Immediately under the bridge there are broken concrete slabs where you can walk or sit or fish from. No one was there of course. But as I looked up again to find the owls, I felt a distinct brushing of my hair and side of my body as if someone just rushed passed me. My entire body jerked, and that's when I saw Adramelech sitting on one of the cement slabs, feet dangling into the icy running creek. Well, as you know from the painting, they're not feet at all, but jagged stubs. I peed my pants, I was so shocked. There was this *demon* before me that looked like a mixture of hard flesh and shards of charcoal sitting in the middle of the night under the bridge, and appearing to me. Wanting me to find it, or him, or whatever, or whomever.

"It got worse. Things always get worse, right, Ronald?" Alice glared directly down to Ronald as she'd approached him while telling the tale.

Ronald actually managed to look up to her, canceling the notion that he'd died. At least at that point. His face looked butchered, as if beaten worse than had a pro boxer come in and worked him over. It caused Stan's heart to skip a beat as he saw Ronald look up to his wife.

Terra just kept her gaze deep into Alice's every move. Her every whim it seemed.

Alice placed her right hand under Ronald's chin as if to give his entire head some strengthening support, then let go, and Ronald's head dropped down again, chin to his chest. She continued the story while walking back to the fridge then around the kitchen island, both her hands locked together, twitching her thumbs together in a nervous tic.

"To each side of Adramelech sat a fleshy dwarf of some kind. Two of them...maybe they were overgrown children. With legs so short and thick they looked more like stumps, each of them the same, like twins. I could see how sickly pale they were in the crescent light. A palish blue flesh that was overly sick, if that was possible. They looked pasty with sweat. I was close enough to see they also had freakishly thick veins, like wet yarn that was moving and pulsing all around their foreheads, arms and hands. I was sure they were demons. What else could they be? They were also eating out of their hands what had to be worms. Their knuckled stubby fingers had obscenely long nails. They were grinning with such weird vileness. I was about to scream with everything within me, when Adramelech spoke with a voice that sounded torn and shredded, like someone I thought would sound like if they had their throat slit and tried to talk. Of course, he told me his name was Adramelech. That he'd also been known as Cain, and that he'd been on earth since time started, and that time was coming to a quick end. That I'd probably read about him when I was a child in Sunday School. Said the Bible lied about him killing his brother, Abel. Told me everything I'd ever imagined possible could all be mine if I'd just keep my eyes open, my wits about me, and to remain patient. He then stood up and placed his torched hands on the things beside him, on the scalp of each of the demon dwarves and with a sudden jerk, pushed them into the creek below. I saw their bodies instantly burst apart in a heaping mess of what looked like jellyfish being blown apart. And then *he* was gone just as suddenly as all the creatures had appeared. I raced up the bank more frightened than I had known possible, certain I'd have a heart attack, ran back to my house and slammed the door, ripped off all my clothes to get into the shower as fast I could because I felt more than just violated. More than just raped. It was like just the sight of him injected me with something that infected my entire nervous system."

Alice stopped and looked at the three of them, looking to Ronald and to Terra and over to Stan, looking at their faces, except for Ronald's, of course, looking for reactions...as if to *seek* reactions.

Stan was mortified in his drunkenness, still too scared to speak.

Terra simply nodded in approval.

"Anyway...a few months later after the new year, I found that painting at a yard sale way up the canyons. Freaked me out when I saw it, had to have it, and ever since I've had it on the wall, something seemed to whisper to me that someday everything would change, and then you arrived with that pendant hanging around your neck. The pendant of *him*. You asked me when Ronald lost his way, when I lost my way. It's not like it happened overnight. Anyone who's ever lost their way will tell you it's a process. Ronald never knew the reality of the painting, or of Adramelech. I never told him the story, in fact I believe I never was supposed to. He just thought it was a cool picture I'd found like so many other things I'd found over the years, looking for treasures. So, as the years went by, and he lost interest in the painting, I guess over time so did I, and that seeing Cain that night at the creek and his demon children...maybe it was just a bad dream. Of course I knew it wasn't, and now I'm sure."

With that, and looking satisfied with what she'd heard from Alice, Terra held the pendant between her thumb and forefingers, not rubbing it, but nurturing it, her head down, eyes fixated on it.

Stan was certain he'd never noticed her wearing it. Or did he and had just blocked it all out back at the bar? When the shifting took place, was she wearing it then?

She looked up and spoke directly to Alice. "You can finish up here then, yes? No need for me to continue?"

"No, I've got it. I'm back again," Alice replied.

"Good, Alice. Good. You make sure there's no fucking trace of him. Perhaps we'll see each other again." Terra then walked past Ronald whose head was then far more than just lowered.

Stan wasn't sure if Ronald was alive, but he wasn't too drunk to realize that what Terra had said to Alice was more of an order, more of a command to kill Ronald if he wasn't already dead.

"Let's go, Stanley," Terra said. "We're finished here. Let's go to your place. I think we both need a few more drinks and I know you're stock is full."

All Stan could do after all he'd just seen was follow Terra in distress out to the Mustang. He was beyond feeling or understanding. He was now simply following. His mind had shut down, as the ghouls had taken over.

***

So Terra Drake and Stan Smitts arrived at his obscenely massive estate built for twenty but housed only himself and his liquor and his sins that ran rampant, as all sins and sickness did, without check without cause without consequence, and as the late day turned to the decaying and frightful night of cold and purity of evil, all the howlings of hell came changing in chorus, came channeling in like the steamy froths of Dante's pitch that rumbled through and through the chanting chanting chanting of a warlock's lock box, with the witches and their brews, which were called upon to dance the silver dances of obsession and compulsion and vileness and vanity that Satan demanded in the wee hours of the nights gone awry, the nights gone south, the nights turning to bleed into the blackness where no sights could be seen but those of the dreadful bursts of blues and purples and the royalties of kings raping the pilgrims so long long ago on Judea's plain when all the world's music sounded like Robert Plant's wailing on about the Battle of Evermore, and the continued dances of the witches with their serpent tongues lashing around the arches of the innocent, lashing and licking and entering their innocence to destroy them forever was such the plan and foreordained agenda Terra couldn't hold back when clamping down on the wasted Stan Smitts, as wasted as the earth that was being ravaged by the savage horrors bellowing beneath us all when she told him it was a night he'd never forget, a night where ruin and carnage would rule supreme, as he knew deep within his entire framework all had changed and was changing changing changing as the fierce pulses of Terminator's soundtrack reamed and ripped and thumped, every living soul that ever walked the earth thought Stan knowing knowing knowing knowing the end of his existence was now just beginning when he thought he'd beat the Covid all he really knew was he beat nothing but fate while his lonely thoughts only wished he'd had one more night outside, the ride of his life, before the virus struck him deep into the new depth of Terra Drake's entrance and annihilation of all that's holy all that's pure all that thought these things could never be real when all it really was was the hypocrisy and flashy façade in the sleepy slow town of Duncan when its world changed and the devils and demons came by her side to play late into the night, late into the portals of all dreams gone bad, all nightmares born from the wombs of all seances screaming and wailing and taunting until the little town of Duncan and all those like it across the earth's scorched surface would kneel and succumb, as Stan knew all too well the ghouls had indeed come to sleep next to every woman, child, and politician of the shadow of Cain.

Dean Patrick

PART THREE

Steve Leaves The Hickory Stack — The Portrait at The Duncan Craft Shoppe — Steve's Dream — The Salon Witches — Burkenstock — The Auction at the County Fair — The Vendor Hall and Alice Goldman — Steve Finds Terra

---

Dean Patrick

I tried to remain as collected as possible when Terra knocked Stan to the floor of The Hickory Stack with an effortless back hand as powerful as if a bear had hit him. I knew he'd been dead already, but somehow his body was just going through the motions. She did him a favor. Still, I wasn't sure if he'd survived it. So, when she told me she was going to give Stan one last good fucking, I figured it meant she still had plans for him. Sensed that he was still alive, no matter how impossible it seemed. When she said I was in it and that I'd needed to make a decision to stay at the bar and all the hell that befell it, or to go with her, I was lost as what to do.

I went with her, of course.

Went with all of it.

Made that decision that so many made when diving back into the endless abyss of relapse when all that slithers around and laces over and under the furious lashes the drink and the drug do to the inner core when it's once again drilled and filled with the strychnine that whips and cuts and slashes apart everything that's ever been and everything that would ever be as the saving grace of Christ is shattered where He was betrayed and turned over to the howls of demons gone mad in their classes and lectures of the unholy dregs of a crying dying ground saturated in blood and filth and vermin weeping and wailing into the nights that would carry on until the end of time.

Seeing how drunk I'd gotten, how much oblivion I'd harvested into my relapse, there was really no turning back.

But we didn't leave together. Terra told me that she was going to stick around the bar for a bit after she was *finished* doing whatever it was she was going to do. I couldn't imagine anything more she could have done to Stan. I didn't need to know, nor did I want to. Said she'd see me later that night, or maybe even the following, but directed me to drive straight home. Said our joy ride had just begun. Regardless of how drunk I was, she told me I'd get home just fine, that she wasn't finished with me by a long shot. That she'd already made sure of it, whatever that meant, and however she did it, who knows. Such drunkenness slobbers nothingness. All the embracement of feeling and being unstoppable on the liquid courage came rushing back to me in a force of absolute locomotive rush.

What else could I do, but as she directed and drive straight home?

I left The Hickory Stack amidst all the mayhem Terra had created. Something she seemed capable of doing effortlessly, but even more than that, she did so with a sadistic glee that you'd only see here and there on film. Oliver Stone's *Natural Born Killers*. Kubrick's *A Clockwork Orange*. Such images and such music that always accompanied such film were all wrapped up into a neat Terra Drake package of violence and ruin dressed as sexually demanding and intoxicating as any young boy's finest wet dream.

To my surprise, I managed quite easily getting back in the Ram, but I did thank God briefly for a touch start because only He knew – and He did – that I would have had issues with keys and ignition slots. Just before pushing it, Terra was suddenly right at my window, a look of sculpted insanity that I knew was her perpetual undermining. Clearly, she wanted to talk further before I left and before the police came. I took a deep breath and hit the automatic window button, watching the window move into its cradle a little too slowly, almost in a trance, all the while looking into Terra's eyes from my peripheral. Then directly into her deep lavender gaze.

"Just a few things before I forget. Wow, what a night, right, Stevie? Not the best for one Stanley Smitts, though, that's for certain. Listen, shit's about to get a lot more real than it already has, so there are some things I need you to do. Want you to do, actually."

I took in a deep whiff of her alcohol breath. It wasn't offensive as so many are when drunk and sloppy. No, hers was that continued sexual intoxication that no kind of liquor could hide or mask. "I thought you were coming over as soon as you could." When I'd heard it out loud, it sounded more absurd than I realized. How was she going to come over later with the police on their way? After she'd beaten my next-door neighbor to death? Or was he actually dead? Didn't matter. I was wiped out and getting more that way by the moment so all I could do was continue moving with it.

"You don't worry about that, Stevie. I'll be along when everything back inside is all nice and tidy, but I can assure you, you need not worry about me. Now here's what I want. First off, be careful. You sure as cock dingle don't need a pulling over. Second, there's a county fair around this area tomorrow that I need you to attend, not in this actual town, but down the canyons—"

"So...you're not coming back to my place tonight."

"No. I thought that was a given. Christ Jesus but I have to *spell* things for you. Can I *not* have to do that so much, please?"

I nodded in agreement, not wanting to press her.

"There's a fair in that town tomorrow, Odella. Kind of a mixture of arts, crafts, even jobs, I've heard, strange as that sounds, but nothing's so strange any longer, right Stevie? Octoberfest environment that's more than just a festival, but a cacophony of booths and activities that surround and highlight the Season. You know about it?"

"Sure. It's a regular deal in this state, lot of fairs around, Why?"

"I want to meet you there. Think it'll be the ideal stint."

None of this was making any sense, so I stupidly pressed her. "How are you getting there? How are you even getting away from here and all the fuck that's happened?"

"With what's happened here and all you've seen, let me fire back at you that *why* don't you see that's not a problem or issue for someone like me?"

"Okay, okay, whatever." I saw the faint lights grow larger and brighter from the local police cars, I was sure, racing in fury to reach the spectacle that had become The Hickory Stack Bar and Grill.

"Listen up and listen closely. Meet me at that fair tomorrow."

"You have a booth or something there?"

"Holy Christ," she hissed again, then reached inside the Ram's cab, grabbed me by the back of my neck, pulling my head inches from her face. "I've still much to show you, much for you to still learn, Steven Paul. I'm going to turn you. You think you've turned now, but I've just started. I've already turned this town more than you know, but you'll soon see, and more than just this town. The Season is here, the Season of all His anguish that once was, that will soon turn to a raging and hateful lyric with no consequence. No remorse. All will be exposed and highlighted for what it truly is—"

"I don't know what the fuck you're talking about."

"You *will*. And what have I said about interruption?" she screamed.

I couldn't believe she was actually thinking about me interrupting her, of all things, of all places, of all circumstances, but was beginning to know that her ways of being particular, as well as peculiar, were as important to her as anything else. Maybe more so.

"Get home safely and meet me at the fair. And get a fucking haircut before I see you."

With that, she released my neck, then leaned her lips into me deeply, licking me so abrasively it felt like a serpent's tongue had laced itself around my throat, razing across it, leaving my skin feeling violently scorched. I slapped my neck in severe pain, feeling my skin so hot it could have been lit coals. I tried to rub out the pain quickly as she then blew me a kiss then ever so gracefully strolled back to The Hickory Stack Bar and Grill as if nothing at all had been going on, to carry on in her ways that I'd wished I'd never seen.

Whatever further hell she was going to reign in was no longer my concern. With the skin on my neck now blistering, it was the further hell she'd have for me that then tormented my every thought, even though while she was doing it, and would do it, didn't matter a smidgen. I was hers, and she knew it better than I did.

***

I fired up the Ram with Ministry's *New World Order* blasting me across the face with yet another bullet of anger from the night's frozen air that was lingering around the bar's bloodbath. I used to listen to it over and over back in college, during times of severe upset and distress. If there were ever such a time that was similar, it was certainly what I'd been going through with Terra Drake. The machine-gun metal of Al Jourgen's monster voice and relentless power chords created the perfect drive into the never-ending night. A song that always had pushed me emotionally into rapid paths of self-destruction, the manic pace and thunderous, endless chants and raves in the background screaming about a world where the president laid out his hollow vision to tunnel the world into dystopian worship.

I followed Terra's first command by backing out carefully from the bar's driveway and onto the main road that led back to my place and the small town of Duncan, driving single handedly as I kept pressure on my neck to relieve Terra's weird licking. It was instantly alarming how clear Terra's instructions were to me to not get pulled over as I put the Ram into Drive, leaving The Hickory Stack in my rearview mirror.

Yet I pressed down harder on the accelerator pedal than ever intended, when, once again as had been the case when driving to the bar with Terra by my side to go find Stan, the night seemed to burst open...burst open in reams and reams of shattered blasts of the crests of magma that oozed and poured and slushed and slashed around and through and under and over the massive truck tires where everything and anything molded from the lava turned to frightening shards of glasslike ice daggers that threatened the very night of souls that seemed to howl that would never stop howling and hissing and that the beggars of the world would hear in prophetic biblical visions of ghosts gone south to play for the winter where that was no longer the case for me as the knowing of Terra's agenda struck not just my chord but I was sure the chord of so many others, so countless others, where all tracks were covered except those tracks of the addict's arms that screamed out in blackened wasted dead crusted blood where it had once flowed into the lives of the hopeful, the lives of the promised, the lives where potential was endless and life blasted out across landscapes of purity and soothing iterations of joy but now had withered and fell prey to the demon Drake, the woman ghoul of a now harlot-infested earth, where roaming had ended of the proud buffalo, where the ends of time now shouted across a landscape, so close it fired rivets into any eyesight where I once had clarity, once adored and took for granted, but now would miss as it dashed itself into bloody pieces of misted horror nuggets that I was sure would never cease their destruction of all that was ever holy, all that was ever real, all that was ever truth, but now wondering if truth was ever defined more perfectly than when spilled from the mouth of Pontius Pilate when asking the Christ what it was, what it meant, and if it ever had any meaning other than just a word.

The whiskey had caned me.

I did all I could to stay focused on the road as it finally, in what I thought would never appear, led to the turn to my place as a welcome relief. I sighed too loudly but felt exhaustion settling into my marrow, wondering how drunk I was as I took the turn that would take me home, thanking God.

It was the absence of life as I drove down State Street, the only real street in all of Duncan, and one that had no stop light from my own home all the way to the freeway, which would take anyone completely out of Utah if needs be. State Street was more than just the pitch of night. It was as if the street itself had cast such a tunnel of emptiness, it was as if the entire town had gone to sleep right alongside Rumpelstiltskin. Only a few business lights remained on as I drove past the local grocery store, the store itself so closed up I wouldn't have been surprised had it been abandoned, never to have a single patron ever visit again to pick up last minute items like milk or bread or beer, by God. The Ace Hardware store and local Tractor Supply looked even darker, deeper, if that were possible. Still, I kept the Ram at the 30-mile-an-hour speed limit, knowing Duncan police were always on the prowl.

As I slowed down and approached the stop sign and intersection where I'd need to take a right on Martin Blvd, my street that led to my place just past the creek several miles down, I noticed the Duncan Craft Shoppe to my left, just before the turn, had its lights dimly lit in harvest reds that glowed outward onto the black pavement like dying embers, giving the patio ground a purple etched effect. There was a large portrait on a thick wood easel positioned directly in front of the store's main window. A portrait of a family is what it looked like, a family of four. A blue, multi-streamed laser highlighted the family members in an eerie, creepy effect one might see on photos taken in the late '70s at Sears or JCPenney's. The family looked strangely familiar, and the store itself, lit up as it was, was such an alarming vision in the frightening night I had to stop, put the Ram in Reverse, to get a better look. With not a soul in sight, and convinced no police were hiding anywhere, I knew backing up in the middle of street posed no threat to anyone no matter how drunk I was.

I backed up to where my driver's door was directly in front of the craft shop so I could get a clean view of the picture. I felt my heart thumping more like a small mallet than the four chambers that kept all the blood in my body flowing in alignment. My breathing shortened as I kept squinting my eyes for better adjustment. I was fairly certain the woman in the portrait was Terra, or at least someone who looked so much like her that whomever it was had to have known Terra and perhaps wanted to dress as her twin. I couldn't make out the children completely, but they looked shifted, tilted. The man of the family was easily a foot or more taller than the woman. He, too, looked way too familiar, but since I couldn't make him out, I needed a closer look, so I backed the Ram up and into the driveway that sat just to the West side of the shop.

The temperature felt close to zero as soon as I hopped down from the truck, shut the door and locked it for good measure, then walked around to the shop's front entrance, walking right in front of the portrait.

As cold as it was, I felt far colder as I studied it. I was trembling, and not just from the cold, as I saw the woman in the picture was indeed Terra Drake.

How? I grimaced. *How could she be in this picture?*

She wasn't wearing anything that I had seen her wear all throughout the night's events. Strangely, I found myself still wondering how in God's name, or *where* is the better question, she'd changed clothes the various times I'd seen. In the picture she was wearing an overly accentuated conservative dress that covered her entire chest to her neck. Nothing that resembled the sexual prowess she so loved to flash around in since I'd been with her. The neckline had a white lace design fitted around her neck so tightly it looked to cut into her skin. Terra's hair was in a bun, much like an older woman would wear just before getting her bi-weekly dye and treatment. She wore makeup that was homely and cheap, lipstick far too red, and far too thickly applied, more like she'd applied it over and over and over again, perhaps in a rage just before the photographer said "cheese." Her entire appearance seemed obscene in its very mockery of women. Her eye lashes were plastered in mascara, her cheeks powdered in a sickly peach that was overly accented by the portrait lights. She looked like she was in some wild trance, clearly not looking directly into the camera for the shot. But it was her. Make no mistake about that, it was Terra Drake in the picture. A picture that somehow had ended up as the Duncan Craft Shoppe's main selling item, of all the places on God's green earth.

I had to actually force my entire trembling body to the right as I continued studying the other family members when "Oh Come All Ye Faithful" suddenly began to play from the shop's outside speaker system. A Christmas carol before All Hollow's Eve. But that didn't shock me nearly as much as the jolt that my nervous system felt when looking at the children. Terra's right arm hung directly down as her left was draped around the two children, children who clearly had bizarre deformities with twisted grins that looked tormented in some way.

They were grotesquely bald. Eyes hollowed out and so concaved I couldn't tell if they had any color to them, just small tube tunnels of emptiness. Each child had cheeks so puffy and egg white I could see every tiny blue vein that look as if they had been crudely threaded into the flesh by a drunken seamstress. But it was their open smiles that I knew I'd never forget. Lips that were not cracked, but more slashed, were surely tortured from the children's teeth that were nothing more than rusted needles, the bottom and top rows embedded with only four or five needles that looked like they'd been used for decades to sew together rags and rotten denim. The children's heads were facing away from Terra, looking to their father who I then began to study, began to see in him what was so familiar that I needed an even closer look. I forced my paralyzed body a bit more to the right.

He had to have stood six-ten, maybe taller. His hair was cut sharp and blocked, his skin looking just as blocked, as if cut from a piece of thick oak. He had both his massive hands in front of his waist, right hand cupping the left, as if about to take a bow. He wore a suit of royal blue that was tattered, almost to ribbons. On his belt he wore a huge pistol, probably a Colt .45. Trousers just as tattered and matching the royal blue of his jacket. He had eyes that looked alive with rage and bright insanity, glowingly hued in a lime green I'd never seen. The man's smile presented enormous teeth that looked more like crumbling dice that had no markings, each blocked tooth hanging from its roof where I could see the roots barely holding each tooth in a ragged place. He wore no tie, but instead a lassoed necklace with a silvery pendant that dangled just past the third button or so on his crimson shirt. That same pendant I knew Terra was wearing in the bar just before she turned to knock all hell out of Stanley, the pendant of the dreaded hooded thing I'd seen lumber across Stan's yard. Yet I could have sworn what had been in the yard, or who, had also worn a gun and belt.

I was so frozen in terror, it was difficult to feel my heart beating. My head felt like it was swelling from some unseen hands pressing into the sides of my temples with the middle knuckles, suspended in a freak animation trick.

Still, I backed away from the portrait with such a heightened awe that it slightly overcame my terror in that I was indeed able to move away, though I realized the fear had begun to take me over in a shock that was more and more taxing my body to exhaustion. All along, insanely enough, I was also trying to follow along to the Christmas carol, but that song, too, took on something that I couldn't quite make out until I started whisper-singing along. "Sing choirs of angels, sing in exultation, sing all ye citizens of heaven above, glory to God, come let us adore him, Christ the Lord." But the song wasn't singing those lyrics. It wasn't singing angels or exultation, or Christ the Lord. It was chanting other words to the same melody, other words that soon became clearly the singing of choirs of hellions...singing in exhilaration...citizens of heaven below...not above...below. And it wasn't Christ the Lord the song kept ringing, it was Cain the Lord. Cain the Lord to come adore and behold. The song grew louder, more profound in its new awful lyrics that made no sense, that spewed out more and more as the singer's voice deepened to knuckled and throaty tones of derangement.

I continued to shuffle away as best I could, when, turning to get to my truck as fast as possible, I saw a huge figure that had to be standing right next to The Ram but was then walking away in impossibly long, animated strides. I was sure the figure wore some kind of tattered suit and had strapped to its side a hand cannon cradled in a thick leather holster. I couldn't make out its head, nor did I care to as I shouted, "Fuck are you doing by my truck?" Didn't matter how big the son of a bitch was, or who he was. Even if he was the freak in the picture, somehow part of Terra's family, or what gun he had, or *it* had, for that matter, I was professionally trained in all acts of fighting, plus the benefit of alcohol drenched veins that I knew would assist in all acts of stupid bravery.

The figure stopped so quickly it looked like it ran square into some invisible wall, then turned to me. Instantly I knew he was the man in the portrait, yet half his head was also that of the hooded darkness I'd seen in Stan's yard. Half his face was that same scarred and wooded blackness I'd seen so clearly, the other half the oak blocked face of the man in the portrait. He had no feet that I could see as his tattered pants hung to the ground several inches longer to cover what could have been feet or boots or whatever.

"That's my song that's playing. I suggest you keep listening. And my time with you isn't here yet. Soon enough, but until then, you follow my harlot. Goodnight." The figure in the tattered suit, six shooter and all, had shouted at me in such a blast of a voice it was more like a sonic boom. Surely, all of Duncan had to have heard it as I actually put both hands to my ears to soothe the sharp cramp that was thumping around the insides of my ear canals. I even doubled over as if someone slugged me in the sternum, but all the while keeping my focus on the figure. Or lack of because just as soon as I had seen it shifting away from my truck, it had now vanished. Or *he* had vanished.

Whoever he was.

***

Once inside the Ram, in a ruffled and hurried mess, I found myself thanking God once *more* for a push button ignition, so trembling were my hands that this time, even pushing it was a struggle. I had to get home immediately to hit the bottle hard enough to pass out. "It's the only way to be sure." I saw my breath hit the truck's window, instantly fogging it. I thought of Sigourney Weaver's Ripley in *Aliens* when she wanted to wipe out the alien beasts by nuking the site from orbit: *That that was the only way to be sure.* That's what I felt more booze would do to my memory of whatever the fuck I'd just seen in the parking lot of The Duncan Craft Shoppe: the portrait of Terra Drake's family and the hooded figure, from all the roots of all Salem's witch graves.

I was home in just a few minutes, as I'd floored the Ram all the way from the craft shop to my driveway. Once inside, there was no music that wailed from all corners of the house. No Nancy Sinatra boots, no Rob Zombie *Dragula.* But the house certainly had been lived in throughout the seemingly endless night. I could smell every movement she had made, every sultry word that crept from her lips as wickedly as her body had slipped around on the bed, and from the couch. I could smell the alcohol as if it was coming from the paint on the walls. Could smell all the senses that had invaded my home and turned my life back to chaos and ruin.

Instead of overthinking the whole weird affair, but still deeply shaken from the night with Terra and the living fright night of the craft shop, I did exactly what I'd planned to do. I drank hard from the bottle of Crown until spitting it back up all over the kitchen counter, stumbled my way to the couch because there was no way I was going to the master bedroom alone again.

I then sank into an oblivion.

It was an oblivion that spun not around, but deep down into the crevices of a landing page where all I could see were the blurs and blotches and wailing pathos of the ancient philosophers ranting on and on about the nothingness of man. No matter how deep the movements of my drenched mind, I somehow knew my body couldn't move a single muscle or ligament in any direction.

I entered a smooth concourse of polished cement, almost ceramic in its finish, that led into a tunneled cave, all surrounded walls painted in this same ceramic finish. It was designed in such a way where sound was so crisp in its basses and trebles that it was nothing less than psychedelic in nature, but supremely opulent in all its presentation. I heard again Terra's lecture to Stan about Joaquin Phoenix's Lecture of the Pigs to the Church of the Elite on stage at the Oscars ballroom. I heard her far more vividly and clearly than when she actually railed-on to Stan, but could not see her. I looked for her with my editor's eyes but found not a trace, and then heard, too, the incessant sound of my father's voice telling me his own pig story. Here I was, trapped in a ceramic tunnel cave, hearing the stories of the pigs from Terra and my dad, unable to stop it as my dad's voice circled around the cave walls, telling me that one day while he was at his farm property, getting ready for the day in one of the trailers on his land, he kept hearing a knocking on the door. He said he had called out several times to whomever was at the door to just come on in, do whatever it was that was needed. But the knocking continued on and on, my dad continued to shout out to just come inside, *for God's sake.* Finally, when he'd had enough of the knocking, in frustration he went to the door, opened it in anger, and found at the foot of the door a pig standing there. A pig of all things. In my own frustration and dismay of the story I asked him why he was telling me such a thing. What was the purpose of such a story? He said to me, I guess there is no purpose. I guess I just had this crazy thing happen, this strange thing I thought was actually a little terrifying and wanted to share it and get your thoughts on what the hell it was all about and how do you think such a thing happened, *for God sake?* I remembered thinking there was no reason, that it was the strangest thing I'd ever heard, and quite grotesque to be honest. Then he said to me that maybe that's the reason. That things out of absolutely nowhere sometimes happen just to see what you'll do, what kind of reaction you'll have, and how you can handle such a thing and keep your wits about you, even when it comes in the form of a pig knocking on your door to see who's home. Back then to Terra, my oblivion continued when I saw her transform into Phoenix on stage who then screamed in a warlike cry that it is the pigs we must worship. We must worship the pigs, for it is we who are the pigs and need to be gobbled up. So fast was my awakening in such a fury of anguish I screamed out loud, "Pigs! Pigs! Fucking pigs!" and fell off the couch onto the floor, trying with desperation to get it together.

I struggled to reach the bathroom, splashed cold water all over my face and hair and body, then quickly decided to take a shower in water just as cold, staying in as long as I could handle it. After I'd dressed and groomed, throwing on a thick hoodie and jeans with slip-on boots, what I thought was at least presentable, I finally looked at my phone and noticed it was getting way too close to evening again, yet still told myself that I'd get my haircut as Terra had asked. Directed, actually, but I didn't care. I'd gone along with her so far, so a haircut seemed the sanest thing that she'd actually requested since seeing her slither around on my bed.

There were only a few places in Duncan to get a haircut, and both of them were just a few blocks from the craft shop, so as much as I wanted to avoid seeing it again, that wasn't possible. It also wasn't possible to avoid hiding my shaken nerves, even though I'd slammed a few shots down before leaving, for Tasha Banks and Danielle Childs, owners of Beauty Us, the place I'd been getting my hair cut since Anna had left me. Didn't matter that I'd shot down the Crown on the way, these ladies knew me well enough to know there was nothing right about any part of me the moment I walked in.

There was also nothing right about them.

Having gone there as long as I had been, I no longer needed to make an appointment, not that they'd ever been busy enough to really require one anyway. Still, walking in and just having Tasha or Danielle take me off the cuff was one of those small-town treasures big cities would, nor could, ever offer. Another one of those treasures was how immaculately tidy their place always was, how fresh it always smelled, how joyful they always seemed, that it was a place always filled with a sense of ease and relaxation.

This time things were different.

The moment I stepped in through the front glass door, as it shut behind me, locking me in, that time I really *did* feel locked in as a stench inside the place was overwhelmingly of rotted meat, or even fish, a stench that plugged my lungs. I coughed a few times to catch my breath as both Tasha and Danielle came out from the back curtains where they had many of their supplies.

"Well, well, well, if it isn't Mister Steven Paul the big city traveler," Tasha yelped out in a cackle that was completely out of her character. "I see you didn't bother making an appointment...*again*, but go ahead and sit yourself right down where you normally plant yourself. Your favorite seat, I know it is, and by God I have to say it should be good to see you, Steve, but I'd be lying my ass off if you want to know the truth." At that, Danielle burst out in a laugh that was borderline hysterical.

I looked at them both, back and forth, back and forth, quickly enough to try and figure out what was going on before Danielle stopped in mid laughter and belted out, "Sit the fuck down, Steve. Didn't you hear her? Let's get on with this."

I'd never heard either of the ladies so much as ever say damn, or hell, or even heckfire, and now the senior partner of the joint was dropping f-bombs in their place of business that smelled as if it hadn't been cleaned in a decade. Glad the Crown shots had hit me quickly enough to where I could deal with it, knowing there wasn't another choice, and that I'd gone along with every other goddamn thing since watching Stan drive off with his mouth ruined and trashed, to Terra probably killing him, dealing with my two hair stylists who were a bit off didn't seem such a stretch.

Except...they were way off.

I sat down in Tasha's stylist chair where she always cut my hair, looked into the mirror in front of me to look myself over as I'd always done when getting a haircut, checking out the length and thinking about how much she should take off, and so on. Tasha was behind me as always, looking me over as much as I'd always looked myself over, and as I looked into her eyes through the mirror I could tell...or at least feel that she was probably going through something much like Stan had perhaps gone through at the start of his demise. She looked as gaunt as I'd ever seen anyone, more pale, more sickly. And I immediately knew she was far more than Covid sick. In my peripheral mirror-vision I saw that Danielle was also going through something similar because she looked the same in her own deterioration.

I looked back to Tasha. "What's been going on around here, because I can see something's been going on. You okay,

Tasha?" I started to understand why Terra had told me to get my haircut. It was making more and more sense in a world she'd created that had no sense, no order, certainly no law.

"Am I okay? Am I okay? Danielle, what do you think? Am I okay?" Tasha said in acid sarcasm, looking over to her partner, then back to me. "You're asking me if I'm okay? Coming in here reeking of drink? You want to come at me that way in your condition? All these years telling us how important your sobriety is, and you come in here like a drunken clown just been tossed out of the carnival. *Boy* howdy do do do, does that stick a ripe pickle up my snatch. How about you, Danielle, that get to your puss, too?" Tasha shouted in a manic tremble.

Danielle looked at Tasha and burst out another laugh, stopping it just as freakishly. "It does indeed, sister. My God in heaven about this earth, it does indeed catch me right where it counts and does a zippy number, that's for crusty sake truth. Jesus lord have mercy on this entire town gone to hell, Steven, you are on a roll here and you just walked in. What else you got for us?"

I stopped looking at the women from the mirror and turned my chair toward them, keeping my hands on my lap but leaning in a bit, steadying myself enough for an explosive getaway if needed. Because it had begun to feel that way.

"Look...you're right. I've been drinking. A lot, to be honest. Christ I've not stopped for days now it seems. And it nearly has been. But I'm not too far gone yet. What's going on here with you two? You don't look well—"

"Whoaaaaaa, *Lordyyyy*. We don't look well. By god, Danielle, looks like this time he's hit the sweet spot, nice and dead on once again." Tasha moved the beauty shop into new territory. "I'll tell you what's wrong with us, Big City. We've been had. All of us. Been duped and cobby hoddled. We've been...been taken to the cleaners with no soap for sale. We have been kursnickered and dumped and seared with a hot iron and branded for a life that's never been worth living."

"Stop it, Tasha, Jesus what are you talking about?"

"No, you stop," she shouted to Danielle this time.

"You will stop and listen to what has to be said. She's right. We have been taken and duped. And now we see it's time to believe, now we see it's time for change. Now we see what we have all along missed so stupid and filthy dumb were our thoughts and actions."

I had to stand up at that point. I needed another drink or else I was going to knock the shit out of both of them, but those feelings of rage turned to ice when I saw hanging on the far wall of the salon a picture, or painting, couldn't make out the difference at that point, of the gunman in the parking lot by my truck, who was also in the craft shoppe window portrait. Only in this one he looked more manicured and tailored with a dignified professionalism that was of that same mockery that Terra was dressed in the craft shop family portrait.

"Where'd you get that picture?" I said with as much ice as I'd felt, which instantly shut them both up from their shouting. Both of them frowned so pronounced I thought the corners of their lips would split.

"You already know exactly what it is," Tasha said. "You already know exactly *who* it is, so the question really is 'why are you even asking about it?' You know what's going on. You've known what's going on—"

"That's right," Danielle screamed. "You have been *with her*. So why are you here? What are you doing here? Why are you asking about everything all of a sudden? You come here month after month and never want to talk, never want to chit-chat with us about *anything*. And now you want to come in here and be all free willy silly? And drunk to boot?"

"It's time for you to leave, Silly Will," Tasha shouted. "Time to scoot, scoot, scoot. That's our picture of Him. That's ours. He belongs to us and we belong to him, and surely you must know something about it all, now *leave*." This time she bared all her horrid teeth that were beginning to look as rotted as Stan's when I first saw him before he drove off into the grand unknown.

I ran out of the salon to my truck and saw it was nearly twilight. The continued endless shocks of what was happening to the little town of Duncan roared right on as Morrison's voice started ringing more than true. Instead of thinking on it too hard, off I drove to the Odella Fair, hoping I wasn't too late.

***

It was indeed dusk nestling in over the mountains, their faces casting long, deep shadows over the highways like giant sashay curtains that were cut perfectly to cover and blanket the freeway system. Temperatures had more than dropped enough to let me know that the deepness of the cold was just around the corner and here to stay, getting dressed in all its oranges, reds, burnt yellows. The dream of the pigs I'd awakened from earlier had also created a dirtiness within me that I hadn't quite shaken, and now was clearly shaken more so from the salon sisters who felt to have come right out from the woodwork of Satan's Den. Women I had known for years, women of innocence and authenticity now turned into whatever it was that was devouring the town.

And still more, there I was driving to the fair where Terra told me to meet her. I was driving south on the big interstate heading into the city, knowing the sun would indeed soon lose its grip on this part of the country, much like sanity had completely lost such a grip on everything around me. Of course, I'd continued hitting the bottle nice and deep to keep things going, not really caring if I'd get pulled over. Not really caring about anything of any consequence, so much so I'd kept the bottle in one of the truck's compartments.

Suddenly, way outside my peripheral, but just enough of a glimpse of clarity to eliminate any doubt, a strange looking bi-plane flew across the sky, low enough that I feared it'd crash directly into one of the overpasses and blow the entire freeway into concrete flakes.

Non-stop fucking insanity continued now in the form of unidentified shit.

Came out of nowhere as if things couldn't possibly get stranger than what had been going on since Nancy Sinatra's boots wailed throughout my living room, just before I found Terra on my bed. In my instant focus on the plane, I followed it just enough to not put myself into any danger as to crash into other cars, or worse, the side cement rails, and even worse, make me look completely drunk as a driver ready for yet another DUI event. In fact, I'm not even sure it was a plane. More like an object that looked somewhat like a double-layered cloud that was shaped like a plane.

Fuck was that, I murmured loud enough to hear my voice sound completely...confused, I would say. And slurred, of course. Though I couldn't follow it long enough to get an actual study, I still knew it was something I'd never seen. It seemed too massive to be allowed any airspace in this part of town, which also eliminated any fact that whatever it was, it was *not* a bi-plane. The longer I eyeballed it, the more crazed it looked. It cast no shadow. Seemed *far* too long for its size, like it was built from a neatly poured, single-piece of soap that lined the bottom of a hundred-foot ancient barge. Not sure if it had wings, but there were protrusions that seemed to stick out that were too short. There were sharp, obscenely bright lights that blinked like strobes, or high-priced sky lights. The edges of the soap-like object were cut in various hard angles that actually moved on their own. And why was it flying so low? Airport was fifty miles outside any distance to land such a thing. Was it going to descend into the nearest neighborhood and wipe out a few dozen homes? Whatever it was, I had to focus back on the road before killing someone.

The rest of the drive to the fair saw my mind strangely wandering back to the thoughts of the cold's too-soon arrival and the level of insanity that scorched the earth every hour of every day. Thinking that surely the faux pas news story that I was then listening to on the radio about a middle-aged man and his thirteen-year-old lover had to be one of the last straws that'd been weighing down every living soul who couldn't possibly wrap his or her mind around just how wrecked our society had become. Then thinking back to the weird plane, then back again to our rotting world, back to the sickened salon sisters, to the beginning of my relapse with Terra, to seeing Stan knocked right out of his chair and on to the wooden floor of The Hickory Stack. Back and forth and back and forth my mind bounced around like a halo pinball as I pulled into the massive parking lot area surrounding the Odella County Fair. All I could think about was finding Terra and what lay ahead.

I pulled into one of the many entrances, was greeted by

a money-taker who looked like one of those trolls who certainly once lived under the bridges, living there to collect coins from children who needed permission to pass, trolls whose only purpose in life was to scare the shit out of those same children so soundly they'd all need permanent psychotherapy. Long burnt orange beard that hadn't been managed in years. Grin that was clearly off and missing a single tooth. Teeth all together hadn't seen a dental cleaning in a decade. Of course, he was mostly bald, and what little hair he did have seemed slapped to the side of his head as if it'd been glued. One of his eyes was a far lighter tint than the other. Right eye, I think. His ragged suspenders held up awfully baggy jeans that hadn't been to the launderers in months.

When I lowered the Ram's window to ask about parking, he didn't seem to care anything at all about where I'd find a decent parking space. Didn't seem to have a clue there was a parking lot at all, to be honest.

And he stunk like rotted meat that made my eyes squint as I saw his name tag read *Burkenstock*. *That was his name?*

"Did you just see that thing fly over a minute ago?" he asked, never looking me in the eye, head gazing up and around as if trying to relocate the object. Or locate something. Hell if I knew, as he continued, voice sounding whistled and broken through his ruined mouth. "Christ all Jesus and holiness, whatever it was...sure looked like it came from everything lacking Christ and all, you follow me, fella? Danged bit looked somewhat like I'd imagined shit all boiled up and brewing from hell of some sorts, what do you say, fella? You believe in hell on earth and hellfire come here to bake us all to crispy shits and giggles? You believe that shit is here right now?"

He was looking so deeply into my eyes with such an intent of wild curiosity that I was certain the swelling veins on his forehead would burst free from all the sickness that seemed to be inside him.

"Think I saw it, yeah...Burkenstock, is it? That your name?" I tried not to sound completely unnerved by his appearance and smell. His sickly voice capped off this showcase of a carnival freak, a voice that was clogged in phlegm and charred walls that had to line his throat. "But right now can you please tell me where to park? I'm not seeing a lot of openings."

"Yeah, yeah. Burkenstock. It's Burkenstock all right. You vendoring here and such? What outfit you with? You with those portrait folk?" He eyeballed me all around as if his eyes were not only moved by his eye sockets, but also greased up with even thicker liquid than his throat phlegm.

"I'm not a vendor, just here to see things and check it all out. What do you mean by 'portrait folk?'"

"God mighty lord have mercy, check out what exactly? All them there inside that come on in to see the *goddamn* world begin its ending? That why you're here? Freakshow fanatic, are ya? Rape me silly, that's what you got on inside ya?"

Far more startled than what I thought, and continuing to thank God I'd been drinking, I told the troll that I just wanted to find a place to park and walk around, that I didn't want any trouble from him, of all people.

But I pressed him.

"Again, what do you mean by portrait folk? I've never heard such a thing or such a group of people."

"Portrait Folk. I think you goddamn do know what I say, by God. Shitheels who come in here with all these portraits of who they call Adramelech, by Christ. Adramelech. Adramelech. You'll soon come to know if you don't already and just here pulling my ying and yang. God lord on high, save us all, and maybe He will. Happen to know what building you're in...or what area your booth supposed to be in? Arena area? Horse track or trailers?" he asked, completely ignoring me about the vendor thing, and switching topics as if I truly wouldn't notice, then looking up, once again avoiding any eye contact.

"I'm not in a building, or have a booth or anything that way. I'm *not* a vendor! Didn't you hear me? I'm just wanting to park. Can you understand what I'm saying? And these portraits or whatever it is you're talking about, about this *Adramelech,* I haven't a clue what you're talking about. Is that okay with you, Fella?"

He looked right at me as if looking inside me to find something that wasn't there, or something that I surely didn't know was there, or that he knew that I'd *known* something, and seen far more than *just* something. He had the look of being able to see things he shouldn't see, and most certainly didn't want to see. Burkenstock, for all his twisted looks and foul smells, also had a deep melancholy about him, like an ancient sadness.

"That's funny. That's a good one. You a mean boy, are ya? You a cowboy? You kinda look like a cowboy, by God. Like you been around the block way too many rounds."

For a minute he reminded me of Brad Pitt in *Kalifornia,* where Pitt played the psycho all too perfectly.

Burkenstock continued looking into me, for whatever it was I didn't know. "Well...don't mean for squatty shit really where you're heading or what area or what not, you can see all over the place all kinds of parking areas."

"But I am *not* seeing any parking areas that are so open as you said." I had grown tired of his nonsense, no matter the slight sentiment I'd had about the troll. Had grown tired of just about everything, to be honest, and all that mattered then was a few more pulls on the bottle.

Burkenstock then looked at me as if not hearing anything I'd said, or not hearing anything at all. "But if you're vending with jobs and such, there's a lot over there by the arena building in the middle, yeah? That's the one by the job booths you just mentioned, and not a bad lot, mind you, since all the nut job booths are just as nearby as you'd love to wander through."

"Goddamn it. I never said anything about job booths, Burkenstock. I am *not* a vendor. Fuck it. Doesn't matter—"

"You didn't think that plane was whack? That thing in the sky?" He spoke meekly and mildly this time as if he'd been rebuked.

I paused for a moment as he asked the question, because looking at him when he said it, I could see that he was more than feeling rebuked for whatever reason, but also deeply puzzled. I then saw too suddenly that complete insanity was raging all around him like a cancerous worm slithering around and eating anything left inside his brain that was still able to determine what was and was not real. Like that object was the most bizarre event that he'd ever witnessed. And *that* part was probably true, because it was something I'd surely never seen. But the Burkenstock Troll had no idea that I'd seen Terra Drake and all that she had to offer, which was every bit as bizarre and more so. He didn't know that I'd seen a portrait of her and this creature figure, or what had just happened at my small town salon. Or maybe he did know. Maybe he knew a lot more about it all, all together. And seeing whatever it was in the sky was now the furthest thing from my own fading mind as watching this troll-like man before me was doing nothing more than reinforcing the fact that everything had simply changed overnight. Everything had been changing on a daily basis anyway, anywhere and everywhere over the past year, that much was certain. The world had gone to ruin, and I was beginning to believe it was Terra's doing, because what had been happening since I'd found her on my bed put all the past year to shame in an endless rearview mirror all around the halls of the ballroom where demons and clowns played dice together, betting everything on their wicked wicked farm.

So...it was suddenly important to show him some respect.

I let out a deep sigh. "I guess that's one way of seeing it, Burkenstock." I looked out and over all the lots in front of me, trying to pick out the one he'd just mentioned, or was at least referring to.

"Yeah...yeah, that's one way for sure. Looky here, free parking's over that way, so have a nice one. Gonna be one of the last days we have before everything turns to ice and gets nice and gone for sure, so enjoy." This time the insanity in his eyes blurred just a tad, looking achingly alone.

"All right, Try and do the same, Burkenstock." I drove off a little too fast, looking in my rearview mirror to see if he was watching me. I clearly heard Eddie Vedder's scraping voice screaming the song by the same title.

Parking was tight as always at such events, but the spot I found was good enough for an easy in, easy out. I walked up to the county fair booth where more money-takers awaited me to open my wallet. I thanked God they were not like Burkenstock. Couple of women buried in their phones absolutely clueless to any surrounding, standing behind a cheap plastic table where an even cheaper cash register sat under a small tarp. Open, of course. Bills flapping up and down barely secured under the metal holders, the ones that look like bent wire coat hangers. To the left was the fair's entrance where I could see a kaleidoscope of various fair events, booths, food stands, all surrounding the Odella Spurred Horse Arena, the fair's showcase of what had to consume the main attractions, and with everything that had been going on, I truly wondered what such attractions could have in store.

There was a black couple to the left of the ticket counter, off to the side of a large tarp that covered the ticket booths (there were a few of them) in the immediate area, engaged in what looked like some heavy shit. They were so out of place in the sea of entrenched Utah bleach, I actually wondered if they felt every living eye was set on them, trying to figure out why they decided to come out to the county fair in the first place. Why not stay home? I put myself in their place with Anna smack in the middle of a black church revival, two lonely pieces of white flesh popping out of slabs of black meat like a couple of raw boils ready to burst all over the large and lifeless concept of reality.

I watched them probably a little too long. They alarmingly became so entranced in their discussion it seemed fierce anger was brewing.

Maybe something a lot worse.

Something more frightful.

I had to peel my head away before turning to one of the white twits still ogling over her device as if she'd never seen such glorious magic in all her live-long fucking days. Didn't take much longer before I lost patience.

"Excuse me. Excuse me," I said, getting their instant attention with my last prompt. "I'm just wanting to pay here, but I didn't think this thing cost any money."

Both of them then looked at me as if I'd just said I'd been recently branded.

So, I said it again, more assertively. More rudely, in fact. "Can I *pay* here? And do you have a wi-fi, by chance? I need the wi-fi that you're using with your phones. And to pay to get into this fair."

They didn't change their looks, didn't seem to budge in any altered profile that would even consider answering the question. In fact, their gazes seemed to just doze away deeper into whatever phone addiction silently screamed at them from their palms.

"Never mind, I'll figure it out, and here, here's a ten. Keep the change, because I know I've got some coming, but you're clearly not able to figure much out." I sounded disgusted. Had I told them to fuck off and ram their phones up each other's asses their expressions would have remained just as oddly stoic and near dead as if I'd given them each a hundred and thanked them for their time.

Maybe it *was* what flew over in the sky that seemed to have such an effect on everyone I'd seen so far, and everything. Or maybe they'd seen Terra and taken her money. Or maybe the two had some kind of correlation with each other. Fact is, everything was getting me wound up. Didn't matter who or what it was, didn't matter how insignificant, I felt I was getting so near the end of my wits that any little irritation was certain to send me into a flying rage, so once again, I also felt the paradox for the bizarre gratitude I had for jumping head first into the bottle.

It was the arena that I wanted to see immediately

because that was the usual area for some decent snacks and a cold beer. The arena also had the special events like concerts or bull rides, and at that particular time, the program had listed some kind of auction was going on, though ambiguous as to what was being auctioned off.

But...it wasn't the first place I visited. No, not at all. It was the tent that claimed to contain The World's Largest Pig, Harmony. In a sudden rush of instant memory of my dream of the pigs and Terra's lecture to Stan on the subject, I had to see *that* before anything else.

I walked right up to a guy I thought to be the pig's owner, a man who looked to be in his late 60's, pure white hair and beard, both long, with a face of severely weathered and leathery skin. He was clearly in shape, probably five-nine or so, flat hard abs, giving me that insight every fighter had when sizing someone up who was clearly able to handle themselves.

"This your pig, this Harmony is it?"

He folded his arms and opened up, surprisingly friendly. "Youuuuuu bet it is, Partner In Crime. Had him for some five years or so. From China, he is. Fucker weighs in at a nice and neat ton, if you can imagine such a beast."

"No. I really can't, but I'd like to. Says here it's a dollar to see it."

"Youuuuuu bet it is, Partner In Crime. One buck O Roo to be exact, and I've got any kind of change you may need, cause you ain't gettin' in without payin'. No one sees the worship of the pig without payment first."

"What do you mean the *worship of the pig*? What does that mean?"

"I'll tell you what it means. I'll tell you..." He paused to rub his chin as if really thinking it over. "You see, you're here to see this pig because it's the first thing you wanted to do. But I don't think that's necessarily true, am I right on the nose there?"

"Why do you say that?"

"Because you're not the type to just wander on over here to see something like this. No sir, you've been going through some shit. Weighing so heavy all over your sleeves looks like that damn hoodie will fall right off you. God haven't we all lately, right?" He slapped his leg at his attempt at humor. "Nooooo, you're here for a reason. You're here out of curiosity for something far deeper than a massive piece of pork and bacon. You're here to witness the grandest spectacle of all, the vilest of *all* the seven deadliest. Greed...gluttony...filth...decay—"

"Filth and decay are not among the seven deadly sins." I'd said it with sarcasm, more from the alcohol than me.

"Oooooooo. Mister Philosophy are we? Mister Retort, eh? Christ on top of Jesus, neither did I say they were, but they're certainly *part* of it *all*, am I right on point there?"

"Look, here's my dollar. Can I just go in?" I'd said that in anger. "You just take my money, and that'll be the end of it. Deal?"

"Hooooooo wweeeeeee. Certainly, certainly, get on in there and see that pig. He's everything you could imagine and then some."

I was already halfway in the tent as Mr. Partner In Crime was still ranting on about absolutely nothing when the stench inside slammed into my lungs, just about causing me to puke up everything that had bottled up deep inside me, including every last drop of drink. When I turned the corner to where Harmony's pen was, I could see why. Harmony the Pig was the most massive beast I'd ever seen, as well as the most horrifying and repulsive. Had to be the size of a small car, its pig nose was lurched into the air with nostrils the size of Frisbees, with all kinds of gore hanging all in and out to where it had looked like it had been flung with violence and repetition. Pig looked like a living dinosaur. All across and gashed in its body were ragged slashes as if the beast had been in a war with swords or large knives or beasts even larger, gashes that were imbedded with maggots and messy insects. Inside the pen was not only piles of shit the size of flat basketballs, but mounds of torn flesh that were bloodied and shredded, flesh that was not only in the pen but all over the walls of the pen and even hanging from the corners of the massive tent as if several even larger beasts had been put through some impossible blender with their remains thrown all about recklessly and carelessly as to create a scene that looked most catastrophic and ruined.

I vomited immediately and continuously as I raced out of the tent, not caring what kind of mess I made on myself. Once outside, I saw Mr. Partner In Crime laughing so hard I knew he'd surely double over.

"Got yourself a real eyeful there, *Pard?*" he roared to me. "You get it now? You now in the *know?*"

I refused to get into it with him, as all I wanted to do was get to the nearest restroom and wash up as thoroughly as possible. I had no idea what had happened in that tent of gore, and at that point nothing mattered to even think it over or even call the police, which I knew had to happen immediately, unless they were in on it all. I just had to get clean as I bolted, still heaving all over myself, to the arena where an auction was underway.

***

Once inside the arena, I found the men's room close enough down one of the long hallways soon enough to where I actually felt a little relief, for whatever reason. I splashed water all over my face and neck, thanking God that Utah water was ice cold no matter what, no matter where. I splashed over and over and washed all the vomit out of my mouth and what had spewed on to my hoodie, looked into the mirror long and hard, trying to get as much composure as possible. Madness had surrounded me and was putting such a stranglehold on every facet and movement of my life that, for one, I was convinced there was no way that I could stop drinking, and two, that whatever had gone on with Terra Drake didn't have any plans to let up any time soon, and three, the entire fuck show that had become Duncan was not only related to Terra in some way, but also to the Adramelech person, or thing, or whatever he or it was, and that he or it was tied to the hooded figure I'd seen in Stan's yard, that it was also part of the picture newly hung in the salon. Both hair stylists that I'd known as friends for years who'd turned their souls over to the sickest of witchcraft also knew about it, and clearly relished in not just that, but every other goddamn thing that I was feeling as I was splashing and washing the vomit off of me in a frenzy. Maybe they hadn't turned over their souls at all, maybe their souls had been taken. Stolen. Or raped out of them. I wondered if they'd even heard wind of the object that flew across the sky. Wondered if they knew a lot more about everything, because I sure as hell didn't know anything other than the fog of chaos that I was fighting for every breath, much like I'm sure Stan had been fighting long before I'd seen him in his truck before driving off into the night that would soon kill him.

After I felt as clean as possible, my clothes far too wet

for how cold it was, I patted myself down and went out to the arena seating to check out the auction, maybe catch a little rest and consider where Terra could have been, or where she'd wanted to meet me because she sure has hell left it as ambiguous as everything else about her.

For a town the size of Odella, Utah, a population of a few hundred thousand...it was massive compared to Duncan. The Spurred Horse Arena was actually quite nice and spacious, with a seating of 6,500. Mostly used for rodeos, demolition derbies, and concerts, it was the perfect venue to showcase any county fair.

It was also the perfect place for an auction, even though what was being auctioned, I'd noticed again, wasn't advertised anywhere, though I was certain it could be pigs or cows. With the horror I'd seen with Harmony, I couldn't imagine the auctioneers doing anything pig related, but maybe Harmony's pen was nothing more than an anomaly that hadn't been dealt with, and the way my mind was deteriorating, the only way I could deal with it was to get some perspective of other fair events, so the arena seemed the perfect place to start.

I walked around a bit on the top level of the two-level building, walked around and looked down on the arena floor as the lead auctioneer walked out onto a platform stage down a wooden ramp that led right to the stage's center area. Though on the upper level, the arena was designed in such a way that any visitor could see everything on the floor with remarkable clarity. He was outlandishly tall, and the moment he started speaking into the podium microphone, his booming voice froze me so stiff I knew I needed to head back to the bathroom for more cold water. But my body wouldn't allow it. I recognized the voice, sat down on the very next seat in front of where I was walking, and focused on who the hell he was. It was the same voice as the figure who spoke to me the night at the craft shop. But how could that be? How could he be here? Why was he here, and was it really him or was I just filled with so much distress I was imagining it, or was I so tired and drunk as to have brought on hallucinations?

As he continued speaking, I leaned forward in my seat close enough to rest my hands on the backside of the seat in front of me since no one was sitting there, resting my head on the backs of my hands, squinting my eyes to get as much detail as possible. His voice was unmistakable, creating within me such a feeling of anxiety and dread every muscle in me locked around every bone.

Then he really turned things up and roared to life like a goddamn monster with a voice ancient and rusted.

"It is with the grandest of pleasure, townsfolk of Odella, the grandest of such rare opportunity, that I come here to this once-in-a-lifetime auction to give you what your great great great relatives must have cherished. You have come here to own another life, another soul. It is now time to do just that. Bring out the first participant." He turned his body toward the back of the stage area, right arm stretched out before him as if to present something spectacular, yet what was brought out was a young girl chained at the wrists and ankles. She was dressed in a ragged shawl that looked more like a cloth sack used for bulk potatoes. To each side of her was a robed man, each one holding the chained girl's arms, leading her to the front of the stage. She'd clearly been tortured and broken, and shuffled along with the robed men without so much as a hair's resistance. I stared at her with an intensity that caused an instant migraine but could not keep my eyes off how disturbing and shockingly awful was the scene. It was as if I'd been shot with succinylcholine and forced to watch.

When she was finally brought to the auctioneer, he leaned down to her head and brushed her hair back, then slapped her across the face so violently I thought it would have killed her. To further the horror, the audience attendees on the floor all shouted out in cheers as if the auctioneer had just thrown a touchdown instead of striking a child slave in chains. Many in the arena seating also cheered on until the auctioneer prompted silence by lowering his hands, palms parallel to the floor. He then moved her directly beside him and spoke with methodical assertive force into the podium microphone.

"Welcome to The Auction of Life. I'm your head auctioneer, Adrian Cain. I've been doing this a long long time in places long long ago, so rest assured I'll take care of all that's needed. As well as all that you need. I am here to whip you into a frenzy, here to divide you so decisively that all that is wrong will be exactly right. As right as rain, dear ones. The truth, by Cain. Now what we have here in this little specimen is the true definition of ripe. This one is untouched by anything morally foul. A chance to have her is a chance for more freedom. For are these not the times that have tried each of our very souls to the bloody marrow? Are we not in it but for *good*? You have come here for redemption, come here for a reckoning, and I'm here to give it. For I am the one responsible for Afghanistan. I am one the responsible for North Korea and China. For California, by Cain. I was the beholden cup of The Crusades, of the fall of Rome. And it is now here, of all places, where it is your privilege to find it all for your own souls."

With that, the arena floor patrons and most of those in

the seats once again cheered as if they were in the middle of a life-or-death 4th quarter game. Adrian Cain raised both his hands high into the air as suddenly, from all corners of the arena's ceiling, dark blue spotlights beamed down and onto the auctioneer, striking and lighting him up in a wild and ballistic aura. I couldn't peel my eyes away no matter the terror that had pummeled the alcohol out of me. With the beaming lights still on his entire enormous frame, once again he lowered his hands to quiet the crowd.

"Now, let's get on with the show just so you know how serious I am. But first, though...a story of scripture, if you will. One that my harlot once told one of her victims down in Texas right before she raped him to death." He paused and looked down to the girl, obscenely towering over her. Remarkably, I could see she looked right back up to him without so much as a flinch. He seemed to have recognized her courage in a way that looked to have startled him a tad, before facing the audience again, this time lowering his voice to a simmering howl.

"*A naught person, a wicked man, walketh with a forward mouth. He winketh with his eyes, he speaketh with his feet, he teacheth with his fingers; forwardness is in his heart, he deviseth mischief continually; he soweth discord. Therefore shall his calamity come suddenly; suddenly shall he be broken without remedy. These six things doth the Lord hate; yea, seven are an abomination unto him: a proud look, a lying tongue, and hands that shed innocent blood, a heart that deviseth wicked imaginations, feet that be swift in running mischief, a false witness that shaketh lies, and he that soweth discord among brethren. My son, keep thy father's commandments and forsake not the law of thy mother: Bind them continually upon thine heart, and tie them about thy neck. When thou goest, it shall lead thee; when thou sleepest, it shall keep thee; and when thou wakest, it shall talk with thee. For the commandment is a lamp; and the law is light; and reproofs of instruction are the way of life; to keep thee from the evil woman; from the flattery of the tongue of a strange woman. Lust not after her beauty in thine heart; let her not take thee with her eyelids."*

"I now set the opening bid at three hundred dollars."

As soon as he said it there was a rapid fire of men and women raising hands that held their auction paddles and numbers, screaming out figures that increased in a fury of desperation to be heard and called upon. I used every muscle within me to stand up and say something. To scream something. To do something, when, just as my body reluctantly began moving, I felt a hand on my shoulder as if to keep me seated. It was Burkenstock.

"Ain't this event a kicker? My god they can put on a show. Never seen anything like this one, have yee? Lord howdy gawd in heaven, you looked like you were about to have an aneurism burst right open and kill you dead in your fetching seat."

I stood up anyway, removing the troll's hand. Looking into his eyes, I saw them ravaged in madness, but there was also that deep, sick loneliness wedged deep inside somewhere that I'd noticed before, so deep no one, not even God, would ever be able to pull it out.

"You're telling me this is all a show? Is that what the fuck this is?"

"You didn't think it was real, did ya? That they's selling off a child slave down there? Is that what you actually thought? Jesus H Christ."

"Yeah. Christ's clearly gone and never coming back," I shouted at him and knocked his hand off my shoulder. "And what's going on down there ain't fake. I could never drink enough to be that blind, so you stay here for the *show*, as you say, you little fucker, but I'm out. I'm finding the police this very—"

"Yes you are out. Now leave this place and never come back. Get out of here before you're the one who's sold next. Think you're impervious to slavery? Now go, you crooner cod." Burkenstock screamed at me with such vehemence and force I thought it would be the last time he'd ever have enough strength to ever speak again.

I raced out of the arena and toward the nearest vendor hall that was probably no more than a hundred feet away, where, of all things, I once again saw the black couple who'd been arguing near the ticket counter when I first arrived.

Christ how long have they been at it?

They were still so trenched together in their talk, I had this shocking thought they'd soon attack each other like wolves or something far fierce. Werewolves? Maybe. Wouldn't have surprised me in the least. When they had then caught me staring, it seemed they even sensed I'd noticed they were actually altering in their appearance so much so they looked like they were about to devour each other. About to tear each other to shreds.

I broke eye contact as fast as my eye muscles allowed, looked down at my own phone to see if I'd have any connection strong enough to call the police as I moved toward the larger metal doors to the vendor hall nearest me, wondering with certain clarity why I'd ever agreed to come to the fair, of all places, to find Terra.

I entered a building that was overwhelmingly quiet. Compared to all the chaos and hellfire of Adrian Cain selling the child in chains as he roared on like a demon prophet who'd come to end the world once and for all, the sound of silence in the vendor hall was almost as deafening. Suddenly, I felt my mind and body move into a loop or a tunnel or even a magician's hall of wax, and the urgency to call the police about the child slave auction started to dissipate in a cloud of laughing gas. All up and down were dozens and dozens of trade show booths with sound so muffled it was like walking on fresh snow during a late fall night just before the dashes of winter's shadows became a perpetual slow melt.

At the same time, I was also terrifyingly aware that I was being watched by every soul in the building. Every eye from every shallow head of every vendor bored directly into my own with such a beading ferocity that, juxtaposed with the tunneling quiet effect, I felt like my insides were imploding.

Christ. Who were they? Why were they here?

It made no sense.

Why was I here?

Clearly this was some cosmic mistake meant for me to uncover and report back to Terra that I wasn't supposed to be there. Not a single booth had any connection or relation to the next one. GE was right next to the local swimming pool builder. Gourmet Coffee from Paris was next to Custom Sewer Drains. Fine China sat next to a local butcher smacking raw meat hard enough to blast fine mists of fresh blood as if shot from an aerosol can.

A migraine in both my eyes then began to thump against the sides of my temples as I walked past each booth. I knew everyone continued to stare at me hard enough they'd surely must have seen the shadows of my bones.

I finally stopped at a booth located at the far corner, the farthest in fact, of the large building hall. It was a local college booth that was sandwiched between the Odella Library and one of Odella's local churches. When stopping, once again I couldn't help but think of Ripley, this time in the third *Alien* film, exhausted and hopeless when knowing she and her ragtag team of murderers and rapists were shit out of luck to ever receive aid to kill the creature.

I looked to the library vendor who was about thirty, maybe thirty-five. Red hair. Red blouse. Red lipstick that was smeared. Too smeared. Mascara looked wet and cheap. I felt a little sick.

"Excuse me. By chance would you know if there's a wi-fi here and password? I'm not getting any service, and I mean none."

Her head jerked quickly enough that I thought some of her wet mascara would flick onto my face. A jerk that seemed to have started and stopped so abruptly it could have snapped something in her neck. Far too similar to Terra's own jerking movements when she looked back and forth. The redhead looked at me with her head cocked and contorted to one side. "I really don't, to tell you the flat out truth of the matter. I really have no idea what it is or even where to get that information. To be perfectly frank with you, I don't even know why you'd ask. We're in a vendor hall marketing our products. We're here doing work and showing work. We're here trying to promote our work, much like you should be doing, don't you think? I mean you're being paid to be here, am I right? Do you really think you should be surfing the net for kiddy porn? Walking around here talking to women like me of all things and places?"

I was certain that I'd not heard a word she'd just said, that she was clearly out of her mind just like Burkenstock, just like Mr. Partner In Crime, and most certainly exactly like Adrian Cain. I paused long enough to show more than just confusion, looking all over her face to study every expression she would want to conceal after making such an abrasive statement sound so casual.

"What did you just say to me?" I asked, instantly scared, but trying not to give her a moment of any leniency. "What are you *talking* about, lady? I'm not a vendor here. I was just trying to get the wi-fi password, and for some reason you seemed the one to have that answer. But I have no idea what the hell you just said about kiddie porn—"

"The city corn," she shouted at me. "I was asking you why you'd want to waste your time browsing about our city corn here at the fair when you should be working like the rest of us. What did you think I said, silly?" She cocked her head even more to the side, grinning forcefully enough to hide her smeared red lipstick. She looked like an Annie doll that had just been slapped, or violently shaken.

"Look. I'm not vending here. And what the hell are you even saying? City corn? You're the library, for Christ sake, and I thought you said something else entirely." I turned away from her ever so slowly, walking away just as slowly. I knew her eyes remained laser-etched on my backside as I turned toward one of the church-going vendors. I could tell he'd overheard the conversation when I asked him about the wi-fi info.

He was full-dressed. Coat, tie, white shirt, manicured through and through. "Hmmm, nope. We've been trying to find it since we got here a few hours ago. Supposedly there's a vendor hall manager or something who comes by every so often to hand out meal tickets, but we've not seen her, if indeed she is a her. Could be an *it*, for all I know. Maybe *it* has it. Maybe she's out at the fair arena not really giving a shit, one way or the other."

It was just about impossible to not laugh, hearing such a

comment come from such a saint, a comment that was as out of place as the troll, the fighting black couple, the lady in red next to him, the object in the sky, and every other goddamn thing that had happened with Stan, Terra, The Hickory Stack. All of it. All of it now seemed to have blended into a concoction that I began to feel was created just for me. Special cocktail from the universe, or God Himself, served up in honor of slipping back into the old world of alcohol annihilation and world fuckary.

"I see. Well, I'm gonna take a walk around and see what I can find. I'll be sure to let you know if I find anything that could help you out here in your booth of Christianity." I'd said it calmly to the saintly man, who also wore a name tag as obvious as the psycho's lipstick next to me who asked about surfing kiddy porn sites.

I walked down another one of the vendor hall alleyways to see what kind of out-of-place-nutshow I'd see next, and then I decided to head out, back to the fairgrounds when another booth vendor stopped me and asked me if I'd like to test one of his massage chairs. He was dressed like a magician, cape and all. Oddly, I actually didn't mind listening to him. If he'd come here dressed up to the nines, I could at least give him a moment, and with what I'd seen so far, he actually looked the most sane.

Still hadn't found Terra, but this would do just fine. At least it'd be a chance to catch a moment's rest.

"You're promoting massage chairs at this event?" I asked the magician-vendor. He stood a good four inches taller than I, skin so pale it looked painted. In fact, was it painted? Some part of his act? The inside of his cape was a deep maroon. He wore black laced sandals where the laces looked more like thick worms than leather.

As he bowed, he held out his hand. "Name's Terrence. You'll not get a better massage by any world class masseuse. Care to try it out?"

I shook his hand. "Sure, why not. Nothing better to do, that's for sure." His grip was so strong I could sense he'd crush my hand like a pack of aged cigarettes, my own grip, one of a boxer's and never one to feel any give, in fact gave into his with such submission I knew then I faced yet one more villain far above my pay level.

"Have a seat, but let me tell you about it first." Thankfully, he released my hand and guided me to a large Lazy Boy that looked quite a bit larger than what I'd expected. The color was a rich velvety black. What was most odd were all the baseball-sized divots that were somehow part of the design, molded into the chair's material.

"What are those?" I asked with genuine concern.

"Please. Have a seat. I'll give you the full presentation."

With that, I moved into the chair as easily as possible without trying to look clumsy enough to fall down. Once seated, I was instantly aware of how every divot seemed to also have some kind of pressure point that dug into every inch of my backside.

"It'll feel a bit uncomfortable at first, but that's perfectly normal. The idea is to let your body completely relax as the pressure points, pressure prods actually, are turned on and begin to memorize the contours of your body. Machine in this thing has an AI engine and literally learns your body's physiology. With every breath, these prods will find the give and take of your natural muscle movement, applying pressure at every point. Won't take long until your entire body is literally plugged with sensations to massage not only every muscle, but every movement. In a very literal sense. Like I said, it'll be a little uncomfortable. Might even feel a little terrifying, to be honest. At least that's what some have told me."

I looked up at him with a hard stare. "Why would a massage chair be terrifying in *any* way? Don't you think that'd make a lousy selling point?"

He smiled at me way too long, a smile that seemed to actually chip away some of the white off his face.

"Actually, you'd be surprised at what a fine selling point such a comment makes. You see, Steve, this chair has a way of creating a physical atmosphere that's similar to a pleasantly mild LSD trip. It opens up the body in such ways that emotions actually trigger, or create...well, visuals if you will. You ever had an acid trip?"

I had, but had never been asked about one by a total stranger selling any goods, much less a piece of furniture, and it was a long time ago. It was a rattling question, but not like the rattle of him saying my name. *Did I give it to him?* I was certain that my teeth were grinding themselves to pieces, knowing I'd need another drink more sooner than later. I wanted to press on and not spend any more time questioning him. "Listen...Terrence, is it? This looks like it's gonna take more than a minute. I think I'll—"

"Relax," he interrupted. "You just told me you had nothing better to do, right?"

"Yeah, I did, but—"

"There's nothing to worry about." He snapped his fingers and the chair came to life.

I wasn't just terrified. I wanted to scream, so sudden was the immediate feeling of the chair and all its protrusions. In fact, I may have screamed, because I had to. The prods, or whatever he'd called them, didn't just press into my muscles, they *drilled* into them, as if to purposely batter and bruise, even rape. The prods drilled into me with such ferocious speed I imagined this was what it had to feel like being shot by a machinegun, only the bullets were not meant to penetrate, just hit like sharp, endless rubber slugs to pound someone to death. I couldn't speak. Every effort to find any wind was mercilessly knocked out of the very pores of my skin. My jaw and teeth rattled and smashed around with such violence I was certain they'd break apart like Lego pieces.

"Hold on," Terrence yelled. "Just hold on to the sides. Let your body give in to the pressure. Give in to the pressure. It's unnatural movement, but your body will adapt. It has to adapt because your mind is telling it to. Demanding it to learn what's going on so your body doesn't shatter to pieces. Feels kinda like that doesn't it, friend? Feels like you're being pummeled into some kind of oblivion. But you just hold on there, champ, doing just fine. Goddamn proud of you, most don't last but a few seconds before begging to jump right off the thing. Not that you *can* jump off, right? Bitch has you cemented in like a monster, am I right? Give it a minute, though. Just give it a minute and let it all go. Let everything go, dear boy."

After a few moments of his roaring on that felt like a week, I knew there was no way I could continue. I was being physically destroyed. Somewhere, I'd once read that when drowning, the body goes through fierce and intensely agonizing pain, violent thrusts and jolts where the lungs imploded with gushing water bursts. This had to be what was being administered to me by this chair, this monstrous, torturous, billiard wrack of certain doom. At the cellular level every fiber of my being was now making a final attempt to find some hint of oxygen's magic. I knew every bone would soon explode apart, not just break. Surely my ribs had gouged to pieces my lung tissue. My pelvis felt shaken as if by giant knuckles trying to tear it apart into boney gore.

I tried looking to Terrence and plead some kind of signal to turn off the chair. That he was killing me. Never had I wanted or needed to scream for relief, but no scream was allowed any escape. I could see he was talking to me while looking down at me, but I heard nothing, and he seemed to not have a care in the world.

In a horrifying panic, I began looking all around for someone else to save me, for there must have been someone in the next booth who saw what was going on. Someone had to hear this. Someone had to see this monstrous event I'd sat myself directly into. And I was right. I could see vendors and patrons all around me. Staring at me in fascination as Terrence continued his direction. Looked like there were dozens of people now watching in fascination. Then hundreds. Then suddenly, with as much shock as when the chair had turned on my body like a starved, rabid giant rat, it stopped. The violent prods stopped hitting me. The pummeling ceased with such genuine relief it felt better and more forgiving than the deepest orgasm. No one was watching me now, except for Terrence, who looked upon me as if he were some magical-caped savior to atone for every sin I'd just had beaten out of me, like a jackhammer baptizing rocks. I was nearly weeping.

"That's it," Terrence said. "There you go. Just as it's supposed to work if you hold on long enough. Just relax and let the chair do its work." His voice was so thick and syrupy, I'm not even sure if language came from his lips, but if it did, those were the words he used. I felt I'd been in the chair for hours when Terrence offered me his hand.

"Well, what'd you think? Quite an experience, wouldn't you say?"

I didn't know what to say as he helped me stand on my jelly legs. I just wanted out. Out of the vendor hall all together, out of the fair to never come back. Away from Terrence and this entire den of wolves into which Terra had sent me to find her, of all places. I wanted to continue screaming for hours to get it all out of my system. I wanted to scream out to anyone who wanted to listen, or maybe even needed to listen: "Run, run for your fucking lives. Get away from this place as fast as you can."

Terrence said, "Get yourself some rest. You'll sleep like a goddamn tomb tonight. I know you've seen a lot. Too much, am I right?" He turned his back to me, faced his demon chair, and began wiping it down.

It was soaking wet.

I gingerly moved one foot in front of the other, looking down to the ground to make sure I focused completely on my balance, wondering if my body would ever recover from such trauma, when, once again, I saw Burkenstock, the orange-bearded troll who'd clearly been stalking me since we met in the parking lot. My head jerked up as if snagged by the cosmic puppet master. "What the hell—"

"Hey, hey, fella. You'd never guess the fuckall this time. I saw that plane again. Thought I'd come in to see if I'd find ya, and here you are as I suspected even though I told you to get out of this place and here you are still. I *knew* it."

I looked into his eyes that continued on in that blaze hotter than burnt orange, wilder than his wiry, knurly, sickening facial bush. Once again, I wondered how *he* knew about me, for he sure as hell seemed to know. It had been only a few hours, yet so much had happened. Clearly, time wasn't doing its trick. The troll still looked just as achingly lonely as when I'd left him in the parking lot and when he had told me the auction wasn't real. But along with that loneliness was also a launching desire to tell me just what he did: it was indeed time to leave. He then looked at me in rage again, but whisper-hissed to me, "Go ahead, go ahead, sonny boy. Go. Leave. You're done here. I think I am, too. Follow me."

As I was about to race after the little bastard, out of the corner of my eye I saw one of my neighbors, Alice Goldman, sitting at yet another booth that was just as whacked out as every other goddamn thing on earth. Surrounding her booth were Christmas trees made of metal, or aluminum, with lights that were all strobing blues and purples. The backdrop of her table was a cloth wall that was completely black. On her booth table were dozens of Bibles of various versions and editions. It was senseless and insane, but I had always thought Alice was gorgeous, so I stopped by regardless of her manic booth.

Taller than most women. Hair always perfectly curled and groomed. A woman who looked many years younger than her age, always incredibly polite and even humorous. Dark eyes, dark skin. Her husband was a complete piece of shit, and I'd found myself wanting to beat him senseless because I'd been told he'd doused her with water on far too many occasions. No one really knew why she stayed with him. Sadly, not many really cared, either. Seeing her, I was suddenly aware of just how fucked up both Duncan and Odella were even when compared to the blatant sickness of the big cities. Seeing her, too, this time, for even a more heightened awareness, everything about Terra began to make more and more sense: why she was here, why she had come into my life, why she had come to Duncan, of all places. Even the terrifying portrait of her and whatever freak family she was with started to make sense. It began to feel like we all deserved it. Deserved everything that was coming to us, and if it was Terra and that figure in black who were here to give it to us, this Adrian Cain, then maybe it was time to just buckle up.

When I approached Alice closer, everything about her reinforced all the newfound senses of awareness I was going through when I saw she was selling miniature pictures of the portrait of Terra's family that was splashed in horror in front of The Duncan Craft Shoppe. As much as I'd seen up to this point, it was far easier to stay in control. In fact, it was Alice who was in far more control, too. She had an instant presence about her that radiated a confidence I'd never seen on her before. I knew she'd also gone through a change before she said a peep.

"What are you doing, Alice? What are these pictures?" I thought that being straight out with it was the only thing to do.

She didn't answer me. She just looked at me. Stared at me without her eyes so much as blinking, as if her eyelids were glued open. Too slowly she said, "Ronald's gone now. Gone bye-bye." She then slowly cocked her head to one side, never taking her eyes off of mine as she slowly lowered her head to the side until I wanted to tell her stop it.

"Well, wish I could say sorry to hear that, but it's probably for the best," I whispered back. "But what about these pictures, Alice?" I asked her again, and again she said nothing. With her head cocked to the side, looking at me just as cocked, she grinned at me, not breaking her lips the further she widened her grin. In one hand she had a remote-control device, and she began clicking it over and over again, turning on and off the strobe lights on the metal Christmas trees. With the other hand, she picked up one of the miniature Terra family portraits and held it to the side of her crooked neck because her head was too tilted, as she'd continued to cock her head until it was completely sideways, all the while never breaking eye contact. Amazingly enough, neither did I, no matter how creeped out I felt from the inside out. Then, as if everything about her couldn't get worse or more obscene, her head completely titled to its side that I thought she'd break her neck, her lips cracked open just enough to where I could see her teeth were not her teeth at all, but the sickening rusted needles I'd seen as the teeth of the demon children next to Terra in the family portrait.

I jumped back and looked down farther from Alice's booth to see that Burkenstock was still waiting for me, and though I had no idea why, I was more than grateful as I raced away from Alice and toward the troll, then out the vendor hall, and into the parking lot to see it was completely empty.

Not a car in sight.

Where the hell is my truck?

I had to adjust my eyes as darkness had settled in. As the adjustment began to move into more clarity I could trust, I stared directly at the center of the parking lot area where finally I saw Terra. She was standing in the middle of the lot, and with what looked like a sliver that opened from infinity, a light was beaming down upon her, and surrounding her in a slow-motion track light. There were also two epic-sized flat projector screens behind her, concert level, which presented her in a shockingly detailed view. Similar to how rock stars are boomed on screen when on stage so everyone in the stadium had ample vision.

The Lady Mephistopheles

How they'd gotten it there, of course, was what first struck me, but at least it struck me hard enough to slap me out of the fright fest I'd just witnessed with my neighbor, Alice, who had gone into Wonderland.

Behind Terra was a chair at least ten feet higher than the top of her head. She was wearing a single piece black dress that looked more like lingerie than evening wear. Deep Vs throughout flaunted her sculpted perfection.

"I guess my little dumpling slave told you it was time to go, Stevie." Her velvet throated voice was as addicting as each part of her physical being.

I should have been speechless at such a scene of visual intoxication, so vivid, so full of more than life itself, but I wasn't. What I wanted was to stop thinking, needed to stop all activity upstairs, but had no option to do so. I found myself wanting to ask Terra what the hell was going on with Alice, but I knew she wouldn't tell me. I wanted to ask her about Adrian Cain and the slave auction. I wanted to ask about all of it when it was she who asked, "Are you ready to turn yet?"

What did it mean to turn? Where did she want me to turn? And to what? Had I not done my part with the relapse? Not followed her every whim?

There I stood before her once again, but not as before as she entered and violated my home she, the woman Mephistopheles, thinking then as I did before when the tale began of the little town of Duncan and its town folk turning wildly into frothed over-psychotics who once were the lovers of God, the patrons of innocence, and those who abhorred the long endless night when carolers did change to warlocks, when streams reversed their course, when now standing in front of her in my aching lonely drunkenness, allowed my mind to at least consider the remnants of what had happened and had been happening, and God knew we all had our turning points, our breaking points, our scouring points where nothing was found but all was searched for, as I'd searched so long for my long lost Anna, my long lost soul, that unquenchable moment as my alcohol-swelled veins slugged along in foggy chaos, when it was all we sought to survive, and Terra knew it as well as the town knew it, as well as we deserved it, and she was what we deserved, now looking at her and wondering if there could have ever been a way back home, a way back to sanity, a way to find that path that always seemed so deeply hidden within the rocks of mayhem, the mud of life, the blood of maggots, the rot and worship of the pigs, the lecture of the pigs, the politics of science, the ruin of the slave, the ruin of the flesh, the abhorrence of the sacrilege of preachers on their pulpits, all coming to that awful ending we never wanted, but that she certainly sought to turn over everything that was ever good, that was ever pure, to turn it all over to her forever.

PART FOUR

Terra Takes Steve Home — Steve and Brother Garret — Terra's Adventure Alone In Town — The Coffee Shop — The Stranger — The Church of Flies

---

erra wanted to take Steven Paul to the place she'd acquired deep into the mountains of Snow Crest City, the tourist ski town about fifty miles north of Duncan. It was a place that had been abandoned over a hundred years ago. An old mining warehouse vast and ominous in its appearance. The front of it looked more like the entry building to Auschwitz than anything else. Still, it was the first place she wanted to take him as she looked at how utterly shaken he'd been from the fair. She knew how much he'd seen, knew that the direction she gave him to go to the fair would be one he wouldn't even consider disobeying, so completely entranced he was with her. Yet she had so much more to show, so much more to give, and, of course, so much more to *take*. It was always her game, always had been her game since her early beginnings of devouring men's souls. Taking from them everything and anything they thought they could ever give, and just when they'd thought they could give no more, Terra always found a way to drain one more last drop of dying blood.

Even though her concert-level arrival was more than enough to snap Steve out of all the visual overload he'd been rammed through, she also knew he wouldn't be able to sustain such a vision for too much longer or she'd risk him completely losing his mind, and that would be no good for anyone, nor for any purpose. She knew how to take until the last drop was sucked out and down, but she also knew that pacing was crucial in order to have any man, or woman, truly turn in the way she needed them to turn. It was different for everyone; she'd learned that long ago.

After giving him a nice long look over as if in review of his complete aura, she turned her head around and gave a signal only she could give, and the massive screens behind her, all hologram in nature, vanished, her red Mustang then the only car in the entire lot.

Ready for more, as was she.

So, she decided in her endless wisdom of destruction to not push Steve any further. Had to feel him out more, and deeper, to get more sense of how far she needed to go with him.

As for Steve, he was in such a state of confusion and near hysteria, when he finally saw Terra after experiencing the auction, the pig, Alice Goldman's frightening metamorphosis, and everything before all of it from Terra herself to the salon witch show and Adrian Cain, seeing Terra in the parking lot in all her demonic glory had some twisted sense of what had become for him rather comforting. She was becoming normal to him as evil becomes normal to the devils roaming the earth.

Of course, she'd taken care of the situation at The Hickory Stack and Stan Smitts, but Steve hadn't heard the hows or the whys, and there were plenty of those. For example, her effortless ability to go back into the bar, pick up Stan from the ground she'd knocked him to, and slam his dead body right back in the chair from where she'd knocked him cold. Her ability to make it all look like he'd drunk himself into such an oblivion because of how sick he'd become from whatever violent illness that had destroyed his body and mind, that it seemed completely natural that he'd died, perfectly natural that she'd hit him in the first place as everyone knew such drunkenness always led to foul and abrasive language, and she was a woman to boot.

Stan had deserved every bit that Terra had laid on him.

Her promise to Steve that she was going to finish off Stan wasn't actually needed since he died on the floor just a few moments after Steve had left the bloodied mess. She'd even taken care of all the patrons inside once she strolled back in after kissing Steve good night and sending him on his way with instructions to meet her at the fair. Took care of them all with her sorcery and black magic witch's brew, her endless sexuality and dry wit that did more than just compliment her entire presence, sexuality and wit that the patrons instantly resonated with, man or woman.

But when she saw Steve's exhaustion when coming to the parking lot and finding her there in all her splendid acid glory, she'd known it wasn't time for Steve to know everything just yet, for no matter what he'd seen or felt or lived through, so much more awaited him.

So very very much more.

Her place in the upper mountains, Auschwitz entry and all, would have to wait.

"I'm not up for anymore," Steve said. "I can tell you that right now. You can do with me what you want, but after all that's gone on, I need some rest, and I need to see a friend." He was completely baffled at the lights and screens disappearing from behind her, just as much as he was when seeing it all just moments ago when finding her.

His body seemed too frail for Terra, more so than she'd expected. Steve was an athlete, older yes, but still trained and strong enough to handle just about anyone, but the man she saw that moment had had his spirit broken. This pleased her because she knew all too well that a broken spirit was quite different than a broken body. To have both broken could be icing on the cake, but it had to come at the right time.

So, Terra looked at Steve with empathy, of all things, as they were both standing by her Mustang, looking like the only two people in the entire region, as darkness was upon them. For all Steve knew they could have been the only two people standing in all of Utah, or the goddamn world.

"A *friend*, you say? You need some *rest*, you say? Hmmm. Actually, I can see that. But what kind of friend do you need all of sudden, Stevie? And one who could replace me, of all people? Haven't I done you well thus far?" There was mockery in her voice.

"Honestly? Honest to God, I'll tell you. I need to see my priest." Steve completely expected Terra to burst out once again in one of her hideous cackles. But she didn't, and that was even more unnerving with all that Steve had come to know about her.

Instead, she breathed in a deep breath, then let it out with a long severe sigh. "I see. Well. Okay, Steven Paul. Get in. We'll do things your way, for a bit, sound like a plan? I'll take you back to your place where this whole thing began and let you get your sleep. Let you see your priest. Not surprising, really. I guess I can even appreciate how you feel, I really can. So just get in and we'll head back. I've got things to take care of without you, for a bit." She looked and sounded every bit as tired as Steve himself.

They drove back to Steve's place in complete silence, only the hum of the Mustang's engine and the raging cold of the night growing more and more fierce in its envelopment with every creeping moment. Within twenty minutes, she dropped him off right at the bank of his driveway, where the Ram was parked as if he'd never driven it.

"How did my truck get here?"

"Burkenstock helped me out, drove it here. I hope you don't mind."

"But I have the key-fob right here."

"Really? You think I need a key?" She snapped her fingers and the Ram fired up, lights came on, like some kind of obedient pet.

All he could think to say was: "Thanks." He clicked his key-fob to quiet and darken the Ram and hoped that Burkenstock didn't put a scratch on it or even change the radio station.

Terra patted his knee. "Get some rest, call your priest, and I'll see you again."

"When?"

"When the time is right and needed."

The sudden submission in tactics from her felt just as off and filled with chaos to Steve that he was convinced it was simply part of her very spirit of hell itself, a spirit and a place that ravaged him with the constant brutality of endless spontaneity that he knew he could never sustain, but also knew somehow he would most likely have to.

***

That very next morning after a sleep that felt what Steven thought people must have felt when awakening from a coma, he did in fact call his priest, one Jonathan Garret. The priest Steve had been seeing on and off for a year or so to deal with loneliness, anger, bitterness, and every other goddamn thing that every person on earth had been dealing with at one time or another. Especially since Covid made it's endless presence known, and Anna the opposite.

"Hello there, Steve. Good to hear from you this

morning. It's been some time." Garret had said this a bit too cheerfully for Steve's liking. But he never liked cheerfulness in the mornings, didn't matter who it was.

"Yeah, yeah it has, Brother Garret. I guess that's why I'm calling you. It has been a while and, to be honest, more's happened to me over the past few days than I ever thought possible, so calling you and asking to see you feels the best thing for me right now, that is if you're okay with it."

"Hmmmm. Interesting out of the blue, that's for sure. But Steve, you know my door's always open. Always has been. Let me open up my calendar and see when I've got something open—"

"You know, Brother Garret, I need to see you tomorrow night, please. I really do. I know that's short notice, but this is important. I'd come tonight if you had some time, but I need some rest, even if just a few hours. You know I wouldn't be this way if it wasn't important."

"You drinking again, Steve? That what's going on?"

Garret had hit a direct nerve, causing Steve to swallow hard, pause even harder.

How the fuck did he know that?

Then he knew how, because the whole town knew he'd been a drunk at one time or another.

"Yeah. I am drinking again. But that's not the only reason. It's not even the main reason, if you can believe that."

"Oh, I believe it. I believe anything. And nothing surprises me. Okay, tomorrow night it is. Come on by the chapel around seven. Fair enough?"

"I appreciate this, you know I do. I'll see you then."

"See you then, Mister Paul. Try to be on time, and do get some rest, you sound a tad ruined."

Garrett instantly hung up without allowing any retort.

So quickly Steve first thought the line disconnected, but just as quickly realized it was just probably Jonathan Garret needing to get on with his night. *I didn't realize it would put you out or I'd not have called in the first place.*

Soon enough, he buried the thought as he found his way back to the kitchen, found an old bottle of wine, and began to pull on it without even thinking about finding a glass to pour it in. He didn't have much work to do, and what he did have he couldn't concentrate on even if he tried, so the decision to start hitting it again seemed the best and most effective way to pass the time along until his appointment with the Priest Garret the following night.

Steve drank all night, hitting wine and some Vodka he'd also stashed. Drank until he passed out, then when waking a few hours later, hit it again to pass out again in a frightening alcohol drowning that could have killed most pros.

By the time a quarter to seven came around the following evening, dressed in the full ink of another frozen night, Steve was more than good and liquored up and ready to face the priest with not just courage and confidence, but veins that were pumping more ethanol than blood into his brain. He took a quick hot shower to dry and mask any of the stench coming from his pores, though useless he knew, it would at least cover it all for a moment or two. He dressed in another hoodie with jeans and the same pull-on boots he'd worn to the fair, jumped into the Ram and was at the local church with five minutes to spare before his appointment.

Garret's truck was parked in the church's lot, the only vehicle there, making the lot and the church seem eerily...alone. Steve parked his Ram right next to Garret's much older Ford 150, white in color, yet plenty worn from all the years of volatile and harsh Utah weather. Garret also owned a Mercedes 600 with the V12 engine straight from heaven, but rarely drove it.

The moment Steve entered the church he wondered if it was the place he really needed to be, a feeling he had always gone through every time he'd been missing church month after month, year after year. That feeling of guilt that always sank in from turning his back on God. There were no lights on. Hallways were as pitch as the night outside and felt almost as bitter cold. He was thankful again for the alcohol ravaging his system, and even more thankful for seeing Garret's office lights beaming out from under a closed door. Steve turned his phone light on regardless, not wanting to trip over his own feet in not just the swelling darkness, but also his own drunkenness.

Just as he approached Garret's office door, Garret's voice instantly interrupted Steve's knocking. "Come on in, Steve, please. Door's open."

Steve pushed the door open and entered Garret's office, one that was plain, but plenty spacious. On each of the side walls hung pictures of Christ, or portraits of what artists rendered how the Nazarene could look, though, of course, they had no clue. Garret's desk was a massive one of particle board designed to look like solid pine. Blue carpet lined the floor with two plush and comfortable visitor's chairs placed a few yards away from the priest's desk, a desk that was perfectly organized with not a hint of clutter. Behind Garret and his desk stood a long, heavy bookcase with various pictures sitting in their easels of Garret's family, pet dog and cat, and few others of people Steve thought looked somewhat familiar, but he couldn't put his finger on them.

Jonathan Garret stood up with a welcome greeting. "It's

good to see you, Steve. Glad you reached out." Garret held out his hand for a shake.

Steve took the greeting in stride, always appreciating the priest for such warmth. He was a large man, six-two, one ninety, lean and strong, with dark skin and a bald head. He had enormous ears that looked like cauliflower blossoms and just as ragged. Steve had once thought Garret had competed in jujitsu, the very sport that created such ears after years of hard grappling. Steve knew the martial art quite well, but his own ears never took enough beatings for the classic look. But Garret never had grappled, or boxed, or lifted weights, just enjoyed running and kept a lean diet.

"Yeah. Nice to see you as well, Brother Garret." Steve shook the priest's meaty hand with just as much strength and resistance that Garret could ever offer. Steve's boxing and grappling training over the many years gave his own hand enough vice-like strength to answer just about anyone's grip. Except for the magician-vendor's he'd felt just the day before, sitting in the massage rape chair that nearly killed him at the fair.

"Have a seat."

Steve did, and the two looked at each other in a long, awkward pause of silence, eye contact that remained locked as if in competition. Finally, Garret cleared his throat and went right to the vein. "What's going on, Steve? What can I help you with?"

Steve continued staring back at the priest, took a deep breath as if to prepare for something formal, yet deeply unsettling, as everything had been since meeting Terra.

"Well, for starters, as you suggested on the phone, I've been drinking. A lot. Fact, I haven't stopped."

"Yep. Clearly. Could smell it before you came in.

Probably smelled it the second you got out of your truck in the parking lot."

"That bad, eh?"

"Just trying to lighten things up, even though things are clearly heavy. Glad you made it in, to be frank. You get pulled over it's not going to be pretty, that's true, right?"

"No, it wouldn't."

"Look. Steve, I'm not here to pass any judgment. You called me, and I'm here. So, what else is it? Besides the drinking?"

"Well, as I said on the phone last night, believe it or not, that's not the worst of it. No, Brother Garret, shit's been a lot heavier than just me relapsing. So much so, I'm a little surprised you've not sensed anything going on around town yourself."

"What do you mean going on around town? Am I supposed to? What is it I'm supposed to have noticed?" This time he spoke with a little more assertion, *or was it aggression?* Garret was also eyeballing Steve a little too deeply for Steve's liking. A little too closely. A little too...quirky.

"I've recently seen my neighbor, Stan Smitts, go through a sickness I know Covid had nothing to do with. Sicker than anything I've ever seen, then after he drove off when he should have gone back to the hospital, I met a woman who's been...I don't know what she's been, to be honest. She's...she's scary. She'd scare you, I bet. And you've never seemed the type to scare easy. Then I've been tormented by the most ugly and vile dreams, and everyone I've seen in this town recently...outside this town for that matter, seem...possessed or something, if that's even possible or even makes sense."

"Possessed you say?" The priest said that rather smugly.

"Possessed. Best way I can think to describe it."

"Hmmm. Well, if it makes sense to you, Steve, then it must be perfect sense. We all have our ways of seeing and feeling things. World's gone pretty south, hasn't it?" Garret sounded amused, which was more than strange to Steve since Garret was one person Steve had known who was always deadpan serious. "Don't take me wrong. I'm not making light of any of this, Steve, especially about the woman. Why do *you* think things have gotten the way they are? Have you stopped to consider that question? And this woman, all of a sudden. What kind of woman is she?"

Steve certainly stopped to consider all that the priest just asked. "Yeah, I don't know, Brother Garret. She's violent, and I know violence. I've followed the world's social studies and cultures as closely as anyone has for years. Written about it, as you know, but why things are so vicious now, I guess people are just tired of everything. And this woman shows up who is a hellcat. Maybe she's somehow the answer to all the shit gone south, as you say."

"Exactly right, Steve. Exactly right. Nothing's really that new. World has gone through cycles of awful events since Adam and Eve. Since she took the fruit and did a number on us all. You've always been a thoughtful man, Steve. Have always been open to some of the things I've tried to suggest over the past few years. Let me tell you a story, if I may. Maybe something that will put things in perspective. About everything you speak about, in fact."

Steve's deepened inebriation wasn't enough to blank out the fact that the priest was speaking far outside what he'd normally spoke about. Talking about Eve doing a number on us all was way outside the normal spiritual lane.

"Sure. Why not. If anyone needs some perspective right

now, I'm the candidate." Steve again scanned the pictures behind Garret, pictures of Garret's family and pets, and one of the pictures of the people Steve thought looked familiar, a picture of someone that Steve knew he'd seen somewhere but still couldn't place it, and though he couldn't, it was a picture that chilled him more than the weather outside. Wasn't one of those pictures that Alice Goldman had at her booth, or the larger one at the craft shop in all its demonic glory, but it was familiar in that same way, getting under his skin almost instantly.

Steve focused on the priest again, not wanting to wander off too much away from the trail. "I'm listening, Brother Garret. Go ahead, please."

"Good, good then. It was one of those days that started out perfectly fine. Perfectly in order, you might say. Evening, actually. It was a cool, yet spectral, early evening as fall began setting in and around the Wasatch Front. A lot like it is now. Maybe not as cold, and God it's been cold early this year, right? But it was getting there. I was with Rusty Taylor. He's another member of this congregation. Do you know him?"

"Not directly."

"Well, he's had problems a lot like you've had. Maybe not as severe, but he's been there. Fact is, I had agreed to go out with Rusty and do some community service with him, as he'd gotten himself into some recent trouble, again, much like some of what you've gone though, Steve. Well, Rusty has never been one to like it when the time changes. Hates it when it gets dark so early. Spectral was right about the night. Keep this in mind as I continue." The priest spoke in more of a commanding tone, rather than just telling a story.

"Rusty doesn't give a shit's smell about religion, or missionaries, or church, or dogma, or anything else related to the deity. *Any* deity. And this time he was forced to go out and do some of this missionary work as part of community service. He needed enough hours to keep him from violating probation, and I agreed to go with him to make sure things went smoothly, and to account for his time to his probation officer. The other places to work for hours were all booked up on this particular weekend. He couldn't pick up trash, couldn't work at the dump, couldn't get a slot at the local library. So, he had pleaded with his PO, and asked about knocking on the doors with a pair of local missionaries, because *that* was always available anywhere, anytime across the entire Utah state, as you well know. But the local missionaries weren't available that day, so, I was happy to do it with him." The priest paused to clear his throat.

A hard clearing of the throat that startled Steve, but not as much as when Garret said "shit" when opening the story, and not so much as how suddenly fast Garret was speaking, as if the priest had knocked back a few lines that Steve hadn't seen. The priest had always been the slow thinking, slow speaking type, always mustering things over before he said anything.

And he never used profanity.

After licking his lips, he leaned over his desk to get a better, deeper look at Steve. At least that's what Steve felt. "Rusty wasn't even convinced that his PO would go for the community service hours spent here with me and going around doing some proselytizing, so I even told Rus that I wouldn't mind calling his PO to verify it was done, to vouch for him. Make things easier. That part was perfect for Rus. In fact, he was more than gracious. What wasn't good...what wasn't part of the plan, was Rusty and I ending up at a home where he felt instantly unnerved. He didn't know why, didn't care why. He just knew from the hairs pricking through his denim shirt that it felt all wrong the minute we knocked on the door of a home I'd gotten a lead on, someone who wanted to hear a good message of hope and cheer. The Good Word, Steve. You remember the Good Word, don't you?"

Steve nodded but now needed another drink and fast, as Garret began to speak even faster, licking his lips all the while as if to fill in any cracks around his mouth from not having enough water.

"I didn't think much of it, to be honest. But I was wrong. I was dead wrong, Steve. I thought Rusty was being paranoid because that's a lot of what Rusty's all about: paranoia. And you talk about me being one to not get spooked easy? I didn't think anything could rattle Rusty. But when the door opened, I think I instantly knew the reason for all his paranoia. Only then I thought he had more of a sixth sense or something. A woman answered the door who looked to be in her late 60s in the face, but mid 20s in the legs and midriff. It was a bizarre look, to be certain. She wore a short wool skirt and heavy-knitted cotton pink sweater that looked weeks from its last wash. She also had on tattered ankle boots as a final touch. Her long red locks of hair looked more like frayed rope strands. Her teeth were browned over in rot spots, at least that's what Rusty and I thought as she smiled wide and silly in a way that made us both feel instantly nauseated. Well, speaking for myself, I felt that way. I felt nauseated, and if I felt that way, I'm sure Rusty felt like vomiting right then and there. I've never asked him since. She didn't open the door all the way, mind you, about a foot or so, so we could see her, but not really much else behind her, and into the home. Her cheerfulness didn't help matters any further as she said, 'Hey, guys, or elders, or priests. Whatever you are, and whoever you are, glad you came by, nonetheless, really happy as a lark.'

"Rus looked at me rather worried, to say the least, said to me 'maybe we head over to the next address. I don't think we have the right place here,' as he then looked at the woman whose eyes seemed to change to this wild look, and far too dark. He was looking at me as if seeking validation. I thought it over a bit. I really did, then said to Rusty that I thought it was okay, that the address was correct and that things would be just fine. I'd seen people with wild eyes before, so I decided to still go with it. She then interrupted any further thought with a 'it's fine, it's fine, it's fine, it's just fine in here. What's your name, sir?' She'd asked the both of us but only looked at me. Her voice was gravely, salty. Best way I can describe it. 'It's Mister Garret, am I right? Ain't you that Garret Priest, or some shit?' she then said, quickly and abruptly, 'Don't worry about a thing. You boys are welcome to come on in and talk church if you want. Talk all about the Lord Thy God, by damn, I don't care a lick or a whistle. And that's the goddamn truth. Or if you need, or what not, to talk over any other things, it's all okay this way.' I looked at Rusty as the woman then turned her attention to him, flashing her wild eyes at him in a strange flutter, then far too quickly subdued them to a droop toward me again. This was one bizarre duck, Steve, I mean to tell you. She said everything was fine, that she had some friends inside, that they were all just having drinks and playing cards and what not. Told us to come on in, to please come on in, to not be shy. To not be rude even."

Garret stopped and looked at Steve in a half-cocked way that made Steve even more uncomfortable. *What was the point to his story? Where was he heading with all this?* But somehow

Steve had a feeling that Garret knew exactly where he was taking the story.

Garret just kept licking his lips, looking more and more reptilian. Steve, needing a drink more and more, decided to say nothing and just hold the priest's stare. It was all he could do, and it was tough work. The walls in Garret's office began to look like they were closing in. At least that's what Steve felt as he looked again behind Garret at the pictures on the bookcase, then back to Garret, then back to the picture that looked so familiar, the picture with a gentleman in it quite beautifully dressed, perfectly tailored in fact.

Steve also thought he began to hear music in the distance. Could have been his alcohol consumption was creating audio hallucinations, but Garret-The-Priest's story had begun to have quite the sobering effect, so music seemed the answer. It sounded ethereal and haunting with a high pitch, but far enough in the distance that Steve couldn't decipher who it was, what band, if it was a band or some solo artist he'd never heard before.

Maybe it's a soundtrack. But why, and what movie?

Such an endless hum and silent roar that Steve wondered if it was actually playing from somewhere outside the church, like a concert.

What concert could be playing late into the evening that was clearly meant to terrify the innocent and provoke the wicked.

Steve continued in his wandering drunken escape.

Suspecting that Steve would continue to wander off in a gaze until he'd fall right out of his seat, Garret continued, but far more slowly in his speech. Far more deliberate.

"You with me, Steve? You still with me?" Garret snapped his fingers before Steve refocused and nodded. "The woman then told us that her name was Misty, by the way, and then opened her front door completely. We could see...excuse me, I could see. I keep saying 'we' but that's a bit rude of me, Rusty can speak for himself if you ever see him. But I could see a dimly lit hallway that was long and dark and smokey. Real smokey. Like the smoke that's been bleeding all over this state and spewed from California, kinda like that, but thicker because it was so close.

"The hallway led to what I could see was a living room area. Three men were sitting on an old couch that was a deep blue. Velvet, or something like velvet is what it looked like. I glanced over to Rusty and nodded that we should go in, even though I was beginning to feel the same as what he'd probably felt before the lady Misty had answered the door. Perhaps that was Rusty's initial concern. Regardless, he took my nod as everything being okay enough to go ahead in.

"So, we followed Misty into the living room that was quite dark, and quite dull even though the room was in scarlets and deep blues that looked bizarrely vivid for so much smoke. Fact, I'll never forget just how vivid. At first, I was also certain that there was some chanting going on, though I couldn't be for sure, and since Rusty didn't seem to hear it, I let it go, but began to feel as concerned as Rusty had felt because suddenly everything about this feeling had begun to be more than just visual evidence of colors and smoke and ambiance. After walking down the hallway, following Misty, when I saw the men, the friends Misty had mentioned, I couldn't make them out with any clarity but could certainly tell they'd been there for a good long while doing far too much of absolutely nothing. Wasting time as if time had no precious meaning or value. Especially value. There were also three women sitting around with the men, all of them sitting around a scarred-up particle board table. Six incense candles were burning on the table's surface. Long silvery strands of smoke crawled up to the ceiling in a slow-motion rhythm that was powerfully trance-like. Rusty kept looking to me for more confirmation that everything was okay, but I couldn't offer that to him any longer, Steve. Couldn't offer that to him at all, because I wasn't sure if anything was okay, to be honest. I wasn't even sure if anything would ever be okay again.

"I looked around the room with more and more...inspection if you will. My eyes had adjusted enough in the dark to be able to see everything with a lot more clarity, and what I saw, hanging on one of the walls in the living room, was a painting of a nude man with an engorged penis. It shocked me cold. Completely engorged to the point that it was painted in a way that you could see semen was bursting out in thick streams of gobby-looking plastic that had hardened and formed into what looked like an infant. A fetus or something. And the fetus was then morphed into a child, and the child into a teenager, and the teenager into a grown man who looked like a demonic figure Michelangelo would have painted. Perhaps he did paint something like it, for all I know. Not really a specialist on Michelangelo. The painting was terrifying, and I wasn't sure Rusty had seen it, but prayed that he did so we could both cue each other that it was time to leave."

Garret stopped and paused again, looking at Steve more severely as if to quietly demand some kind of response. Steve looked back at the priest in utter stillness, having no idea what to think of such a thing, such a story, such a *scene* in such a story, and wondering with even more intent why in God's name a man of God was speaking about such an insane moment. Why hadn't the priest known all along what a terrible idea it was to go into the house in the first place?

Steve knew he had to say something as the music from the distance seemed to intensify, if just by a hair. Had to say something to either end this meeting or find out what was next. He needed a drink more than anything, so he started there. "I'm not even sure what to think, to be honest, Garret, but I'm drunk. Been drinking as I told you, and from the sounds of this story, I think I need another."

"Just hold on, Steve. I'm sure you're feeling that way, I'm sure of it, but just hold on. Can you hold out a bit longer? Let me finish? It's important, and I'm sure you're sensing that, so just stay planted right here with me for a bit more. Can you show some discipline?"

Steve took a deep breath almost in anger, but held on as asked, nodding for Garret to continue. Garret took just as deep a breath, then let it out nice and slow and heavy all the while continuing to hold Steven Paul's drunken stare.

"The painting was shocking enough. Clearly, right? I hadn't really noticed what Rusty was doing or thinking or how he was reacting. Just that he was mingling with Misty and her friends, not really looking around the place as I had been doing. And then I hear someone else in the house, in the kitchen area. Someone we'd not met or seen before. The kitchen was just off to the side of the living room. Whoever it was, was making quite a bit of noise, almost as if on purpose, to get attention or something. Banging pans and turning on the water full blast. When I looked over at the kitchen area there was another woman. She was dressed only in her underwear and a thin t-shirt. Quite erotic, to be honest, but also dirty in a really dirty sort of way, like she'd not bathed in a while, like every other person in the place. Taller woman. Skin alarmingly white. Couldn't tell if her hair was black or a deep red. Pulled tightly back in a fierce ponytail. Her body was hard, like she worked out every day for hours.

"I noticed that Rusty had noticed her, too, and when he did, he made it a point to get up and ask for a glass of water. Glass of *something*, I don't remember. As he entered the kitchen area, he was instantly startled that a few children were crawling on the floor around the woman. Wearing only diapers. Filthy at that. Fleshy to the point of obscene. Oily and bluish. Looked like they were actually nibbling, or even biting the woman's ankles, they were so close to her, crawling around her as if she was something foreign. *That's* what I saw and was probably far more startled than Rus because I was still sitting and had a better view of them, noticed the crawling naked children were also hideously deformed in the mouth. I stood up immediately, my own skin so unnerved I did everything I could to keep from looking like I'd scream. I raised my voice to Rusty that we needed to leave immediately. He moved quickly enough to cause the woman in the kitchen to giggle. Not even sure it was a giggle, but she didn't make it easy for him to get past her, using that body of hers to be an obstacle, to say the least. She giggled more as he got past her and actually stepped over one of the children on the floor. Misty then laughed like a hyena or something wicked. 'Don't want to stick around with us good folk to talk church and God? Don't like my friends, is that it?' She taunted us both. The woman in the kitchen stared at me with eyes so wide and purple that I couldn't stare back for more than a moment as Rusty was then by my side, grabbing my arm and telling me it was indeed time to get the hell out, and get out fast."

Garret stopped so abruptly it was almost like his voice cut out. He placed both his hands on his desk, intertwined his large fingers together and moved his thumbs around and around, cocking his head and licking his lips more gamely than he'd been doing throughout the meeting. The walls in his office continued the odd vacuum movement, at least that's what Steve continued seeing as his alcohol crave became painful and gnawing.

But Steve held on, still holding off on saying anything, waiting for Garret to continue on. So, Garret did, with his mouth opening wider and wider as if to really consider what to say next. "All this making a bit more sense now, Steve? You came in here and told me you wondered why I hadn't noticed things changing around town or feeling that things had changed. That's what you said, right? And that you'd met someone. I think I met her, too. Maybe we've all met her. Maybe you've been right all along, Stevie Boy."

"I'm done with this, Garret," Steve said, with as much force as he was able after hearing such an obscene tale, standing from his seat in front of Garret's desk. "Done with your psycho story, Jesus God." Steve said it in a whisper-shout that sounded like it could have been the last speech he'd give for months to come. He still managed to stand up completely with an air of dignity and composure for someone who'd been drinking non-stop for days.

Garret waived his hand to the side as if to dismiss the entire scene. "I know you're shaken, Steve. Course you are. Let me ask you something before you go because you've been eyeballing my pictures ever since you stepped inside my office, reeking like a dead bum who'd soaked himself in gin." Garret turned to the bookcase and grabbed the picture that Steve had tried and tried to recognize, then turned back to Steve with picture in hand. "You recognize this gentleman?" He handed the picture out for Steve to take. "Go ahead and take a closer look."

Steve was more than disgusted with all that had been said, horrified even. Couldn't believe where things had turned. Still, as he thought it over in his drunkenness, he really had no other place to be, or to even go. So, he took the picture from Garret's hand and gave it a nice long look over. The face was unmistakable, as was the makeup. Or paint, Steve couldn't tell even looking at the man in a picture. There was no cape draped around him, but the picture was certainly that of the massage chair salesman who said his name was Terrance, who placed Steve in the massage chair and turned on hell itself.

"Met him a while back. Sells massage chairs, being a masseuse himself. Fine looking fellow, wouldn't you say, Steve?"

"When did you meet him?" Steve looked Garret dead in the eye as if in combat mode.

"Couldn't say really, but he did capture my fancy. Never thought I'd see it coming, to be honest. But things happen to people, right? People change. Things take place that suddenly trigger something deep within you that you never knew you had or even knew was possible to exist. Least that's how I see it. You meet someone or see someone and something awakens inside of you."

"*Fuck* are you talking about? You've not made any sense since I came here, and now you're rambling on about someone that I actually met at the fair yesterday. And he was more than just a furniture salesman."

"Right? You are so right. He is so much more than that."

"I've had enough. I'm out, Garret. I've nothing more to say to you."

"Then off you go then, Steve Paul. Hope to see you at

church, because if you think about it, that's really the place you should be. That's the place I should be. Even invited him to come on out. It could be a real fine event of healing and transformation, Steve. Best not miss it. I'll be looking for you." Garret was just as deadpan and combat ready as Steve was, the two of them locking eyes, wondering what the other knew, knowing that what the other knew was far more than the exchange that had just taken place.

Out in the parking lot of the church, after rubbing his hands together quickly for heat, Steve jumped in the Ram, fired it up with his hands trembling as he grabbed the comforting leather-wrapped steering wheel. He took a few deep breaths. More than a few. In, out. In, out. *Steady does it. Steady does it and don't get pulled over.*

He continued that thought as he pulled out of the church's parking lot and was back home in what he thought was less than a minute, but also more than a few hours, his mind racing and wondering and thinking and believing that all he'd ever known and all he'd ever believed had been shaken more than to his root, more than to his inner coils that were now all bundled and strapped and ready to unleash in a fury that he'd been feeling and dealing and rolling around in with the woman Terra, the woman alive, the woman somehow his priest may have seen and ran away from the moment her wild-eyed monster children gnawed at her legs in the house of Satan that should have never been visited with all that Steve could muster now back in his home, back in the living room where it all started for him, where it all ended for Stan Smitts, where Steve dropped down on the living room floor and passed out for what he thought were days and nights gone by, when his cell phone rang and screamed into his ears as he answered it to Terra's voice wailing and demanding full attention.

"You up, Stevie Boy? You get your rest you so deeply needed?"

"How long have I been asleep?" Steve asked, hearing how it stupid it sounded but couldn't take it back.

"Ohhhh my, my, my. It's been many many days now, if you can dig it, Steve. Since I dropped you off. You been asleep that whole time passed out?"

"Jesus, no of course not, didn't have any idea that much time's gone by, though. I need a shot. Now."

"*Of course* you do. Been drinking yourself to absolute annihilation, haven't you, dear? Get up and grab your bottle and pound down some more, can't stop now. No, no, too much time to catch, too much to do."

"I don't know what you're talking about."

"Well, let me catch you up, Stevie. 'Cause it has been a bit. You have a minute to talk on the phone? People don't really talk on the phone anymore. Notice that?"

"Yeah, I guess so." Steve was now up on his feet, thinking exactly where he'd left his last bottle in the house, remembering it was in the freezer to keep it nice and wicked cold for easy go-down. Vodka at that. His favorite, of course, when the drink really began to have its way with him. "Let me get a few down and we can talk all you want."

"Do that. I'll wait right here on the phone with you."

Steve knew she meant it, so hanging up and having a little peace with his liquor was out of the question. He took the bottle out of the freezer, didn't bother finding a glass and pulled a few slugs right then and there, instantly feeling the heat from the freezing Vodka bath that settled his inner demons that had gone stark raving mad, of this he was certain.

"Feel better?" Terra said with comfort behind her acid.

"Yeah."

"Then keep hitting that, and let me fill you in. Get a comfy spot and tell me when."

"Already there." Steve sunk into his leather couch, his favorite spot where he loved to watch the big screen late into the night, always deeply missing Anna at such times.

"After I left you...well, dropped you off that is. Felt like I left you. Didn't like leaving you, to be honest, but after I drove off, I headed back up to the place I have here in the upper mountains. Place deep behind the resorts of Snow Crest City. You know the town, I'm sure. Town full of sickness and vile, perversion and hatred. Do-gooders who think they do better than the rest of everyone around them. You know the type. Old miner building I happened to come upon some time back. Abandoned and gutted, filled with the anguish of dead spirits. I'll show you sometime, Steve, but up here I went to pepper things up for a few more outings to your little town of Duncan."

"You're in Snow Crest City right now? That's where you are? Never mind...then what happened? Peppered things up to do what, exactly?" Steve was quickly growing sarcastic as the Vodka began to settle in, hard and stony.

"Course you've not been watching television the past few days, maybe you'd already know where I'm heading with this story. Even if you had been watching the big screen, stories from the source are always finer tuned than what's on the screen."

"Jesus. What did you do? When? What is it this time?"

"You like Type O Negative, Stevie? The band?"

"Sure." He sounded impatient.

"Have any of their work handy?"

Steve did in fact have a few of their CDs, *Slow, Deep and Hard*, and *Dead Again*. He'd always appreciated their heavy, death-like sound, with Peter Steele's sultry, throaty voice of someone who sounded like the dead would sound if they could sing rock-n-roll. "You want me to put something on, is that what you're saying?"

"Do, yes. Please and thank you, dear Steven."

Steve put on *Slow, Deep and Hard*, sat back on the couch, continued to hit the Vodka. "Okay, Terra, I'm all ears."

"Good, good. Fine then. What'd you talk to the priest about, Steve?"

"I thought you had stories you wanted to tell me."

"I do. But I want to talk about the priest first."

"Well...I don't really feel like talking about it. I was drunk and shit wasn't making sense. He ended up telling me some strange story about a visit he made to a house he shouldn't have gone to. Had some bad shit in that house. But he went because he was helping out another member of his congregation. The meeting didn't end up how I wanted, and it seemed like a long time ago." Steve actually was trying to remember the whole meeting with Jonathan Garret, as well as avoiding the part about the woman at the house who could have been Terra herself. All of it was beginning to mix around Steve's mind in one sluggish, endless cocktail at the end of his brain stem. "So...can I hear your story now? Please?"

'Storrrrieeess, Steve. Stories. Most certainly plural. Sure, we can go that way. Talk all night about them. We can talk about the priest later. When I see you. Sure you haven't seen any of the news?"

"No. And I'm afraid to." He gulped more Vodka.

"Maybe that's how it should be. Keeps you fresh, fear

does. I'm getting ready up here in my Snow Crest City pad, thinking about walking around the main street and dash around all the fancy shops and people-watch all the fancy pants who really are nothing more than whores and freaks, but I decide to go back into Duncan to fetch you, of all things. Few days ago, in fact. It was around two or so in the afternoon. I'm heading down the street that leads to your place. School had been just let out, as kids seemed to be everywhere. I slow down to be careful. All that's been going on, always good to be careful, right Stevie?"

No comment.

"As I'm driving past a few kids that look more like teenagers, I give them a look over. And you know how I look. Doesn't matter what age, I bring out the carnal in everything with a cock. Same with these kids. Except one of them is far older. Clearly the leader of the bunch. And as I look back in the rearview mirror, I can see that he's not only the leader, but also a piece of shit bully. He's berating the others, or even worse, the more I watch, I see him shove a much smaller kid, a girl she was, then he catches me looking back, and decides to flip me off. Sticks his hand straight into the air with his middle finger fingering the breeze. I wasn't really thinking much of it, but the more I looked in the rearview mirror, the more the bastard kept jamming his hand into the air, as if his middle finger could reach me and plough my ass. The younger ones look a little relieved, as his beratement had been taken from them and put on me. I could see it. Shit triggered me, the brash courage, so I slam on the brakes and hit the Mustang into Reverse hard enough to spin the tires, then slam on the brakes and stop right beside him. The whole group steps back, but not the bully.

"I roll down the passenger window, all the way down,

lean way over the passenger seat and ask the Finger Shooter what he thinks he's doing. He's probably nineteen, twenty tops. Wiry. Cocky. A real bad ass, he thinks. Hotshot shooting the bird as if he's the first one who's given the gesture, then suddenly laughs out loud and tells me, 'Fuck off, lady. Get the fuck out of here.' He's clearly being the showoff in front of the youngsters, who by that time had completely distanced themselves. I put the Mustang in Park, open my door, walk around to where he's standing, walk right up to the thug who now has his mouth open, rather than the finger flying. Of course, he's got nothing to say, as I'm right up on him, looking him dead in the eyes, as he's my height.

"He's clearly never seen a woman like me and can't take his eyes off my cleavage. You know about that, don't you, Stevie, except you did nothing about it. Anyway, this punk's getting a nice long eyeful when I raise my hand and arm all the way back and slap him across his face so hard it splits his cheek open. The youngsters take off running in a dead sprint, and it's just the bully and me, his face bleeding, my hand cocked back to strike him with the thunder of Cain, by God. But he looks at me with defiance, maybe to let me have a go at it, but I can see he's thinking it over as if it's a standoff. I settle down a bit, tell him to get in the car, but to keep his mouth shut. Of course, he's leery, so I grab him by the front of his shirt and give him a little direction. Some of us need that, as you know. He doesn't put up much resistance as I get him in the passenger seat, get myself in the car, and off we go down the main street right on past your place where I pull over about a mile or so down the road. Past Stan's place, past the Y. Pull over, stop the car but keep it idling, really getting his attention.

"I look at him up and down his entire body, and I mean

I really look at him, Steve. Look at him long and hard. Look into his eyes, forcing him to not take his eyes off mine. Forcing eye contact. Then I look at his neck, his chest, his groin and cock in his pants. I keep staring there until I know he's uncomfortable, embarrassed even. I break that stare and look him dead in the eyes again. What do you think I did next, Steve, any idea?"

Steve took another deep pull on the Vodka bottle, not saying a word, then he took in a deep breath. Something he'd been doing a lot of since finding this monster of a woman on his bed, slithering around to Nancy Sinatra's boots made for walking. He let it out slowly. "I have no idea, actually, but if it's on the news, I'm sure it wasn't the best outcome for the bully."

Terra broke into one of her frightening cackles. "That's exactly right, Steve. You cracked shit open again. No sir, it didn't turn out well for him at all. What I did, Steve, is ask the fucker his name. He cautiously lets out 'Davis,' or 'David,' or something with a D. Said his name as if he didn't want to give it out then followed up with a 'fuck you, bitch.'

"'You mean...with this?' I asked and grabbed his crotch. He jolted back at first, but then kinda pushed up into my hand as if things were changing in his favor. So I gave him what he wanted, fondled him, stroked him, and when I thought he'd come in his pants, I reach down and grabbed his balls, then squeezed them in a vice-like grip so hard they made a crunching sound. Blood gushed all through his pants. He opened his mouth to scream, but in so much pain, he couldn't belt out a single noise. With my free hand, I slashed his throat open nice and wide with my fingernail, and before he could spray blood all over the Mustang's interior, I reached over to open the door and pushed him out onto the road where he rolled into the gutter to bleed out and die. That's where I left his body to rot, for all I cared. Police are still looking for his killer, but since it happened in the middle of the day, and that this Davis or David's group had run off long before seeing me drive away with him after I'd slapped the shit-heel silly, the small-town cops are clueless, don't know what to think about how the bully got done in so grizzly like. Never happened here before, nothing even like it. And that's where we are right now, doing story time again over the phone. Should I continue?"

"Probably Davey Butler," Steve whispered holding his phone to has face far too tightly and taking yet another Vodka pull.

"So you knew him?"

"He's a piece of shit, I'll give you that." Steve realized that he knew a lot of people in this small town, but really didn't know anyone personally. *And why was that?*

"So good riddance, right?" Terra mocked.

"The cops are going to find you eventually."

"Maybe Stevie, maybe. But not until the time's right, and time's not right yet. We've still got things to do together. Do you want to hear the rest?"

"What else is there? You murder anyone else, cause now you've killed two people I know of, making you a serial killer."

"Not a soul in this town can pin anything on me for ole Stanley Smitts. Everyone saw what happened in the bar. He drank himself to death. Or did he?"

"I know what I saw." Steve knew it was useless to argue with her. Fact is, her story was so fascinating in its detachment for horror and mayhem, he actually wanted to not believe her. All the violence and alcohol was making yet another cocktail of life's downward spiral that was becoming more intoxicating than any drug-induced night Steve's past had ever produced. But his inability to debate her held true enough that indeed she did go on, but not long.

"Let me just say that after my rape and pillage of the bully Davey, I made a scene at the local grocery store, getting so damned impatient at the incompetence there that I shouted down one of the cashiers in such vile hatred and anger that she began weeping in hysteria. I then slapped the shit out of her, and hit another retailer, the hardware store, and became so disgusted with one of the shoppers there who had brought his toddler in to look for car wax, or car soap, or some damn car wash item, but instead decided to act out with such debasement and obnoxiousness because he was clearly coked out or meth'd out that he needed everyone to pay attention to him and his insane laughter. Assholes like that need such a good raping themselves that it's a damn shame they don't get it that way more often. Dry fucked up the ass and left for dead. I grabbed a hammer from the tool aisle then got the piece of shit's attention by burying the hammer in the top of his skull. Did him in right then and there, turning the toddler into an instant government project. That's what's been going on since you told me you needed to be left alone, that you needed to see your priest, and you've been passed out for God knows how many days, out on your living room floor until I called to rudely awaken you."

"I don't know if I believe you, don't know if anything happened that you said did. You're a liar, right? I just don't know. You can't lay that all on me."

"What you think doesn't matter one bit. News has it, just click around. Click around, dear Stevie, click around and see for yourself."

"So you called just to fuck with my head?"

"I'd like to meet you at the coffee shop, one that's down by the liquor store. I need you to meet me there, and it's in your best interest to do just that. You're still safe for now, but time's running out. Be there in thirty," she commanded, then hung up as abruptly as when she called to awaken him out of his unknown days of drunken slumber.

Steve stood up from his couch with a warm glow all inside him from all the fresh, icy Vodka. He stumbled into the bathroom, splashed his face with cold water, ran some through his hair, and brushed his teeth, then grabbed a long sleeve shirt and jacket. In the living room, he turned off the stereo and turned the television to the local news.

All over his massive television screen were blaring chyrons that read:

"local police still in shock and
confusion over gruesome discoveries..."

It was clearly plural. Stories, not just one. Steve slammed home more Vodka and headed out to the coffee shop, most certain that his drunk driving couldn't possibly bring him any attention now that the police were trying to clean up, and figure out, all Terra's bloody messes.

Duncan's coffee shop—like everything else in the town, its name was in it—was unlike most small-town coffee shops spread out across the state, in that the Duncan Coffee Shop had splashed all over its open bay windows Gay Pride flags and colors, something that had become quite shocking to the local residents who walked around self-righteously pretending such things shouldn't exist in their town. The inside of the shop was enormous, more so than one would think when driving by. Huge, spacious living room area to the left of the entrance even housed generous sofas and love seats, all positioned around large glass coffee tables, large enough for endless place settings for drinks and pastries. To the side of this living area design were various racks of tourist glasses, clothing items, an abundance of health foods and snacks. The coffee bar itself was designed as exactly that: an impressive, modern bar made of steels and fancy linoleums.

Steve had been there many times to just sit and relax and enjoy the high-speed internet that his home didn't offer. After he'd parked his truck next to Terra's red Mustang, the instant he entered the coffee shop he knew everything was different for one reason: the patrons were sipping on their brews and casting about idle chit-chat that Steve knew instantly had nothing to do with anything good. On one sofa sat the black couple he'd seen arguing at the Odella Fair, the couple who when he last saw them looked like they were about to tear each other to shreds. They still looked that way. Sitting on one of the love seats was the owner of the largest pig on earth, or so he advertised at the fair, Mister Partner In Crime, who was chowing down on some beef jerky, or what looked like it, really getting into it. He was filthy and had what Steve thought certain were pig guts or shit all over his jeans. And Alice Goldman was there. Alice Goldman who last time Steve saw her had ruined teeth and her head cocked to the side, so far to the side he thought she'd broken her neck. He was relieved to see she looked better than at her nightmarish booth showcasing pictures of Terra's demon family. But he couldn't see her teeth, so he remained most cautious, especially since sitting next to her in another love seat was Burkenstock the Troll. He was looking down into his lap as if in another world all together. Sitting at one of the corner tables of the coffee shop, alone and to herself, playing with a large ball of twine that looked more wire, hands bleeding, was the child slave (Steve thought for sure) who had been sold at the fair. Instead of any last moment of defiance she'd shown to Adrian Cain the Auctioneer, she looked utterly defeated and hopeless.

Of course, Terra was there.

Also, alone. At one of the booths next to the coffee bar, clearly waiting for him.

As he approached her, he saw she was dressed in a midnight blue denim jumpsuit, clearly fitted to highlight her every flawless curve. She had some kind of animal fur jacket next to her, though Steve didn't know which animal and was terrified to ask. Her hair was pulled back in a ponytail so tight he could see her forehead skin stretched to the point it looked like it could tear from her scalp if she moved her head too abruptly. Lipstick and nails painted blood red.

"Steve," she said, almost as if she'd truly missed him, "wow, it is nice to see you. Sit down. We have so much to talk about, and I know you don't want anything here to drink or it'd do a real number on your alcohol level, right?" She set her elbows on the table, fingers intertwined, and leaned over in her booth seat, looking up at Steve.

"Yeah, you're right. Nothing here interests me. I see your gang's all here." He nodded to the living room area, then slid into the booth seat across from her, shrugging in his coat to get comfortable.

"That's very very funny and cute, Steven Paul." Her eyes were deadly striking, but with a murderous rage so controlled and stiff it nearly sobered Steve at the quick. "Glad to see you've got your wits still moving along up there in that wet noodle of yours. They're not all here, but that's not important right now. And not to worry, Stevie, look what I've brought." She seemingly pulled a flask out of thin air. "Filled it just for you."

Steve was relieved, and it showed all over his face.

"Here you go, dear, have a pull on that." She handed him the faux alligator-wrapped stainless-steel flask.

He did as she'd commanded and was relieved it contained Vodka. Terra knew exactly what he needed.

Of course, she did.

She then leaned back and motioned to the coffee bar attendant, a woman Steve hadn't even seen when he came in. He looked back over his shoulder in the general direction, seeing a woman who looked strung out, to say the least. Ratted hair. No makeup. Trashy hoodie and jeans.

"Misty, can you turn that song up please, set the tone in here."

The name *Misty* chilled Steve right to his drunken marrow. *The Misty? Misty of Brother Garret's home visit? The Misty who hosted the warlock home?* Wide-eyed, he looked back to Terra.

She instantly noticed his shock. "Want to tell me more about your talk with the priest?"

Rob Zombie's *Dragula* filled the entire coffee shop like a heavy-metal concert in low volume. "This is our song, Stevie."

Zombie's tormented voice grew in loudness, pulsing throughout the walls. The song took him back to his bedroom the night he found Terra on his bed with such vivid awareness, for a moment it felt he'd never left with her.

"Do you agree?"

"I thought Sinatra was more you. At least the boots song." Steve held Terra's lavender gaze.

*She's stunning...the most stunning woman I've ever seen...if she is
a woman.*

Terra stared deeply into Steve's eyes. Her mind was
moving into his own. She pushed out her thoughts like an
invisible tunnel fueled with the emotions and passions from
the depths of hell itself, and all of hell's knowledge and
understanding burrowed its way through the flesh of one and
into the flesh of another. Steve felt sinking sinking sinking as
his thoughts were vacuumed away and the hounds of Terra's
endless lash of terror ripped another gash across the last
backsides of sanity in smalltown America.

She leaned over the table toward Steve, lifting her hips
and ass from her seat, leaning over close enough where she
could wrap her hands around his head, grasping the sides of
his face and pulling his lips to touch hers, long and hard. She
kissed him deep with a seduction and sexual prowess he'd
never known, never knew he could know. She let her hands
go from his face and placed them at the end of Steve's side of
the table as to have the clasp of power to pull herself into
him with such strength and aggression he'd be pinned to the
back of his own seat, forever etched in time. He didn't know
what he was feeling other than the cascading notions of
arousal and dismay fused together as something more potent
than mescaline, more inebriating than a hundred shots of
single malt, more intoxicating than all the velvet whores in all
of Babylon.

She released him and sat back in her seat with the same
sharp jolts of assault she'd just dealt to his mind and body,
moving her head side to side in slow motion, never taking her
eyes off his own. "Are you falling in love with me, Steve? Are
you falling so hard in love you can't focus, is that what's
going on?" Her voice sounded so sultry and soothing he

wasn't sure if it had been recorded with Zombie's own sound in stereophonic.

"I don't know, Terra. Probably. Hard to tell the difference between anything real or not." He'd slurred those words, completely unable to focus on anything but what she was doing, how she was doing it, and everything around her she seemed so effortlessly to command and control.

But then something quite remarkable happened, so remarkable *its* very nature overshowed the very *nature* of Terra's horror show, when the coffee shop's entry door opened and in walked a stranger of no consequence, no self-importance, no air of anything other than what felt like the literal air of everything that ever was or ever will be again.

Steve and every single coffee shop slave of Terra's in the living room area (including the child slave herself) saw the stranger enter with such a peculiar stride of confidence and compelling grace it caused them all to feel a sudden current run straight through them that was so dramatic it almost felt familiar enough that everything else going on was forgotten, as if it never happened...if just for a moment.

The stranger was dressed in a world-class wool suit that looked so comfortable and tailor-fit it had to have been made somewhere far far away from Duncan, a suit so pure in its ivory color it glistened. He stood just a tad under six feet, with deep almond hair that was tussled and thick from years of fine vitamin nourishment. His skin was weathered and sun drenched. Though walking in with such grace and confidence, the stranger also looked more than just weathered, but quite possibly exhausted, though completely at ease with any worry weighing on his broad shoulders. As he walked toward the coffee bar, he didn't afford a single glance to those on the sofas and love seats, yet each of them who were talking, especially the black couple, instantly fell silent as if their vocal cords had been cut. Burkenstock and the child slave actually looked up to the stranger from whatever they were thinking or doing, and looked at him as if he was unconditionally unique. Steve could see the man's eyes were emerald, so green and vibrant they looked more like solid glass marbles. Though Steve couldn't help but place a hard stare on the stranger, in his peripheral, he saw that Terra's reaction was that of measured concern.

The stranger didn't stop to order anything from Misty, who had her gaze down to the floor, but instead walked over to Steve and Terra. "Pardon me for interrupting, but you look familiar to me, kind sir. Have we met somewhere before?" The man looked directly at Steve with eyes so focused they could have been emerald lasers.

"I-I don't think so," Steve spluttered. "It's possible, I guess." It wasn't that the man didn't look familiar, but everything about him felt familiar, familiar in the way that one suddenly remembered something that was surely once warm and soothing.

Steve also realized the music had stopped. It hadn't just stopped but had been cut off with such a subtle permanency that maybe it had never been on in the first place.

"Noooo, I think we've met before. You used to be with a woman named Anna, am I right? Anna Layton?"

Her name took Steve instantly off guard. In fact, Steve almost felt wounded by the sound of her name. He swallowed hard. "I did, yes. Long time ago, but yes you're right."

"I thought so." The stranger looked at Terra.

Steve also looked at Terra, and what he saw was something he never believed possible with her. She looked nervous. Worried. She shifted uncomfortably in her seat as if suddenly needing to use the ladies room.

"You also look familiar," the stranger said to her. "Do I look familiar to you?" The stranger gazed at Terra with such a confident aura Steve knew instantly that he was a man who feared absolutely nothing.

At that moment, Terra had an opposite aura, if that was possible.

"I'm sure there's something familiar about you. Sure," she said as if really working on holding her own, but Steve had no idea why.

"I'm Steve Paul, this is—"

"No need, Steve," the stranger quickly cut him off. "If I need to know her name, I will ask it, and she would have to tell me. But that's *not* something I need to know right now. And as for familiarity, sure. We all have aspects within each of us that feel or look familiar. Maybe even smell. We all do. Don't we? Within each of us is something we all cherish in some way or another. Like we were all once connected. At least that's an outlook I like to take. Keeps the edge off, and things seem to be quite edgy lately. Do you mind if I join you for a minute? Warm up for a bit before heading back out again?" He kept his laser focus on Steve, completely ignoring Terra and her flawless beauty or her endless sexuality that was eye-addiction, but he looked at Steve as if staring right through his corneas, all the while smiling with an expression of authenticity Steve had seen only a few times in his life. A few times from his mother when he needed her to hear him out. And, actually, plenty of times from Anna when he was saddened and fearful and she was there to comfort him. Then from this total stranger.

"No, I don't mind." Steve looked to Terra for

permission, as he'd done so many times since knowing her. He could tell she was instantly put off, if not disgusted, but said nothing, only nodding in approval. Except it was an approval that she didn't seem to have control over.

Instead of sitting next to Steve or Terra in one of their booth seats, the stranger walked over to grab an isolated chair from the coffee bar area, dragged it to the end of the booth table where he could sit and see both of them.

"What are you doing here?" Terra hissed, finally breaking her silence.

The stranger turned to her as if feeling her anger, but completely subdued in his control and reaction.

And why was she angry in the first place?

"I'm here to talk to Steve, if just for a minute, and while I'm talking to him, I would prefer you not say anything. In fact, it's best if you stay completely silent." The stranger spoke to her in such a command of authority, Steve wasn't sure what had just happened.

Since the moment he met Terra Drake, Steve was immediately convinced she was someone whom no person on earth could ever match up against. Not in any way. Not intellectually. Not physically. Not emotionally. She had proven to him to be a physical force of impossible energy and power. Yet at that moment when a total stranger had told her he'd rather not have her speak, she didn't. She stayed silent as the stranger had asked her to do.

"Listen, Steve..." The stranger let out a deep sigh as if suddenly all the power he'd just displayed had been acknowledged. "I know that you're not in the best shape right now. Could smell the booze leaking out of your pores the moment I walked in. Smelled it over the brewed coffees and pastries. I smelled you first. I know you've been going through it, if I may say so."

"How do you know me from Anna? Anna told you about me or something?"

"You know, Steve, I'm sure Anna is always with you in some way. That she's even watching over you, if that makes sense. But I'm more of a messenger. A friend. You can have a little peace knowing that I'm a friend. And as such, I don't have to tell you that you're not heading in the best direction. I'm sure you realize how completely off everything has been, how really terrible it has all been. Because you've seen it and been part of it, you have to see that this conversation is as completely real as is all the bad you've seen. Even though it's...*off*, maybe it's not as off as you'd have once thought not too long ago, right?"

Steve leaned in closer to the stranger, looking into his eyes just as profoundly as the stranger had been looking at him while speaking. "Yeah. You're right. Nothing really shocks me anymore."

"Well, I'm going to leave you with this last...suggestion, you might say. Last tip, if you will. There are things that will continue to shock you, even if everything you've seen, hasn't." He turned toward Terra's gang sitting in the living room area, his hand outstretched as if to highlight them. "It's a funny thing that we can adapt. No matter what's placed before us, if you think about it, we can adapt if we just let ourselves. You're a lot that way, Steve. Better than most."

"How do you know that?"

"You've been in jail, haven't you? Rehabs?"

"And how do you—"

"Steve, it's not really hard to see such things, or to know such things. I see your state right now, your condition. It's not hard to see all that could have happened in your life. All that has happened. Doesn't matter that I know, or that anyone knows. What matters is that you've been there. You've seen things in places where you had to adapt, and you did. In fact, you've adapted perfectly. So, everything that's been going on since you've been with her, yes, it's been harrowing. It's been dreadful. But you've adapted, even if it's been through using the wrong means. Things will get worse, Steve. They always do, they always will. And you will adapt. You must. You've been one who does what it takes. So, do that. Steve. Do that. Now, I need to be on my way." The stranger stood from his seat, still looking down to Steve, then to Terra.

She didn't say a word, but she looked back at him with her eyes locked and loaded to his, the stranger looking back at her with just as much fervor and determination as hers, if not a tad more. Steve thought the two of them looked upon each other as if to stare down the other until the end of time. Steve's drunken state had snapped to an alarming awareness, watching the stranger and Terra interact in silence as if in combat, then the stranger turned to Steve, bowed his head a few inches, placing both his hands over his beltline, and walked out of the coffee shop without another word.

Terra looked at Steve across the table with her jaw clinched as if grinding her teeth. Rob Zombie's *Dragula* pierced the air again, but quietly.

"I think we both need to go to church after that gig," she said, gaining back her composure, then quietly laughing, sick humor clearly being a defense mechanism Steve hadn't yet seen, hadn't seen because she'd never shown him the need to do so.

Steve took a deep pull from the flask, the only way to get his composure back, then: "Did you know him? *How* did you know him?"

"I know of him, Steve. I know of him."

"Who was he, and how did he know so much about me? He sure seemed to have your number."

"You will keep your mouth shut about that," she yelled, loud enough for everyone in the coffee shop to hear and look over at the two of them. She calmed herself, but her eyes remained clearly furious. "Nothing he said will ever make a difference."

"A difference in what, exactly?"

"In *anything*,"

"You'll never quit drinking," she hissed back. "I'll see to that, but one thing that bastard said is true. Adaptation. We all need that, Stevie boy, that flexibility. I'm leaving. I thought today would be different. You stay here and polish off that flask. You can give it back to me when I see you next time." And clearly she was disgusted. Getting up from her booth seat, she grabbed her animal-furred jacket, slung it over her shoulders then glared down at Steve. "I've got things to do, dear."

"W-where are you going?" Steve managed to say.

"Get to church on time. You don't want to miss it." With that, she pulled her coat more tightly around her body and left Steve sitting in the coffee shop to drain the flask.

He watched her race out of the parking slot, wondering what he was going to do for the next several days until it was time for the Sunday Sermon with Brother Garret. More than that, he wondered what had just happened with the stranger, thinking that the man came straight from Robert Heinlein's strange land. As Steve polished off the final drops from the flask and wondered if the entire world had slipped so far off the edge of the universe that no amount of *adaptation* could ever save it.

***

Duncan, like every town in Utah, small or large, had a church on every other corner, every church looking almost identical to the next. The location of Brother Garret's congregation was nestled in the comfort and protection from the outside world in one of the most wealthy estate settings in all of The Wasatch Front. The congregation was some one hundred fifty strong. At least all attendees thought they were strong. They were more than just the elite of the area, but the finest in all the worlds of wealth and power. Yet what Steve remembered most about the congregation didn't come from any one of its members, but from what Garret himself once said, that every single one of his congregants had issues and problems just as bizarre and weird as anything Steve had ever gone through. And a lot worse. At the time, Steve thought this quite odd. He'd always had issues with people of money going to church and truly believing they were better than others, that they believed they were born better. Garret's crowd probably had enough money to buy off small countries, or large courts, whatever worked best for them. Now, looking back at what Garret said about their strange issues, it all made a lot more sense. They easily had far more issues with access to funds to buy any sick, twisted depravity their entitlement could fancy.

Steve arrived a little late that Sunday afternoon. The weather had moved into deep coldness far too early for everyone alive in the Utah mountains. He saw Terra's red Mustang parked away from the various exotic cars: BMW, Ferrari, Porsche, and even a few Maserati dotted the manicured parking lot.

Steve pulled right in next to Terra, instantly feeling his truck, even though as new as it was with all the latest features, fell far shy of the leopards in the field. He'd dressed casually, but nice enough in denim jeans, fitted shirt, leather jacket, and alligator boots. No matter how cold it was, he felt the need to dress more hip than spiritual.

These elite motherfuckers can kiss my ass.

He opened the glass entrance doors that led to the chapel. As frozen as it had become outside, the heat inside the chapel was blistering. When he opened the chapel doors, he saw a congregation of worshippers who looked literally beat down by the heat inside. Steve took off his jacket immediately, trying to not draw attention to himself as Brother Garret was on the stage speaking, though Steve couldn't figure out what Garret was speaking about. The priest seemed irritated and harsh, visibly sweating from his forehead and neck.

Steve took a backrow seat, of course, and scoped out the chapel worshippers in attendance. The chapel was far from full, Covid and all, and he couldn't see Terra anywhere, as he scanned for her, first and foremost. Quickly, he rolled his sleeves up, feeling the discomfort of the heat.

Why had Garret set the thermostat up so high, better yet, why the hell hadn't he turned it down, or off?

He looked around the chapel, up and down and across each aisle, not surprised that Burkenstock was there, or Mister Partner In Crime. What did surprise him, seeing them yet again, was the arguing, angry black couple from the fair. They looked to still be at it, harshly whispering to each other. They were a few rows back from Garret's podium. On the stage area with Garret stood the child slave, this time dressed in a pure white gown that was also torn throughout, exposing skin that looked scabbed and bruised.

Steve wanted to stand to say something, and the eight highballs he'd downed all morning gave him plenty of juice to say whatever was on his mind, but he decided against it when he noticed, to the other side of Garret's podium, Terrance, the massage chair salesman from the fair and from the picture in Garret's office. The masseuse was dressed in similar fashion as he'd been at the fair: Royal purple jacket and slacks, polished black boots so shiny they looked blue, but no cape draped him. He had the same lacquered white painted face and hands, but the paint was clearly dripping due to the hellish heat. Steve didn't know what to say or think as he didn't want to stare at Terrance long enough to make eye contact, so he continued looking around the congregation. He recognized a few people here and there but felt his heart thump hard when his eyes caught those of Tasha and Danielle from the salon. They were sitting so close to each other it looked like they were joined at the shoulder blades. They were giggling obscenely. Though Steve couldn't hear them, he could see it all over their faces as they'd turned toward the back row when they'd heard him walk in and watched him take his seat to look around at what was becoming a spectacle.

They kept looking at Steve and he couldn't force himself to look away. He could see both of their now completely ruined mouths. Their hair was ratted in filth and grease, and there were a few large flies buzzing around them. In fact, Steve noticed several of the same rather grotesquely large flies in his own immediate area, so disgusting it caused him to lose attention on the salon witches, no matter how ghastly their appearance.

The Lady Mephistopheles

Repulsed and angry—for Steve hated flies more than any other insect (any living creature of any kind)—he swatted and grabbed at them fiercely and even stupidly, but regardless of how large the flies were, or how slow, they still easily maneuvered away from his futile efforts to kill them. Instead of continuing to swat at them, he sat back on the plush bench and tried with all his might to focus now on what Garret was rambling on about.

And he was indeed rambling. Not about scripture, or God, or Christ, or the Virgin Mary, but about the rise of decadence and immorality of the flesh, and not that it was a sin, but something to embrace and feel the power of its instant pleasures and soothing comforts in a world that was dying anyway, so why fight it?

The longer the sermon droned on, the more Steve felt his mind slipping away so far from reality he wondered if that's how it felt when Alzheimer's first crept in to start eating away the brain. He swatted at more large flies, which were increasing in number, slamming his palm to his neck in near rage as he was sure one of them landed on him and took a deep bite.

Of course he missed, as *shits* and *fucks* hissed from his mouth, but he leaned forward anyway to do his best at hearing more of Garret's sermon.

"We are all sinners, brothers and sisters. We are all latherers of the flesh. Each of us a walking representation of worship, but what do we worship? As the elites, it is our right to worship what we please. Is that not what we believe deep inside us? Deep in our core do we not only come here to feel some form or glory from the days of our womb when all was truly righteous and whole? Of course we do." Garret's voice boomed from his podium as he began to really work himself into a frenzy. "We believe, because, if nothing more, we believe in a *borrowed* testimony, but we've never seen anything that saves or glistens us with rapture. At least, that used to be the case. Things only moved along in our senseless, bubbled lives with each of us walking around in a pretend world that had very little truth to it. Until now. *Now*, I say to you. You've all seen it. You've all felt it. Change is ripe within the fold, and Oh, Oh...is that Brother Steven Paul I see in the back? Brother Paul who came to visit me so desperately in need of atonement. Welcome, Brother Steven Paul, everyone, of course you remember him. Didn't think you would make it out, Steve. So filled with joyous rage to see you." Garret thundered in his nonsense, looking directly at Steve.

Steve felt every sick and bizarre eye of the heathens in the chapel turn to him in a glare of such a shock that all the eyes together looked like the face of a massive fly lurching toward him as if to suck on the sweat now streaming down his temples. He wanted to scream, but Garret continued before even a breath of relief could escape.

"Do not mind him, brothers and sisters. Leave him to his own thoughts, as each of you have your own." He roared on as the congregation did exactly as they were told and looked again toward the raging priest. "*Pay* attention to your own sins this day, this I tell you true. This day...on this day you have come here by direct invitation. Not just by me. You have felt the invitation, for even I was invited to come for this Sabbath chant." He glanced over to the child slave dressed in torn white, then to Terrance, where the priest stopped and kept his stare on the massage master. "Please, please, do come up. It's no longer my time." Garret walked to where Terrance was sitting, and as Terrance stood, he shook Garret's hand, then walked to the podium.

The Lady Mephistopheles

Terrance stood before the congregation and put his arms high above his head, as if he wanted to touch the ceiling even though he certainly knew he couldn't. Suddenly, he twisted his body in spasms...controlled spasms, shaking his arms, pummeling his hips back and forth, the whole of him looked as if he was being violently shaken by an unseen force, or that he'd been drilled by a frightening current from the floor that ripped straight through the arches of his feet.

Steve looked on with an awe that was just as strong as his fear, and more flies swarmed in and buzzed around the entire chapel. Fierce, large flies that were clearly on the hunt for whatever was in their way, grew in such a number Steve could hear them as loudly as he could hear his own struggling breath.

Terrance continued in the spasms long enough to where Steve thought the masseuse must have been feeling the same way Steve had felt when being tortured in the man's massage chair at the fair. When Terrance's convulsions finally subsided, he grabbed the microphone from the podium and began walking around on stage with plenty of strength still remaining. He looked wild and beastly as he spoke, sweating huge drops of white paint.

"As Brother Garret said to us, dear church goers and do-gooders, we have been invited today to be filled with the edification of He who will make things right again. In fact, He already has. He who now reigns, and He who no one knows. And I wish to give great thanks to Brother Jonathan Garret for opening up his chapel and providing this Den of Thieves the finest of offerings. I give grand thanks, my fine Brother." Terrance looked over to where Garret had taken his place. "Come to me. Let's you and I thank them together in our unity."

Garret arose and walked back to the podium where Terrance was standing with microphone in hand. Terrance then embraced the priest, wrapped his hands around his head and pulled his lips to his own, kissing him deeply with ravaging aggression.

To Steve's horror, yet to the congregation's twisted glee, Garret kissed him back with just as much aggression and force. The two men continued their carnal deviance, kissing deeper and harder, grabbing each other's asses, forcing their pelvises violently together as if to fuck each other in anger and obscene passion gone deeply awry into the backs of the crevices of all that ever burnt and scorched the walls of every inferno that blasted magma and tormented coals from the bowels of Satan's hallways where the screaming never stopped, where the raping never stopped, where the jaundice of every cracked sore ever oozed out the endless writhing of maggots to create the endless swarm of flies that grew and burst apart from the insides out, spewing their millions of eyes that would never sleep.

Steve used every ounce of last physical strength to stand, to run from the freakish scene that would never right itself. But just as he stood, Terrance and Garret released each other, with Terrance speaking once again in his rhythm of gore. Steve noticed the black couple had stopped fighting, that the salon witches stopped laughing, that the child slave stood from her stage seat.

"That is all we have for you, brothers and sisters, that is all Brother Garret and I have to show and to say, as it is my pleasure to now give you our final speaker, Father Adrian Cain."

The entire congregation then stood in unison and roared out loud in a chant and rant so disturbing they no longer sounded human.

Steve remained standing where he was and watched the Stage Left door blast open to let in the hulking, towering Adrian Cain. He strode across the stage, to the podium, and snatched the microphone from Terrance. Cain was dressed in a suit so white it looked more like chunky white noise background among the swarm of flies now buzzing the entire stage area. His hands were obscenely long, with fingers even longer, not looking at all like fingers, but more like wretched twigs. He had on the same heavy leather belt and six-gun Steve had seen in the portrait that awful night in front of the Duncan Craft Shoppe, as well as the creature he'd confronted in the parking lot. Covering his face, Cain wore a mask of a fly's face and eyes of such intricate detail that it looked surgically attached to his neck. A hood covered the top of his head, and Steve knew it was the same battered hood he'd seen on the figure that had shuffled across Stan Smitts' yard that fateful night when Terra had appeared in Steve's bedroom. There was no reason to believe the figure on stage was Adrian Cain, other than his introduction by the massage master. As the filthy scene of obscenity continued, Cain then leaned down to kiss Terrance. But it wasn't Cain's kiss; it was the fly mask that kissed him, the fly's spongy structures of its labella and proboscis that sucked the face of Terrance. Cain then moved to Garret with the same dreadful greeting, and finally to the front of the podium, his knobby hands and fingers placing the microphone back in its stand. He raised his arms at the elbow joints, splaying his fingers apart on each tortured hand, then spoke without removing the mask or hood, his voice muffled and echoed, but filled with volume.

"I want you all to stand, and remain standing, as our final offering will soon come to you all, a final offering that will be all that you could have ever dreamed in your darkest holes. It is my honor to offer each of you, as a whole unit, a *complete* sacrifice, an eternal sacrifice that only I am able to offer. I give you my very own Harlot, *thy* very own Harlot, The Lady Mephistopheles who also gives you her very soul. Come to us *now* my Whore of Babylon," Cain screamed, now lowering his fly-masked face into the microphone with such rage Steve thought his own ears would shatter, as the back doors behind the back pews burst open with such force it sounded as if they'd been blown off their hinges.

Terra Drake then entered the chapel completely naked but for a pair of golden leather sandals. The entire congregation had turned toward her entrance as their voices awed out in a low, deep synchronicity. She walked right past Steve, not offering him even a glance. Here entire body was the skin that Steve had always seen as sculptured ivory. Her body was flawless and hardened like stone, breasts more like muscles, legs honed to a chiseled perfection. Her jet-ink hair was hanging low and heavy from the deep sweat that was dropping from her head, neck, shoulders, all down to her backside. Steve thought she was sweating from every pore as she walked down the center aisle of the chapel toward the stage, the priest Garret, and the child slave who now crawled on her hands and knees to finally kneel in front of the horror of Adrian Cain's hooded fly creature.

Bizarre, melancholy themes swooshed from the organ to accompany Terra as an anomalous compliment as she continued her stark-naked, drenched stroll to the stage. She looked exhausted, beyond human endurance, yet what distracted Steve even further was actually trying to focus on the vastness of it all, over the rising and sickening sound of the buzz of flies that had begun to overwhelm the chapel, swarming and lashing about at the benches and walls, everyone in the congregation slapping and swatting at them uselessly as Terra made her way to the stage to face them all in her depleted, yet spectacular beauty of mockery and bewilderment. Steve noticed how the flies avoided her, as if her demonic beauty repelled their insect evil, a paradox that seemed to Steve, a scarce deformity that had given the space-time continuum a split in its endless seam that could never heal.

Once on stage, she faced the congregation, spread out her arms, making her entire body an ivory-flesh crucifix.

Cain went behind her and effortlessly picked her up high above his masked and hooded head, placing her on top of the podium's oak wood surface.

Her body arched backward and she kept her feet together and her arms outward as if her own body worshipped the fly-infested ceiling.

Cain moved to the side of the podium and looked up at Terra's outstretched form, then bent down to his knees, looking up to her as she balanced herself perfectly on the podium. Her body and soul were the complete mock crucifix, a betrayal for everyone on stage, and for the congregation, a warning to either bow down and worship, or (Steve was convinced) be executed; every last one.

Garret and Terrance were on the opposite side of the podium from Cain, embracing each other again, holding onto each other, two demon lovers bewitched and entranced, in absolute submission to Terra's mock crucifixion. The tattered child slave walked directly to the front of the podium, her back to the audience, fell to her knees, raised her arms and placed her hands on top of Terra's feet. She then looked up to Terra, her arms remaining outstretched with her hands and fingers widely opened, as she was completely and wholly welcoming and embracing the congregation as if they were her very infants just learning the truest and most defining moments of an atonement so deeply entrenched in the myth and façade of the universe's betrayal. Terra looked down to the child slave as if to tell her...to direct her...to command her to behold the fainted world.

It was the orchestra of chaos as Steve watched in paralysis Terra Drake standing on top the podium with her apostles from hell worshipping her Naked Crucifix in absolute unison as they all moved from their seats, onto their knees, and began to chant. Chanting in the tongues of the ancient mariner, the long-lost ghosts of ships buried deep in the ocean's blackest dreams. Some even howled a howl so hallow Steve believed it was their souls crying out their last moments before signing off forever into Duncan's newly dug grave.

Steven Paul did not take a knee. Did not bow, as he was the only one, yet he could not peel his eyes from the contemptuous scorn on center stage of all that he had ever known to be holy or pure. Instead, he stepped into the middle of the aisle Terra had just walked to her Calvary. He looked upon Terra's soaked body, wondering how long she could possibly stand upon the podium so outstretched. He thought that her insanely sustained pose had turned her to stone. The music thumped forward in new and brazen melodies, and everyone in the congregation and on stage stayed exactly put, not daring to move until given permission to do so.

Terra opened her eyes, beamed her glare dead center into Steve's forehead, and winked her left eye. He felt the very strands of his stomach lining so stretched in tension that he would surely never think another wholesome thought as long as he lived, wondering how he would ever live, how he could ever live, was there anything left to live for, was all life as he'd ever known it gone forever more into the deep deep endless night of chants and wails and witches howling and heaving and spewing out the lies that would never end, the betrayal that would never stop, the realities so shattered that nothing real would ever come forth again, to ever breathe again, the light of hope of chastity or virtue as it was all slammed against the walls of the church of flies where death rested easily over the floors and seats and royal chambers of when Steve found the Lady Mephistopheles rolling around her bedroom chamber as his world in Duncan fell prey to the starving wolves of laughter and abuse of every golden hour that seemed to have stopped forever.

PART FIVE

*A Brother's Phone Call — Steve and Burkenstock Meet Again —
Doctor Jacquelin Pinault and Ballroom A — Houston's Radar —
Steve's MRI — Steve and Marion Talk Again — Terra Drake's Utah
Pad — The Turn At the Odella Hotel — Steve's New World*

Dean Patrick

I couldn't bow. Couldn't even suggest that I'd bow to her. When I stepped into the center aisle that led to the church's stage area where Terra was standing on top of the podium, transfixed there, her body positioned as a human crucifix...when I had seen all that I had seen since I'd met her—found her, actually—on my bed that awful night when Stan Smitts drove off to his death at one of his favorite watering holes, I had to make a choice to at least attempt to show her I was able to *portray* defiance, for I had surrendered to her every whim and scent.

Everything that had happened at the Black Sacrament came down to what I knew was an evil that had overcome not just my own small town, but every small town that had been the last pillar of resistance against the very nature of evil itself.

I also knew Terra wasn't done with me, and when I'd seen her open her eyes while standing on the podium, naked, sweating such heavy drops, all of her ghouls of worship surrounding her, with Adrian Cain who'd somehow unleashed the Jihad of gore, it didn't matter how drunk I'd gotten, or how long I'd been drinking, or how constant. It was most important to make my own final push toward re-finding my own defiance that alcohol had always given me the edge to survive no matter how much carnage was being chucked at me from every goddamn direction that God allowed for whatever His unknown sick reasoning demanded. I had to avoid her, but how to do that was another thing, and for how long I could was even a further unknown. Or an unknowable unknown, as my boss in Houston, Dr. Marc Lucas, had written about in a book he was writing for his children. A book titled, of all things, *An MBA for Children*. He wrote a chapter called Unknowable Unknowns, where he discussed unknowable unknowns as the uncertain future that produces anxiety, lack of predictability, and lack of stability in decision making.

I was certainly in Lucas' complete world and realm of unknowable unknowns.

Maybe it had something to do with the stranger who came into the coffee shop who possessed the kind of power over Terra that I'd thought was impossible. Or maybe it had something to do with the stranger knowing about Anna, and maybe even where Anna was, or at least to where she'd moved on.

What I did know was that Terra had indeed torn out the hearts and souls of Duncan, just as I'd said she did when I started this tale, that she had had those hearts and souls hand-delivered to the church that Sunday, right to the base of her naked body, forced to worship or suffer a fate far worse than what she'd already inflicted. Neighbors had been turned to monsters, priests into warlocks, and ghosts were endlessly and freely roaming the streets with no place to go but deeper inside the dying world of our own souls' blood that was bleeding out with such acceleration, it seemed pointless to ever consider again fighting back against anything. Before long it would be Christmas, and I was certain all the carolers would come by chanting witchcraft while all the town's lights burned red.

As I mentioned, it was a story I had no other choice but to tell, and a story that continued as I looked up to Terra's eyes when she'd opened them while posing as her self-induced crucifixion. It was that moment when she opened her eyes and winked at me that I wanted to find out why she'd come for me, why it was me whom she had so carefully plucked out of the cold universe's low hanging fruit tree to do with what she pleased. What was her purpose with Adramelech, or Adrian Cain, or whoever he was, and was he somehow the figure I'd seen all along? Was he, hers? Or she, his? I was sure it didn't matter, but I still wanted the answers to those questions; demanded them. The whys and hows of everything not only I had seen, but clearly every other goddamn member of the community, town, state, country, and world.

I *was* falling in love with her, as she had asked me so amorously, yet also with a disjoined sexuality, as I sat with her at the coffee shop before the stranger came in and rattled her cage. I was falling in love with everything about her. Of course, her looks. She had an unmatched physical prowess. Yet her ability to control and out-maneuver anything that crossed her sight, outmatched such a prowess. Except the stranger.

She had consumed my mind, yet I had no idea how to get into her head or even how to guess her next thought or reaction, much less the whole of her thinking. Even though I'd seen her murder my next door neighbor, or that she'd somehow turned my hair stylists into a Duncan Witch Duo, that my dreams were filled with pig visions and violent ruptures of anything I'd ever believed sane, I had to remain standing because *that* would be the only possible way to even have a scent of a chance of surviving her. Surviving her meant I had to stay away from her. Somehow avoid every move I thought she would make or could make.

I had managed to do just that for a few months as

Christmas approached the world with one last push toward a hint of valiance so desperately needed by the world as a whole. With just a few days until the celebration of what most considered a dead God, the world of the new Duncan had me in full alcoholic throttle.

Not only was I still in such a throttle, drinking so much that alcohol pumped through my veins as freely as blood, the severe migraines I'd been fighting since Terra kiss-licked me just before I'd left the Hickory Stack the night she backhanded Stan into the next world, had grown far worse. Not only that, I was also experiencing severe vertigo several times per day. I knew something had gone terribly wrong within me just after the beginning of my perpetual relapse. I didn't know if it was something Terra actually had done to me, but how could I be sure? She'd only kissed me a few times, but that last time, just before discovering the horror portrait of her, Cain, and their demon children, her tongue had raked across my neck and caused such a shocking pain I couldn't help but wonder if she'd left a wound that not only wasn't healing, but perhaps progressing into something deeper than just a wound.

I kept thinking over and over again what she meant by "turning" me, and was it this turning that she'd done to all those who had fallen in line to worship her with such absolute resolve. Was that how she turned Stan, or was Stan, in fact, actually resisting her to his very death instead of giving in to her, or turning for her?

It was also unclear if it was I who managed to avoid her over the eight weeks or so after the Black Sacrament, or was she avoiding me. Because everything about her, the fury and chaos that was her inner core, was perfectly strategic and agenda driven. Because I knew that much about her, it wasn't important the reason why I'd not seen her those few months. What *was* important was finding out if I was heading into an oblivion that I'd never escape, and that, I was convinced, would have to begin with finding out what was happening inside my very brain.

The best thing that I could think of in the endless inebriated state that followed my every breath, was that I needed an MRI for more clarity. Utah wasn't the place to do it, in my opinion. Not for me. It was time to head back to Houston's Medical Center where I knew that Dr. Lucas, the man I'd been working for over the past several years, writing many of his medical white papers, presentations, and editing his book, would connect me with the best brain specialists in the world. I called him a week before Christmas, asking if he would set up an appointment for me. He told me to catch the next flight out, that he'd have it all scheduled, no questions asked. He was that kind of friend, not just an employer.

I booked the flight right after we hung up, then decided to call my brother, Marion. The only family member I'd had left, as both my parents had died, and our only sister had gone missing just as Anna had. I hadn't spoken to Marion in several years, but he'd know the second he heard my voice that I'd been deep in the trenches of yet another alcoholic binge. The last many trips I'd taken to Houston I never saw him because he himself had been going through his own shitshow of a police force meltdown as Marion was an HPD homicide cop who'd gone through a god-awful blood bath shooting that wrecked him to the point where he'd separated from his wife, June, and their family of four. Still, I needed to see him. Needed to tell him what had been going on, what I'd seen, and yes, that I was drinking, but that the dark forces surrounding Duncan were far more the issue than my own personal collapse, that I was coming to town to get an MRI to make sure I wasn't on the fast track to the morgue.

Had to tell him all about Terra.

Before I called, I slammed home a pint of Gray Goose, and put on Nine Inch Nails' *The Downward Spiral*, making sure to play *Hurt* a few times on its own, as it was *the* go-to song I had so delved into during my darkest binges. Trent Reznor's anguishing cries and lyrics of hopelessness and despair set the perfect tone for two brothers deep within their own anguish.

> STEVE: Hey, brother. Thought I'd call with a bit of Christmas cheerfulness to brighten your day. Hey, it's Steve—
>
> MARION: I know who it is, Steve, what's up? Drinkin' again? Because I'm sure not in the mood for it, brother.
>
> STEVE: Christ that didn't take long.
>
> MARION: Known you since birth, think that one'd slip by me? Me of all people? Steve? Really?
>
> STEVE: Yeah...well, I know. I know. But you just picked up the phone for Christ sake.
>
> MARION: Think a phone call's going to mask it? Thing is, think I need this shit right now?
>
> STEVE: Not calling to give you any shit.
>
> MARION: Oh. Okay, Steve. Hadn't spoken to you in, what? Year now? More? And out the clear blue moon an obnoxious call about Chris-Fucking-Cheer?

A long pause takes place across the lines of the two brothers as they enter a verbal sparring match, feeling each other out for the most

The Lady Mephistopheles

vulnerable openings. Steve begins again after letting out a long sigh.

STEVE: Well, listen. I'm really not calling to give
you any shit or grief. I'm flying down
tomorrow and will be there for just a few
days, wanted to maybe see you. Not
maybe, I do what to see you. I'm getting
an MRI to be honest. I've got...I don't
know what I've got. Something, I don't
know. I called Doctor Lucas about it and
he thought it mandatory, you could say.

MARION: I see. Well, Steve, as much literal shit as
I've got going on myself, you're still my
brother and I guess I could be there
when you get it done. What's been going
on? What is it you think?

*Another long pause takes place as Steve knows he needs to get
right to the point with Marion, because even though Marion's a hardcase
cop, Steve knows Marion can pick up on bullshit faster than a fly can
smell it.*

STEVE: I don't know exactly what it is, Marion.
Honestly...it could be a woman. I think.

MARION: HaHa! Of course it is. When has it not
been a woman with you? Christ, Steve.
What about Anna?

STEVE: She's gone. She's been gone. For a while
now. Don't even know if she's alive, to
be perfectly honest.

MARION: Jesus. Well that explains why no one's
heard a word otherwise, and you're
already with someone else? Jesus, Steve.

STEVE: It's not like that.

MARION: It's always like that. You're telling me you
              don't even know if Anna's alive or dead,
              and it's not like that?

STEVE: Can I just say this, please? Just tell you?
              Can I get a word in?

MARION: Sure, Steve. Go ahead. Tell me all about it.
              Or whatever.

STEVE: I found her in my room a few months ago.
              Literally. Now please listen before you
              just cut in. Please. I found her there. It's
              too long a story to cover it all over the
              phone, and you'd need to see me to
              know I'm not shitting you. I'd just come
              home from a trip when it started, was out
              shoveling snow of all things that early in
              the season, and after I saw my neighbor
              for a few minutes...who, by the way,
              ended up dying that same night...I went
              into my house, and she was in my
              bedroom on my bed. No sex. Nothing
              like that. It was far different in that she'd
              come there for a *reason*. Like she came for
              me for some reason. I ended up...I don't
              know...going with her, I guess you could
              call it, going with her and being part of
              this strange world she seemed to have
              created all around the entire goddamn
              town, Marion. And the last time I saw
              her was at church of all places, and it
              wasn't just because it was church, it was
              what *happened* there. Like a scene out

Dante's goddamn Inferno come to play itself out on stage in real time. And I've been getting worse ever since. Not just the drinking. Like I said, my head. Migraines, dizzy spells. I'm not doing well, and I'm coming down to get it checked out, and I just wanted to let you know.

Marion doesn't say anything for the longest time as he takes the phone away from his face and looks at it as if it's a foreign object, but also one that isn't lying. He takes a deep breath as he hears Reznor's voice continue as his brother's background white noise.

MARION: I don't know what to say, Steve. Honestly. You're clearly upset. I see that. I hear it. Sorry it's happened, whatever it is. Don't know what I can do about it, but look. I'll meet you where you're getting the MRI. Just text me or call me with the time and address and I'll be there. We can talk about everything.

STEVE: Alright. I'll do it. Thanks, Marion. I mean it. There's no one else to talk to about this. Sure as hell not telling anyone else in the family but you.

MARION: We don't really have much else in the family, do we? I understand. Look, I gotta run. Give the time and place and I'll be there. Love you. Talk to you then. Have a safe flight.

STEVE: Thanks. See you.

And that was that. Not word for word, but that's how I saw it play out, and I was more than glad I'd called. Marion always had a way of providing calmness that was chilling to watch when under severe pressure; who knew if the pressure I'd seen would become one for him that would make all the years he'd spent raking the landscape of Houston's underbelly something rather tame and manageable in comparison.

***

I'd never had an MRI.

Had no idea what to expect.

I'd heard they were terrifying because of the sounds and the fierce anxiety that could be brought on like a catapult into darkness and stillness while the noises burrowed inside the tunnels of your mind. But there was something troubling me equal to the headaches and the fear of getting the procedure: the anxiety of seeing my brother while in the middle of the worst alcoholic meltdown I'd ever delved into (and I'd had plenty over the years before this one had begun) just in order to survive all that Terra had done and shown.

Mostly shown.

I'd done nothing but drink those eight weeks before the yuletide carols were to have their moment under the bloodlust moon, nothing but do everything possible to drown it all out. How I managed to keep my work afloat was beyond my understanding. Even more odd was the ability to keep boxing and training whenever possible, though filling the gym with stench at every visit. On top of it all was the constant nagging literally *inside* the migraines that kept drilling me with "what does it mean to turn?" What did she mean by turning and not yet turning, as she had so taunted me over and over again where it became as constant a thought as was my drinking.

Everything about me had become nothing more than a pure sense of dread that had become the lingering of evil over all of Duncan that I could see hovering over the town like a rotted fishnet that stretched from the county line to the Duncan Craft Shoppe where Terra's portrait remained in full display throughout the pitch nights of a cold bleaker than Terra's demon children.

Even though talking to my brother took a bit of the edge off as I booked a flight to Houston's George Bush Intercontinental Airport later that same evening, there was no way I could sleep no matter how much I drank. I didn't want to pass out, so I did the normal pacing of shots that kept the shakes away, but the energy riding freefall on fumes, then headed out into the rotted town's filth and despair to fill up the Ram's bottomless gas tank so I'd be ready the following night for the airport trip.

It was lightly snowing and the storm was supposed to get a lot worse, so being gassed up was always the best plan. Something that Anna had always told me to do, and God how I had wished she were around so that I could have at least called her for some piece of advice that she would surely give me to make it all seem better. But that wasn't to be as I put on a heavy jacket and snow boots, fired up the Ram and headed toward one of only two gas stations in the entire town, both of which would require me to drive by Terra's portrait from Hell. As I did just that, *It's Beginning To Look A Lot Like Christmas* started playing, and I didn't have the heart or the nerve to listen to it, for all I knew the lyrics would change in real time to some sick, twisted shit written specifically for Cain, just like what happened that night when

I saw the demon leader standing next to my truck.

I shut off the stereo without a moment's pause.

Soon enough, I pulled into the 7-Eleven station located just before the freeway entrance and saw, of all people, Burkenstock also gassing up. But he wasn't gassing up anything he had driven, but an old banged up and rusted out Jeep Cherokee I had sold to one of Duncan's favorite freaks, one Jack Wiggins, a hoarder and fellow creature of the night. At least that's how I'd always seen him.

Wiggins was an old man in his early 80s, had a few strands of sickly hair that he never bothered cutting, or grooming, just let them flop about and stick wherever the wind slapped them down on his pasty head. He stood about five-five, weighed easily two-twenty or more; had a mustache so thick it looked like rusted cut wire; all his teeth gone except for a few on the bottom row; skin a constant yellowish hue that made him look just as constantly ill. I had sold him the jeep a few years back when I no longer needed it, though I'd put a few grand into it because I had loved the damn thing. I kept it clean and manicured. Wiggins let it go right to the same shit he had let his entire life go. Every time I'd see him riding around in the jeep, back and forth to the store and whatnot, it looked worse off with each passing, always filled with boxes and boxes of endless junk that made Wiggins look like he was hauling around enough worthless shit to donate to every child in Duncan who went without whatever it was they were without.

I decided to drive past the two of them as Burkenstock was finishing up and putting the gas cap back on, certain he'd not seen me, and even more certain that Wiggins hadn't seen me, as he was looking in the review mirror and picking around on his gums for god knows what. I stopped right by the carwash directly behind the store, maneuvered the Ram in position to where it would be simple enough to follow the two of them back to where ever they were going. When Burkenstock got in the passenger seat I found myself actually snickering at how obscene and unruly the two creepy figures looked sitting next to each other as Wiggins pulled away from the pump and back on to the main road leading back to his place, which was not more than a mile past mine. Looked like he was heading back there as I pulled out of the carwash and hit the accelerator pedal just enough to quickly catch up and get right behind them, no longer caring if they'd seen me or not. I wanted to know what they were doing together. *Why* they were together, and what kind of information I could find out, if any, about Terra's inner sanctuary. Her den of fuckery.

Wiggins drove exactly the 30-mile-an-hour speed limit if not a bit slower all the way to his place, which sat up on a mound of dirt and rubble about an acre or so in size. He lived in a shack that looked like it had been through a machinegun war. No grass anywhere, just dirt, busted rock, and dozens of torn up tires, broken lawn chairs, trash cans, and a slew of metallic objects that once belonged somewhere long long ago in a time that was filled with hope and promise and majestic opportunities that had since been stripped naked to the hallow bones of a town that had sold its soul.

I pulled in the ruined driveway right next to the old jeep as they were both getting out, slammed the Ram into Park and hopped out, ready to get it on nice and ugly, plenty liquored up. Burkenstock turned to me looking just as saucy and a little freaked out.

"Whooo eee, what in *gawd's* name you doin' up here, fella? Comin' up on us like a bat outta Creepy Ville?"

"I followed you to ask the same thing, so just stand

back so I don't bust the shit out of you and the old man." I took a few steps back, caution in stance that would brace me for a fight, though I doubted it would happen with a sawed-off troll and an old man with a few straggling, rotted teeth.

"Saaaayyyyy, I know you, sunny boy. From the fair and the church, by Lordy."

"He's fine, he's fine," Wiggins said. "He's the fella that sold me this jeep, ain't that right, Hickory?" He was looking at me with as much friendly order as he could. He'd always called me Hickory since the day I sold him the jeep. Had no idea why and never bothered to ask.

I ventured a peek into the Jeep. "Christ, Wiggins, what do you have in the back there? Looks like piles of rotted cardboard. Jesus. Disgusting." I looked at Wiggins as closely as my drunken eyes could focus.

"I don't know really, Hickory, to be fair. Just stuff I guess." His eyes now looked crazed and lost.

I looked back to the troll. "This your new hangout, Burkenstock? Your new guest house?" I felt far more at ease as I saw their vulnerability.

"Ha, Ha! That's a good ole one on ya. I guess that's a fair 'sessment," he yelled. Almost hysterical. Almost sounding like my dead neighbor and friend, Stan Smitts, when I saw him just before finding Terra on my bed.

"You want to come on in and catch some warm-up inside, Hickory?"

It was snowing harder, which made it less cold, and much quieter. Everything was suddenly far quieter, one of the little marvels of a Duncan winter when life was sane and controlled.

"Not really, Wiggins. I don't like your place, to be honest. It's a shit hole and I can't see a minute in there that could warm a cold worm."

"Then what in *gawd's* name are you here for, you scallywagger?" Burkenstock shouted. "You don't want to come in, but you follow us here? What gives?"

"I wanted to talk to you, to be honest."

"Me? Good mighty sunny Christ. Why on this dying planet would you want to talk to me?" He looked up to me with genuine curiosity on his crooked brows.

Wiggins huffed. "Looks like you two have some recollections you want to go over. I'm just gonna head back in and fiddle around with all my own...recollections." He walked away from Burkenstock and headed up the rubble to the carnage in which he lived.

I didn't pay him a wink's attention as I kept looking at the troll. "Why are you here with him? What gives? I mean, the two of you make quite the fine pair, but what brings you to him? To *here*, of all places?" I yelled as the sounds of winter's beginning grew more and more silent, yet more and more invasive.

"Why don't you ask me what you're really wanting to get at, you kicker you? Cause it sure enough ain't about that ole hoarder in there and why I hooked up with such a devil. And he is, make no mistake, a devil. Most are who've been touched by her. That's why you're really here, and make no mistake about that, you wanna ask about her. I can see that as giddy on up as giddy can take me by my beard ends." He was growing more agitated and hysterical.

"I don't have a fuck's clue what you're talking about, Burkenstock, but you're right on one thing. I do want to ask about her. Who knows why, or how this moment brought me here, but you're spot on here. Give you a prize if I had one."

"Then *git on* with it, you fishy scallywagger. What's you

want to ask, ask it. Just spit 'er on out, *by gawd*." His face had grown redder than his beard, so I did as he ordered.

"What does she mean by turning? To *turn* someone. You're still alive, and you're here with Wiggins. Strange choice, but you're not with her, so does that mean you've not turned? Whatever the fuck that means."

Burkenstock then looked at me as all his anger and hostility seemed to have instantly vanished, as if depleted somehow, then sat directly on the snow-covered messy Wiggins driveway. Sat down with his legs crossed Indian style and looked up to me, whispered to me to sit down with him. I looked down at him as if he'd gone completely mad, but again, did as he said, not caring about the mess the ground was becoming, sitting as he sat, facing him as he faced me, leaning into me with more whispers, then speaking with such clarity I was completely taken aback. Sounded like the gentle thump on a Waterford crystal glass had replaced the sound of a thump on a metal can.

"It means something different for everyone, Steve. It means something for everyone that's tailor made just for them, and them only. For you...who knows what it is, what it could be. It's not the drink, that's clear. You've had that one around your spirit long before she came into your life."

"Yes, but I was with her when I relapsed," I said, also whispering, locked in complete fascination as Burkenstock's voice and tone remained all his, but how he spoke had changed so dramatically, all I wanted to do was stay down on the ground, sit with him, and talk about all the secrets of the universe that had remained secret for a damned good reason until Terra Drake forced the universe's hand.

"That's completely irrelevant...whether it was with her...*happened* with her, it was something that you had all along. Alcohol had already taken you long ago. She wants to turn you with something you've not known, or done, or felt. That's what it's all about, Steve, and maybe you have felt it before deep within a place that you couldn't entertain completely." He looked at me with genuine concern and compassion.

How was that possible? What had taken over the weird creepy troll and turned on such a switch?

I was awestruck, felt in the wideness of my eyes and the heat in my cheeks. "And what about you? What about now? How is it you're now sitting here with me on this snow-mudded ground, suddenly coherent and thoughtful? Is that whole troll sound and feel just an act? And why haven't you turned, or whatever the hell it is she does?"

"Who says I haven't?" he snipped, cutting me off, looking at me as if to search my face for any hidden agenda, searching my eyes as a new detective would, as if he were reading my thoughts, and how did I know he wasn't? "Let me say something, Steve. It's like this Covid thing, this Delta variant that's now being spread all over the place and spewed on about. She's like that. There is no predictable outcome with her. There is no strain of her that can be isolated, studied, and figured out. Haven't you seen that? Haven't you tasted it? My God we've all probably been infected by her. Her infection comes from touch, at least that's my own take on it. But this turning you seek or want to understand, that's her Delta, and you can be certain it's not the only one. She's the ultimate terrorist, the grand swindler, if you will. You'll never be able to guess what's next. Or who is next, if you follow. Notice that, too? All the psycho-dribble that has come into your life and all the lives of others?"

Burkenstock looked up to the falling snow after he

whispered his confusing tale that actually began making complete sense inside the wreck of my own dying mind, then back to me in that same almost overly authentic concern.

"Grand swindler. That's perfectly said, Burkenstock. Have to hand it to you. Reminds me a lot of *The Grand Inquisitor*, you know the tale?"

"Dostoyevsky. *Brothers Karamazov.* Best part of the book. Who knows, maybe we were both thinking it before I called it out—"

"Yeah. We were both thinking about Dostoyevsky and his relation to Terra Drake." I snickered.

"Why is it so out of reach?" he shot back.

"Okay. Okay. Maybe it's not. Grand Swindler. I guess it makes as much sense as every other psychotic nuance Terra struts around in." I didn't want to get the troll wound up more than usual. I had no idea how long it would take before the lucid troll would be replaced by the little monster I'd met at the Odella County Fair.

"And you remember the nature of Dostoyevsky's part?"

Yeah. I remembered it. "The nature of the devil is what made it so powerful."

"Right. Exactly right. The nature of the devil. That the only way to freedom and atonement is to live by the devil's rules, the principles of evil are what will ultimately lead us to salvation."

"Then I guess we can go to Hawthorne's *Young Goodman Brown*," I interjected. "Doesn't matter what story we find, or character, or thinker. It's all the same. I know what you're getting at. Jesus, I should have seen it more clearly when she was ripping into Stan Smitts about pigs and Marxism and Joaquin Phoenix's lecture."

"It's like her understanding of darkness is so complete,

it's useless, even futile, to go against her." Burkenstock was really giving an effort to figure it all out. "Then again, what if you'd somehow turned as she wanted, but you quickly sacrificed yourself so she couldn't have you. Maybe that's how you win." His voice grew much quieter at the dreadful thought.

All I could do was look at him in disbelief as we sat there together with the snow covering us in a blanket of iced cotton.

I was clueless as to how to make it out of this mess alive.

***

I ended up leaving Burkenstock while he continued sitting on Wiggins' broken and then snowed-over driveway, not bothering to give him a hand up or say goodbye, not giving a shit that he'd changed so dramatically in his speech and tone. Because I'd probably see him again in some other bizarre setting just like he'd said about the whos and the whats that kept coming at me like a carnival sideshow served up from Hell's Master Chef. I left him there because yet another migraine had begun to put another stranglehold around my skull, and I needed a few shots to make it ease up, if just for a moment.

I could feel everything within the marrow of my bones achingly tell me that I needed an MRI, and having Dr. Lucas recommend it made the ache all the more nagging. And like I said at the beginning of this tale, I was finding myself closer and closer to not having much of a choice of anything other than to tell it all. Spew it out. Give everyone a good nice yarn that would keep them up into the ugly ugly nights of winter's discontent when the howlings never ceased nor ever ceased to amaze everyone who was lost in all the laughter of a world gone so awry and so south that deep travels would only continue deeper south until hell itself arrived in an almost pleasurable sense with Satan at the doorstep, creaking the old oaks of hell's gates just a twitch enough open to see inside where the dances of the devils and their delight in those dances their delight in all the carnage and wreckage and ruin cast upon the innocent whose souls anguished in the deepening and endless nights, crying in vain and vanity to a God whose ears were plugged so tightly shut no cries no prayers no wails no anguish no relief would ever be provided for again by His warmth and glorious bathing of forgiveness that had seemed so long ago and so far away, it was a wonder if anything ever existed from before the beginnings of the black holes and luciferic worms.

After gassing up the Ram, which had been my original intention, I drove home, logged into the Delta Airlines website, booked my flight for the very next morning, and drank myself to sleep after setting my alarm to a full blasting sound of my phone's most obnoxious ringtone so I'd be sure to awaken in plenty of time to hit the juice enough to be perfectly numb on the flight to Houston. With all that had been going on over the past few months while locked in a perpetual relapse, I cared not one wit's end to make one more drunken drive across the frozen grounds to the Salt Lake City Airport.

The flight took off without a hitch and arrived in Houston ten minutes before scheduled. The rental counter was surprisingly empty, so I rented what was available, also surprising in that I was offered a Dodge Charger at the price normally charged for a Ford Escape. Even more surprisingly still was no one at the checkout counter said a word about what must have been a thick alcoholic stench vaping all around me. At least that's what I thought until the front desk lady got a little chatty, if not a bit flirtatious.

"Seems you're in the place I'd like to be after work, you make sure you're careful, now, you feel me?" She leaned across the counter to purposely show off a cleavage that any woman would be honored to own. She was dark skinned, but not African American or even Spanish or Mexican. Perhaps from Brazil or Venezuela, but she was stunning enough to take my mind off everything else, and that was a feat in itself. She was probably five-nine, short cropped black hair, maybe twenty-five at the most, and making the most of the standard issued Hertz Rental uniform. I decided to entertain it as I could see the look in her eyes was perhaps more than just curiosity. Plus, I was drunk.

"And what kind of place is that?" I said, turning back to her and leaning back on the counter to face her, probably no more than a foot from her head and shoulders.

"Well...I think you know, Mister Paul. I'm not gonna say anything, even though I'm supposed to," she purred. At least that's what my inebriated ears heard.

"I appreciate you keeping this to yourself, uhh, what's your name? I can't see your nametag." I peered down her opened blouse again, looking at her necklace and pendant as much as her cleavage, grimacing at what I thought the pendant looked like.

"That's because I'm not wearing a nametag, Mister Paul, and if I was, it would be higher up than where your eyes are peering." A small clearing of her throat was a signal to not stare, as it wasn't polite.

I took a deep breath and looked into her eyes to show

good faith. "Of course. Sorry about that." I straightened myself up to stand upright, shaking off the pendant thought. "Maybe I'll see you around, who knows, right?"

"No need for apologies, Mister Paul, and maybe you will indeed see me around," she said, more friendly than what seemed appropriate, with a smile that opened more wide than appropriate, showing teeth and gums that were not nearly as polished and white as I would have expected from someone so beautiful and exotic. In fact, her entire mouth looked parched, with a gumline that looked to be in the beginnings of something that was probably causing her a lot of discomfort, but she certainly didn't show it as she continued to smile. I couldn't hold her stare as I backed up cautiously. She saw this and giggled. The pendant dangling from her neck, too familiar, but I had to focus.

"Make sure you watch where you're going, 'specially in your framework, Mister Paul." She stood straight again, showing off her body as much as possible from behind the rental car counter. I felt a little nauseated as I couldn't stop staring, not at her, but at her necklace and pendant that seemed to have started dancing, looking then as the one Terra had worn at The Hickory Stack, which had suddenly seemed a lifetime ago.

"I never got your name," I said, still backing up.

"Do you really want it?"

I decided to go with it as I'd gone with every other goddamn thing, except taking the knee at the Black Sacrament. "Sure, what is it?" I said more acidly.

"It's Joy, my name's Joy. See you around, Mister Steven Paul." And with that she turned to head back behind the scenes to do whatever it was that rental car attendants do when wrapping up a customer transaction, leaving the paperwork, on the counter for me to grab.

I followed the lanes and signs in the rental car lobby that led to a vast and open parking lot filled with hundreds of vehicles, following every sign that led to the spot where a white Dodge Charger was waiting for me, keys in, ready to roar. It had a blower hood, and looked like it was speeding just sitting there.

It was close to 11 am and even though check-in wasn't until 3 pm that afternoon, I'd stayed at the Houston Downtown Marriot enough times over the past few years that the hotel manager had become a business friend, always making sure that no matter what time I arrived, check-in for me was always welcome and available. The hotel was located in the center of Houston's fabulous skyline, my room always the same one on the 31st floor with a spectacular view of the entire surrounding skyline, with the Galleria of Houston and The Houston Medical Center (both areas of town large enough and impressive enough to serve as any city's actual downtown) providing a backdrop that created a dazzling and massive megaplex of modern city greatness only equaled by the likes of New York, LA, Paris, or Moscow.

I parked the Charger in my usual spot always held for me when staying at the Downtown Marriot, checked in quickly as everything was arranged and set, spoke briefly to hotel staff, whom I didn't recognize as they were clearly new, but still knew all about me, treating me with complete distinguishment. I asked them to say hello to Brenda Winston, the manager I knew, and as I was about to head to my room to unpack my bag, shower, and slam home a few of the mini-bar's vodkas, with cranberry, Brenda sauntered out from the back of the front desk area to say hello. I turned back to say hello as I heard her cheerful voice.

"Haven't seen you in ages, Mister Paul, and it is truly so gooooood to see you." She was as perky as she'd always been. Perhaps too much so.

"Hi, Brenda. Nice to see you as well." I said it with as much restraint as possible to not slur. Not that it actually mattered, but I always liked Brenda and respected her and her work ethic, keeping shit together during the Covid fuck show.

"Come on over here an' give me a hug, Mister Handsome Man." She made her way toward me from around the front desk counter.

So, I did.

Brenda was probably in her mid fifties, stood five-ten or so, skin and bones, native Houstonian, African-American who'd been working at the Downtown Marriot for over twenty years, and she loved customer service more than any one person I'd ever known. Every time I'd given her a hug I wondered if she'd ever eaten anything other than popcorn, or celery sticks. It was no different that time when I pulled away from her to get a better look, noticing to my concern that she was even thinner to the point of exhausted gaunt.

"You look...tired, Brenda," I said as politely as possible.

"Tired? Tired? Good hell, son, I'm peaked, let me say it. Peaked out, you hear me?" She drilled me with eyes that looked as if they were in the beginning stages of glaucoma. "Come on over to the desk, Mister Paul. I gotta show you something, gotta *give* you something, actually." She turned back to the front desk, grabbing my hand, giving me no other choice. I didn't say anything and just followed along.

She walked behind the front desk, to her check-in station, fidgeted around various papers in front of her, shuffling them about until she found a particular sealed envelope. It was the envelope itself that looked so peculiar, as if it had been mailed from a different time period, a place long lost in time with a blob of wax that had it sealed shut. Just as she was about to hand it to me, or what I thought she was going to do, to the far left of me in the marbled lobby area just in front of one of the tailored dress shops of the hotel stood a woman dressed in a fitted red mini dress. Vampire red, with black stiletto pumps, and she wore a wide-brimmed black velvet hat. I could tell that her head was shaven, that her skin was so white it looked more like the polished wax mannequins that were built for the finest boutiques in London or Paris. Her arms and legs were just as white, long and slender in perfection. Her fingers I could tell looked almost too long, making her look so shockingly produced and beautiful she could have easily been mistaken as an expensive Christmas display designed to bring in the richest of shoppers and guests. It was only her walking around that gave her away that she was, in fact, human.

Brenda cleared her throat a few times loud enough to know she wanted my attention as I found myself almost entranced by the wax-white woman. "You're married, Mister Paul, but you lookin' over at her like you're not."

I took a deeper breath than expected. "I've not seen Anna in quite some time, to be honest, Brenda. Fact, I've not seen her since the pandemic hit, come to think of it."

"Sorry to hear that, Mister Paul. And here we are now in irony."

"What do you mean?"

She handed me the strange envelope. "These are tickets to a presentation that woman over there is giving later this afternoon. Thought you'd be interested in goin'. Didn't know you'd be alone, so there's two tickets, but here you go, make no never mind."

"Thank you, Brenda. Who is she?" I was completely intrigued.

"Don't know much about her. Name's Doctor Jacquelin Pinault. Some kind of art critic is all I've heard. But the presentation seems like something I thought you'd enjoy, so I was able to get you tickets. You know, just in case. Always looking out for you, Mister Paul."

"Very nice, Brenda."

"She sure caught your eye, I'd say." She followed that with a weird giggle.

"She has a different look, I'll give her that."

Brenda suddenly broke out in a laughter I'd never heard from her, nor would have ever expected. It was almost too over-the-top.

"Thanks, Brenda, really. Thanks for this. I need to head up to my room and clean up. Long flight and all."

"Again, don't you never mind, Mister Paul. Always a pleasure seeing you. You go on up now and do more than just clean up. Get yourself a little more of that something you may be needing right about now."

By that time, I was sure she'd smelled the alcohol spewing from me in all directions.

"Yeah, Brenda. I'll probably see you later." I backed up and headed to the elevator tower that led to my room, more than relieved that Brenda didn't say anything further. I turned to look over to where Dr. Pinault had been walking in her black wide-brimmed hat, but she was gone, so I quickly opened the envelope, peeling off the wax seal, to see what she was all about. For the first time since I couldn't even remember, I wasn't thinking about Terra Drake. This Dr. Pinault, whoever she was, maybe didn't quite rival Terra's physical prowess or beauty, but how she wore that fitted mini dress, with what seemed like all her hair shaved to the bone white skin she had, was certainly quite the visual I needed. And even though Brenda had so gently reminded me of Anna, Anna had been so far estranged, or even dead for all I knew, my drunken stupor had to allow for such women as this Pinault, perhaps all that she could offer.

I thought about calling my brother, Marion, but since he was going to meet me in a few days for the MRI, I decided against it, as drinking, of course, was more critical. That, and opening the sealed envelope from Brenda, which indeed did have two tickets to Ballroom A, featuring one Dr. Jacquelin Pinault, who would be speaking on the lost manuscripts of what could have been written by Michelangelo. It sounded far too bizarre to have any truth to it, but as I continued to walk around the hotel's stunning lobby and ballroom areas to kill a little time, awed by the stunning beauty and sophistication of the hotel's Christmas lighting and décor, I also couldn't stop thinking about how to kill the headaches that seemed to be growing more intensely as if the bone of my skull was penetrating the surface of my brain.

On one of the walls of the massive lobby was a gorgeous poster that advertised a variety of events going on throughout the city's immediate area. Houston was known for nightlife, entertainment, and dining that provided offerings that were an eye feast to any world traveler. I scanned the details of the poster, not taking but a few seconds before I found exactly what I wanted to do after the Pinault presentation. More than that, exactly what I needed for the frame of mind I was in that was doing nothing but spiral into places where only something hard and wild could perhaps contain it. Place called *Under the Radar*, or *The Radar* as it was known to Houstonians, a psychedelic dance club and bar that was four stories high and deep enough to land a plane in.

But first I had to see what Dr. Pinault was going to say about Michelangelo. I headed up to my room with the fabulous 31st floor view of downtown Houston any pro photographer would envy, slammed a few mini-bar vodkas, showered, and changed for the rest of the day and night.

When I took one of the interminable elevators down to Ballroom A, I immediately took notice that not only was I the only one on the elevator going down, but when reaching the massively spacious waiting area that fronted the ballroom entrance, I was the only one there, as well. At first, I wondered if it had been all the alcohol I'd consumed over the past months and that what I had just drank from the minibar had been the final drops that finished my brain's ability to know what was real and what was trying to be real.

The double doors to Ballroom A had to be at least twelve feet high, maybe taller, were heavy oak and deeply carved in intricate details of different histories of Houston: Sam Houston Monument, Old Spaghetti Warehouse, the beginnings of the Ship Channel, Gilley's Bar and Grill where *Urban Cowboy* was filmed, The Astrodome, Buffalo Bayou's Park Cistern. Rich brass handles were the final touch before entering. But before I did, I walked around the waiting area to make sure I truly was alone. While doing so I couldn't help but remember the scene from *Vanilla Sky* when Tom Cruise was walking down Main Street in Manhattan only to find in his own dream-like horror, he, like me, was absolutely alone in a place that normally housed thousands of visitors and guests of all walks of all nations.

But I wasn't in a dream as Cruise had been, though I wasn't so sure about the film part as I opened the ballroom doors and beheld an audience of probably two hundred or so guests all seated for Dr. Pinault's presentation. All sitting upright. All dressed in light yellow straitjackets.

It had to be a film.

I slowly glanced around the ballroom audience, back and forth each of the rows of chairs, every single person stitched into their own straitjacket. Not one of them turned to look back as the ballroom doors shut soundly and tightly behind me as I moved a few more feet forward.

Dr. Pinault was onstage, talking about something that made absolutely no sense, and certainly had nothing to do with Michelangelo, talking about what seemed like someone's misfortunes and mistakes, and not those of the ancient master artist. The stage itself was as grand and impressive as any I'd ever seen in any Houston arena rock concert, easily a hundred feet across and five feet high, making the ballroom's appearance so large and open its design seemed more appropriate for the likes of a Kiss reunion, or even an Ozzy Fest. But on this massive stage was only the lone figure of Dr. Pinault's shaven white head and black velvet hat, this time poured into a satin green dress so deep and vivid it looked as alive as her body. She was walking back and forth in a slow-motion stroll where long deep echoes penetrated the ballroom with each of the heavy clicks from her stiletto heels that tapped the wooden stage floor, making it the perfectly bizarre compliment to whatever she was talking about.

Click.

Clock.

Click.

Clock.

Click.

Clock.

The chairs in the ballroom had been set up to where the audience was divided perfectly in half, with a large center aisle that led to the stage, an aisle that was directly in front of the entrance doors. I didn't know where to sit, as every seat was clearly taken, but I continued looking all around the entire scene, thinking that it had to be a literal movie set, but I saw no camera crew, no director's chair, no story boards, no extras, no gaffs. I felt a panic attack coming on as Dr. Pinault stopped her melodic stroll, placed both her hands on her hips as if in irritation, and spoke directly to me, with not a single straitjacketed guest turning back to look at me, every one of them still riveted forward in what looked like an audience paralysis.

"I see you've found your way here. Would you please come forward?" Her voice filled the entire ballroom as if it had metastasized into a single speaker that presented her voice in such clarity that I felt drugged.

"Excuse me?"

What was she talking about? Have I found my way where? Why was she addressing me as if she'd expected me?

I thought so quickly, in such rapid-fire succession, I felt almost as instantly sober as I'd just felt drugged.

"I said would you please come forward. Would you mind, please? Please come forward." She pressed me with complete authority.

It was pointless to retort, as this was clearly her world, and I suddenly felt even less important than any of the other visitors sitting before her in those obscene light-yellow straitjackets.

I walked down the aisle to the stage, down an aisle that seemed as long as the stage was wide, feeling my legs and body weaken on me. I couldn't tell if it was fear or anxiety or everything that had been happening to me over the past months that had just then come together in one colossal moment of insanity. I walked up to the stage as directed, not looking at the audience, not even glancing for fear of who those people were and why they were there the way they were. When I was a few feet from the stage, looking up to Dr. Pinault, she walked directly in front of me, looking straight down to me, my head completely tilted back. With effortless movement she sat down on the stage, almost plopping, her legs dangling, her high heels dangling from her feet.

"Take a look behind you. At your audience, if you will, for you are the only guest here today, my dear one." Her tone was so thickly smooth it sounded just as *produced* as her very appearance, making her an entire holistic walking and talking vision of a beauty, an enticement that was designed and created, never actually born and bred.

"What do you mean I'm the only visitor here? *You're* the guest speaker." My defiance, I could see, she instantly appreciated.

"Who told you I was the guest speaker?"

"I have this ticket that was given to me at the front desk. Well, from the manager, actually. She's a friend of mine, as I've come here quite a bit over the past few years. She gave me the ticket, you see. Here." I offered her the ticket Brenda had given me.

"I don't need to see it. I understand. Doesn't mean anything, though, as I am clearly the one in charge here, so it's kind of my show. Now, look around at your audience. Please, and thank you."

I did as she said.

Everyone seated in the audience in their tightly stitched

straitjackets had their eyes and mouths also stitched open so wide and stretched I felt an instant sense of pain and dread, wondering if their skin would rip apart. As this awful sensation overcame me, what was equally as curious was the whos and the hows of the makings of this awful scene.

Who had done this awful deed? How was it done in such perfect organization of horror and controlled pain?

A thousand pried-open and tortured eyes and mouths glared at me with such a shocking display of an open-wounded welcome that I felt I'd just shoved my entire hand inside a live circuit box in the middle of a rainstorm. My own eyes slowly traced back and forth and up and down each row of seated, living, life-size voodoo dolls who were all forced to stare into every facet of my being.

"Each of them represents a section of sin you've delved into throughout your life," Dr. Pinault said in a velvet whisper.

I turned back to her as she stood up and stepped back a few feet on the stage, her heels doing the clicking that created the sharp echoes I'd heard when walking down the aisle to her.

"That's what I was lecturing about when you arrived." She began pacing back and forth on the monstrous stage. "Curious as to how you didn't hear that, or recognize it, for I was giving unto them all that you had given unto the world. You have seen so much, haven't you, especially as of late. So much, so much. You have within you a fortress of sin, so it was my duty, my obligation to share with each of them what you have done." She stopped pacing and placed her hands on her perfect hips to glare at me like a scolding mother.

I felt reprimanded. All I could do was stare up at her in awe and fright, completely unable to even think of a retort no matter how much I'd drank, no matter how much I wanted to drink so much more. I wanted to ask who she was, why she was here, wanted to turn back again and look at the audience that had somehow been elevated right out of Dante's seven terraces of The Inferno. In fact, looking up to this overly-produced woman of pure shaven white, I felt I was being transported through all of Dante's *Divine Comedy* where surely the whole of earth must have been passing through since Terra Drake had arrived in my bedroom to the sound of Nancy Sinatra's own walking boots.

But I had not bowed to Terra while in her mock crucifixion. I did not bow to her when everyone around me seemed to have lost all choice. It was that instant memory of courage that gave me just enough strength to now face this new hurdle of demonic effeminacy.

"I don't know what you're talking about," I whispered, knowing she could hear me with crystal clarity.

"Oh quite the contrary. I think you know *exactly* what I'm talking about. And if your claim to know no such things, let me provide a little synopsis for you. A soliloquy as each of them has already heard the terrible tales. The terrible acts.

Deeds! Done! Dirt! Cheap!

"You know the song, that's rather obvious, isn't it? What else could have caused them such perpetually etched startlement?" Her voice elevated to a new pitch. "Look at their open torn puzzlement. They have heard the terrible tales of your mistresses in the dark, of your lonely lonely nights, seeking out the pleasures of the whores on earth to tickle your every fancy. They have heard the tales of your fraud and deception, of how you stole from savings accounts of the old and feeble who had no means to fight you back. The tales of your fierce and furious anger toward your parents. Your violence toward them. Your stealing from them, robbing them blind. Your lies to all your lovers, all your friends, all your family to where every last bridge was burned down to the ground in embers never *forgiven*.

"I told them all here today that you are nothing if not worthless because you never had the courage to do anything that was right, never had the courage to face any of your fears, never had what it took to make yourself better than just the lowly scoundrel drunken fool you've always been. You are a cheater. A *liar*. You are an addict and thief. Never to be trusted by anyone. These are the tales I gave this audience who are now *stuck in terror, so foul your sins are to them*." She outstretched her ivory white arms and hands toward the audience as if to give them some kind of comfort from all she'd told them, as if for them it was the first and only sin they had ever heard since being born.

She stopped again, hands back to her hips, while I looked up to her, wanting to never again see that audience of stuck repulsion. She walked to the very edge of the stage and looked straight down to my face while I did all I could to hold her eye contact, knowing she was fully naked under the lively emerald dress. Her black eyeballs moved around in such fluttering circles, it looked like utter madness was settling in nice and deep within her.

I did not turn back to the audience but placed my hands on the edge of the stage to brace my body with as much strength as possible.

I held her glare...

And whispered again, knowing full well she'd hear my words clearly. "Why don't we go ahead and finish this."

She placed her hands to her mouth when I said it, as if to cover herself from being slapped, then composed herself just as quickly as she stared down to me. "Seems you have gathered enough courage to do just that. Well done. Well done, indeed. I guess we're finished here, then, and I thought we'd just gotten started. Seems you've been underestimated. Shame, as I thought I'd have you all to myself."

"You don't. And I'm out." My defiance was growing in strength, knowing full well who she was talking about, and even why. With that, I turned back to exit the ballroom, and actually ran down the aisle, feeling it best to get out as quickly as possible, hearing Dr. Pinault shout at me that things were not at all over, that she'd see me later, that the sin gatherers in the audience had not heard the end of my final tale.

***

The Radar was the only place that seemed logical to run to after I had indeed ran out of the ballroom where I did everything possible to counter Dr. Pinault, or whoever or whatever demon she was from Terra's own cauldron.

Who else could have sent the good doctor my way?

I asked myself that question over and over again in sick and drunken sarcasm as I raced to the hotel's parking lot, fired up the Charger, and headed out into the Houston night, as indeed the night was quickly approaching, just a few nights before my MRI, and yes, believe or not, that was just as much on my mind as the freak show in Ballroom A at The Downtown Houston Marriot.

The club was a terrifying place at first entry. The four-floored bar was more a venue for pure hedonism than anything else. The layout. The music. The volume. How people acted. It was like walking into a massive hall of ghouls and warlocks so much like all that Terra was about and had most likely been about since whatever it was that created her had placed her on the earth from the beginning.

Designed as towering hallways—each the size of a small arena, with four enormous stages that each could hold its own concert—each stage had women dressed as scantily as if working as strippers, guitars strapped onto them as they power corded their way through heavy music and wild rhythms in mock gothic rock seduction and worship. The walls were designed in the golds and purples of the Taj Mahal, with ceilings portraying all the works of Michelangelo, which caused me instant wonder if cosmic irony had just played its last hand for me. I hadn't been there in years, and the moment I walked in I remembered how overwhelming it could first seem with what looked like thousands of witches dancing all over the floors. It was a rock and dance club designed to rip out one's throat.

Cypress Hill's *Rock Superstar* was playing at full throttle, hitting on all cylinders from an amplifier system that sounded powerful and crisp and loud enough to fill the entire city of Houston, much less the club. The song's ferocious bass and cellos in the background that wrapped around Sen Dog's and B-Real's metal rap voices and lyrics hit me like a blasting furnace of rage, as the entire floors of dance looked like one lit up, entranced monster insect with a million wired legs.

As soon as I hit one of the floors to voyeur over the many guitar-strapped floozies on stage, I suddenly found myself having no idea why I decided to go to *The Radar* other than I needed something that pushed everything to the max before going in for the MRI, something to also push out the awful living Voodoo Doll Presentation of all my sins from Dr. Pinault. For drowning out hell, it seemed best to enter another one, and *Hard Radar* was the perfect venue for an alcoholic as ferocious as I was to find all the vacancies inside my tortured mind filled and plugged with the most decrepit and vile acts available.

The first thing that raced across my mind as I began to wander and mingle my way through the maze of dazed bodies on every drug known to humanity, was the never-ending question of whether or not Terra was there, somewhere, lacing in and out and around the dancers and drinkers like some orchestrated sashay that perfectly blended everything together.

But she wasn't there as the heavy music pushed onward in an endless god-like pulse and thump from Cypress Hill's merciless pounding about wanting and needing to be a rock star. Maybe that was the reason I'd turned to *The Radar*, to briefly live out a fantasy in a fantasy world that took me away from the reality horror of the world gone wrong.

As I continued moving my way through the wave of the living dead, my head began to ache again from yet another migraine and severe dizzy spell, and not one induced from the club's extreme noise levels. I also needed more alcohol and to sit down. The club had hundreds of small tables and bench stools splashed everywhere and nowhere in as much chaos as everything else in the place. I found a two-seater located close enough to one of the bars to where I could easily order drinks without having to move around more than necessary, yet didn't need to order anything myself when a waitress came right to me the moment I sat down.

She was probably twenty-years-old, dressed only in short-shorts, bikini top, and a belly bag where she carried her tips and pen and paper and so on. I couldn't see what colors she wore as the club's lighting system was designed as thousands of strobes and lasers that pummeled the club in vividly colored lights that looked like a million beams cascading together like endless spiderwebs of virtual kaleidoscopes.

She didn't take my order, but she did sit down right next to me, looked me deep in the eyes and shouted at me. She had to shout as did everyone else to hear each other. And the shouts were not nearly loud enough to clearly understand anything said, creating even another layer of mayhem. I couldn't hear her, so I shouted back at her, using my hands to animate that I couldn't hear her. She shouted louder, and I still couldn't hear her, giving her further indication what she was shouting was still being crushed from the music's overpowering reverb. She then stood up, opened her belly bag, and took out two sets of miniature headphones, placing one on her head, and giving me the other, signing to me with her hands that this was how we'd communicate.

She sat back down directly across from me. "Test, test, one two, one two, can you hear me now?"

"Yes." I was astonished by how clear she sounded, how all the noises and sounds from the club had completely disappeared as if the entire club had been clicked off with a single switch.

"You need to leave. You shouldn't be here. There is nothing for you here. You need to leave now. I tell you this, as a friend sent me here to say it." She leaned over the table to get as close to me as possible. Though dressed in almost nothing that was clearly meant to only entice, everything about her lacked any eroticism or seduction.

"Excuse me?" I didn't know a single other word to say to what she'd just told me.

"I'll say it one more time. You must leave. Now. A friend sent me. A friend of yours, as well. You may know him." She sounded filled with genuine concern and warmth.

"Who? Where is he?"

"He's probably left by now, but what I say to you is true. It is time for you to go, Steven Paul. Please follow my direction, as I have been directed. Please. And you were right when you said it's time to finish this. It is, just not here. I must go, and so must you." She stood up, kissed the palm of her hand then placed her hand on top of mine just for an instant, as if just tapping my hand.

She turned around and disappeared into the wave of wild patrons.

I was speechless yet again.

I stood up and did what she said, never to see *The Radar* again.

***

When I awakened the following morning after nearly forgetting I'd even been at the club, nor had ever seen the scantily dressed saint who told me I needed to leave, it was still another day before the MRI, so I decided to spend the entire day at the hotel doing nothing but drink from the minibar and lay around the room, get on my laptop from time to time to just browse, and do nothing all the way until the evening when I simply passed out and slept straight on through to the next day, waking up again even more in a stupor than the morning after *The Radar*.

I slammed a few more shots, showered quickly, dressed even quicker, and drove to the facility with a BAC level three or four times over the legal limit.

It was as cold and as clinical as any medical facility I'd ever been to, and for an MRI procedure that would be my first, I instantly found myself in desperate need of some warmth and comfort the second I entered the building. My brother wasn't there yet, making it all the more despairing. I was then fiercely drunk, and still dealing with all that happened with Dr. Pinault, both in the ballroom from her demonic presentation designed and produced somehow specifically for me, and then approached later that night with a warning about finishing it all being the right thing I had said.

Pinault had to have known Terra Drake, that much at least *seemed* clear, but how well she knew her and how deeply wasn't something clear at all. As for the bikini saint, all I could think of was perhaps she knew the stranger who'd come to Terra and me that day at the coffee shop. Stabbing Westward's *Shame* that had rattled the walls just before I left the club, was still doing the rattling inside my head as I walked to the counter and checked in with the receptionist who looked far too young to be working at an MRI diagnostic imaging facility.

Christ. Are you old enough to work anywhere?

She greeted me with such enthusiasm, it was a bit alarming. "Welcome. Welcome. Welcome. How is everything today, Mister Paul? You sure don't look like you're ready for this, now do you?"

I looked at her with such curiosity, she picked right up on it as she cocked her head with a jolt. She picked up on the drink as well. "I'd have to have my nose completely plugged with a cork screw to not smell that stink coming right out your pores, Mister Paul. That much is for certain, but think nothing of it. The machines here will sift right through all the wet clouds in your noodle-noodle, rest assured. Rest, rest, rest *assured*."

I couldn't reply. *Who could?*

The door that led to the back opened. A male nurse stood at the ready with yet another overly-cheerful greeting. He looked even younger than the receptionist, possessed the disturbing appearance of a toddler's face on a man's body. "Mister Paul, come on back. Let's get you started. And settled, for that matter. So dearly glad you are here. Don't mind Virginia there, she's rather new to all of this. Noodle comments and all."

"I haven't filled out any paper work or any—"

"Not needed, Mister Paul. Doctor Lucas has taken care of everything for you."

I looked at Virginia once again, then back to the nurse, too tired and too drunk to argue with them, especially since Lucas had it covered. "I need to call my brother first. He was supposed to meet me here."

"I'm sure he will be here, Mister Paul. Let's go ahead, get this moving along now."

"I need to call him," I demanded, my voice raised. I was feeling quite upset at the pace of how this was going, as I hated to be rushed to do anything, especially medically and feeling quite vulnerable and deeply alone all of a sudden.

"No need to be so snippy, my, my, my. No need to be a snapper head. You go ahead then and call him." The nurse had replaced his smile and cheer with a frown so quickly and effortlessly, I had to turn away as I dialed my brother's number. He answered on the second ring, told me he was running late, but that he would be there shortly. I decided to not wait, turned to the nurse again, and followed him to the back, where he looked at me in anger.

The back area was designed more like a locker room than anything clinical or medical, in fact, there were lockers lined up and down the walls in the room just before the entrance to the MRI machines. I looked at the nurse's tag to finally get his name, Todd Carol, as he gave me a key to one of the lockers where I put my phone and wallet and locked them in.

"How long you been working here...Todd is it?" I asked him.

"Doesn't really matter now does it?"

"Listen, Todd, didn't mean to get off on the wrong foot with you, but this is nerve wracking enough, okay?" I sounded just pitiful enough to where the nurse gleamed at me once again and suddenly looked like a machine himself, his face morphing that obscenely.

"I truly understand, Mister Paul. Let me give you something to help you relax during the procedure. I'm sure you'll need it. Am I right?" He looked at me with such pity I wanted to grab his neck and strangle him right then and there, but instead opted for whatever he was giving, which ended up being a mild dose of valium, along with a pair of insertable ear plugs to muffle the noise. At least he said it was valium. I followed him into the MRI room, laid down on the machine's long mechanical plank that would take my head and brain into the enclosed area where it would be scanned for any possible issues that were causing my head to split in pain, along with dizzy spells that threatened to take me to my knees at times.

"Okay, Mister Paul. Let me tell you about the experience so you don't panic or anything, which that pill should take care of real quick like, but this is HIPPA regulation and all, and this being your first time, you should know what to expect, which isn't that big of a deal, unless you enjoy the sound of jackhammers in your ears and head banging around." Todd chuckled.

I didn't say a word as I lay on my back.

"Just rolling along here to lighten things up a bit, okay? It will sound like a jackhammer, though. That's the best way to describe it. A jackhammer rapping the insides of your skull like it's being raped or something. Least that's what others have said about it."

"Wait. What? What are you talking about? Rape? Did you say *raping my brain*?" I jolted up quickly and braced my body on my elbows in defiance.

"Now, now. You just lay back down there like you're supposed to, okay, Mister Paul? Let's not make this any more difficult than it needs to be." He placed his hand on my chest to push me back down, with a strength that was suddenly scary. I made an attempt at some resistance but it was futile as I could also feel the pill kick in with just as much strength as the nurse's arm and hand.

"Don't resist, just relax. I'm going to place some vice-like devices to your temples as to lock your head and neck in place so you're unable to move your head, which would really screw things up." He bent down low enough to place the devices to my head, making me feel instantly trapped and even paralyzed.

As he tightened them to my head, he also placed another similar brace on my forehead and tightened it down, securing my head in such a way it would be impossible to move it.

I felt abused and frightened, but also knew this was part of the procedure and clung to that knowledge as to keep my sanity when Todd breathed out a long sigh in disgust before speaking again.

"As I said, it's a loud jackhammer sound, which is why

you have the ear plugs, makes sense, right, Mister Paul?"

Of course, I couldn't nod any kind of affirmation, so I just stared at him as the medicine he gave me continued to increase in strength, eliminating any thought that anything "mild" had been administered. "Let yourself just ease into this deal, it's about an hour and it can feel like an entire day if you let it, so don't, you catch me?"

I stared back uselessly, feeling more and more defeated. I then felt the drug take a sudden quick dive as I felt I was falling into the sunken place from the movie *Get Out* when Catherine Keener's character placed her victims into an otherworldly place that was far more real than just trance-like, and hating Keener as an actress anyway, the feeling that came over me was all the more worse.

I tried to keep my eyes adjusted and focused on Todd, as I could see he was then looking across the way and speaking to someone else who had just entered the procedure room, a woman I could sense as I moved my eyes to the other side of the room as much as they could roll, when I saw who he was talking to was probably another nurse, or even a doctor, but was wearing a worn-out red dress that completely covered her body right up her neck to her chin, her hair in an old-style bun, her makeup looking far too cheap and far too familiar. Before I could move my eyes back to Todd to give him the signal that I was indeed alarmed, I was also frighteningly aware that I couldn't speak, that my vocal cords had gone into paralysis as much as my entire mind and body were heading. As I tried with more effort, the MRI machine's conveyor system began to move me into the encapsulation area where my brain would be scanned and imaged.

Whatever medicine Todd had given me was plenty enough to keep me from going into a full blown panic attack, and for that I was at least a little grateful when the conveyor system stopped, the lights went out, and the jackhammering began.

I kept my eyes closed and wondered about all that had been going on and all that had been seen and all the deepening frustrations that I was battling and how the rest of the world had to be feeling the same things going over them in their own minds as their own worlds were probably in just as much a free fall into the hells of their own, but that Terra had come into my own as a designed personal assistant to guide me through a specific hell where she wanted her victims to turn and to turn to what and how it was going to happen no one really knew as I could hear the direction of Burkenstock just a few nights back on the ground in the snow, preaching to me in ways he never portrayed when the jackhammering kept the hammer down loud and melancholy almost in some symphony of utter chaos that made only sense to the demons and howlings from the ceaseless evil that came rapping rapping rapping on every chamber door...then it stopped as insanely as it had begun.

"Mister Paul. *Mister* Paul, hey. You're okay. It's over. It's all over. You did such a fine job." Todd helped me sit up to catch my bearings, even placing his hands on my ears to help take out the ear plugs. I knocked his hands away as I sat up from the MRI conveyor. He flinched back quickly as if to defend himself. "Hey, hey, sorry there, Mister Paul. Lordy it's okay. Just follow me back to your locker and we can get your things and you'll be on your way. Your brother is in the waiting room."

I brushed down my clothes and body as if it would somehow make things better and more clean, less violated. "Who was the woman you were talking to just before the procedure started?" I asked him with as much assertiveness as my medicated brain could muster.

"Woman?" he said with innocent ignorance. "There was no one else in the room but you and me, sir. No one at all."

"That's bullshit and you know it, Todd. Who the fuck was she?"

Todd reacted as if I'd slapped him. "No *one* was here, Mister Paul. It was just the medication doing its thing. Sometimes it causes people to have mild hallucinations, it affects everyone differently so sorry this has been such a bad experience."

"Yeah right, Todd. I could see her plain as day and..."

"Yes?"

"She just reminded me of someone way too familiar is all."

"Here here, Mister Paul, come on now. Let's get you on your way, and you can forget about this entire ordeal. You'll have the results in a jiffy, that much should give you relief." His soothing voice sounded completely insincere.

"I'm done here and with you. I can see myself out, thanks." I walked back to the locker room area as quickly as possible, got my wallet and keys, then thrust open the door to the waiting room so hard it slammed against the wall. My brother was indeed there, and he saw instantly how shaken up I was. My relief to see him must have been so acute, he stood up and rushed toward me as if I was about to topple over.

Never in my life had I been more grateful to see my younger brother, Marion, the moment I saw him stand from the couch where he was seated in the waiting room. Never had I wanted to tell him every last syllable of all that had not just gone on over the past few months, but what had taken place just the past few days in Houston, and what had just happened with the MRI.

I was heavily drugged, hung over, and completely filled with anxiety and dread. So much so I felt more unstable than I'd ever felt, and I knew that Marion would be the calming voice to help me wade through all waters of not just discontent but malevolence.

Steve and Marion are at Marion's townhouse. It's late at night. Steve is exhausted from drugs, alcohol, no sleep. Marion is even more exhausted from working another shitty Houston homicide case. It's quiet. The lights are low. Marion has put on a 90's greatest hits album.

STEVE: I swear to God, Marion, I swear to Christ I am losing my mind and it's not just the drinking.

MARION: I can see that. What *is* it, exactly? What's been going on? I can see a lot has.

STEVE: I'm sick. I can feel it. Not from Covid, either. I know something is wrong with me, something in my brain is not right. Hasn't been right for months now, and I am dead certain it's because of this woman. And now at the hotel there's another one I've met whose part of the whole fucking thing I swear to *God*—

MARION: Hold on, hold on. Just slow down. There's no rush here. Take it a piece at a time, brother.

STEVE: Okay. Few months ago, as I was telling you on the phone the other night before I got here, there's this woman in my room of all places—

MARION: Right. Right. In your bedroom, no sex, whatever. Got it.

STEVE: Yeah, well it's a lot more than just that. Before I find her in my room, I was outside talking to my next-door neighbor as he'd just gotten out of the hospital sick as shit from Covid. Almost killed him. And when I saw him, he looked worse than death. Like he had rotted away or something. Well, that very night as I begin to get...involved I guess, with this woman, we end up at a bar where my neighbor is. Stan's his name. Stan Smitts. Or was his name. She ends up killing him, Marion, I swear to God. Ends up hitting him so hard it knocks him off his chair to the ground.

MARION: Okay...

STEVE: I know how it sounds, but shit gets a lot worse as I start seeing her everywhere I go. Like a *picture* of her that's outside the main window of the local craft shop. Her and a couple of demon children and an even more awful husband, or partner. Whatever. Late at night I see this guy or thing or whatever the fuck it is, as I leave the bar scene. Not only that...but, wait. *Before* all that, as I was saying, I see this freakish...thing. That's all I can call it when I saw it, this freakish looking thing that looks like an apparition that's been made of scarred and knotted wood, draped in a cloak and hood. Lumbering across Stan's yard just before I go inside and find the woman. Her name's Terra Drake, by the way. And this thing turns out to be someone who goes by the name of Adrian Cain. Same guy in the picture. As time goes on, and it goes on fast, brother. Light speed. I find out Terra has what you'd call a following of some of the most frightening and sick twisted beings you'd ever want to meet, but more than that, characters that you'd never dream to meet—

MARION: Steve, hold up. I don't think this is all the booze talkin', but it's not making a whole lot of sense.

STEVE: Course it's not making sense. Think about how it's been *living* it. I mean, Christ, Marion, I end up going to one of the county fairs that's not far from my place, and at this fair I see a pig that's the size of a car. Bloodied and scarred and living in filth. I see one of my neighbors become someone who looks possessed. Woman who's lived with an abusive piece of shit guy I heard was also killed same time this is all going on. I go to an auction at the fair where child slaves are sold. I go to the women who've cut my hair over the years who have been turned to witches, for Christ sake, and just when things can't possibly get worse, I go to church one Sunday and Terra ends up on the church stage naked and posing as a mock crucifixion scene, where she's lifted up by this Cain character, with the church filled with flies the size of roaches. You think any of this makes sense? And now I'm here spilling it to you and I *hear* how fucked up it sounds. It's not even all of it, not by a long shot.

MARION: Look. Just hold on, brother. You're gonna cause me to have a drink and I've never drank.

Steve and Marion now look at each other as both of their levels of exhaustion have reached pass-out levels. Steve knows how things sound. Marion knows whatever has happened, has happened because he sees it and feels it all through his townhouse as if what his brother has said has entered into the walls and begs to be heard in real time.

STEVE: I know you're trying to lighten things up. But there isn't any light, Marion. Can you feel it? I mean, have you felt it? We have seen how bad things have gotten in the world, but this is the next level. And everything that's been going on that I've seen, yeah, it's a small town, but can't you feel it's now in every small town all over the earth? That somehow everything is now or never?

MARION: Maybe you're right.

STEVE: I think I'm right. As trashed as I've been and even now am, I think I'm right.

MARION: So now what, brother? What are you gonna do when you get back?

STEVE: I'm going to find Terra at her place. Place up deep in the mountains behind the ski resorts of Snow Crest City. Told me she has a place there, of all things. Nothing surprises me anymore, but I'm going to find her, especially since I've been avoiding her the past eight weeks or so. Find her before whatever I have in my brain kills me. Or before she turns me.

MARION: What do you mean by that, turns you?

STEVE: Something she's said to me since I've known her. Talked to one of her minions about it and it seems it's different for everyone she contacts, so I don't know what it means for me. I don't know what it is.

MARION: Alright, Steve. I hear you. And I mean it. But I think right now you've got to get some sleep before your flight tomorrow. I'll take you. I can always get your rental car back for you, if you'd like.

STEVE: No, Marion. You've done enough by having me here. I'll drive myself, doesn't matter that you're the law and all, I doubt you'd arrest me in this case.

MARION: Let's get some sleep.

That was it that night with my brother, as we both fell into a deeper sleep than we probably had ever known. Amazingly enough, I was able to get up the next morning to my phone alarm, quickly get ready and head to the airport as Marion was still asleep. I didn't want to wake him, but as I left, I prayed it wasn't the last time I'd ever see him.

The flight back was an easy one, and as soon it landed, I headed straight for my truck. No stops at any of the airport bars. Drove straight back to Duncan to get my free alcohol going. Hard and fast. I stayed home alone for Christmas, called Marion and spoke briefly. Our parents had passed on years ago, so the loneliness that night felt entrenched and permanent. It felt too sad and depressing to move into anything long and heavy with my brother after what we went over that night at his place. The sadness felt so thick I decided to drive into Odella and stay at one of the local hotels there, a place that Anna and I had always loved as a weekend getaway. Historic hotel by Utah standards, the Odella Majestic had been around for over a hundred years, and many claimed it was haunted due to a few suicides that had taken place on the hotel's top floor.

Maybe it was haunted, but I knew it sure hadn't seen the ghastly undertakings that Terra had tossed around in complete manic glee, so the hotel was the perfect place away from my Duncan home. I stayed at the Majestic all that week before New Year's, pacing my drinking just enough to have whatever edge I still possessed in preparation of finding Terra Drake once again, at her place, far north of Duncan, much farther north than Odella, in Snow Crest City. I meant what I'd told my brother. I was going after her this time, not the other way around.

Whatever the result.

That, and finding out my MRI results were indeed positive, that there was something growing and tearing my mind and brain to pieces, was the final nail in the coffin to get things all wrapped up.

***

Whatever had attracted Terra to come to Duncan and begin her annihilation of all that was ever sacred or holy, it was Snow Crest City that was far more her venue. A town known for its level of elitism and sophisticated sin and all manner of depravity, it was just as well known for its ski resorts, shops, bars, and prime real estate where most who lived there had second homes and apartments that sat vacant all summer as if to flaunt useless expenses for no other reason than to define flaunt itself.

I had always hated the town. Hated it for its entitlement. For its hypocrisy. And for its drug court program that attempted to save my life, but clearly and utterly had failed as I was preparing to face the Lady Mephistopheles as rip-roaringly drunk as one can manage without alcohol poisoning, though I was sure my BAC level was close enough to killing me off, thinking I'd rather have *that* do the deed than whatever it was inside my brain that was growing and eating it alive. I didn't bother going into any of the details when Todd the nurse had called me back, believing he was a part of everything from the get-go.

I remembered one night when Terra had told me about her place that was nestled deep behind the main ski resort, an old mining warehouse. I knew that many such places were still intact within the outer boundaries of Snow Crest City, had seen many photos of them in coffee table books that were always lining the walls of the town's shops and coffee bars.

But I'd never been to one of those mining houses, had

never wanted to see one. Yet I still had an idea where her place was located as Anna had showed me the area once while we were riding up and down the gondolas that led to the peaks of the resorts in the summertime when it seemed we had the whole of the mountains all to ourselves. I found myself missing her with such a longing that I grabbed my vodka bottle and pulled home a few slugs down the hatch to get the courage juices nice and fired up again.

It was New Year's Eve.

The cold so sunk in and settled it was unthinkable that summer had ever been a part of Utah. I left the hotel just before eleven that night, grateful it wasn't snowing because it was too cold to snow. The roads up the canyons to Snow Crest had been completely salted down as to make the traction as safe as possible, making it also possible to arrive in less than an hour, the Dodge Ram effortlessly eating away the time.

The town itself had one main street, called Main Street, that was literally polluted with shops of so much variety it had more of a circus feel than an actual tourist attraction. A few streets north of Main was Cherry Blossom where I knew I could park in the town's library parking lot. As I did just that I noticed another vehicle parked there with its lights on full bright. I decided to park right next to it as I was then drunk enough to start up a conversation with a complete stranger just before heading up the trail to the place where I was certain Terra resided. I parked the Ram and shut off its engine, got out and walked around the truck in time to see the door of the rental car open, and I could now see the driver lean out to push the door full open. Blasting from the stereo was The Beastie Boys' *Sabotage*, and the driver was none other than my brother, Marion Paul.

"Marion? What the hell, brother? How did you find me here? *What* are you doing here?" I was completely shocked, but also just as completely relieved that the universe had somehow placed Marion, the bad ass cop brother, right on center stage of what I could only imagine would be my own final showdown in a world that had recently died.

"I turned on your phone's share location option when you stayed with me. No way I wasn't going to know what-was-what after all you'd told me, Steve. And here we are in the middle of ice-cold fucking winter about to go to God knows what or where, but I can see this shit is real. I could feel it. Flew in last night." He cupped his lips and face as his frozen breath blasted across the frozen night. "So where is it we're going, brother? What's the plan? Or do you have one?"

"Terra's place is supposed to be just up that way behind the library and the last rows of houses, I don't know exactly where, but I have that feeling. And I don't have a plan." I pointed directly behind the library. "Won't take long to get there. Got no idea what to expect when we get there. You have a plan? I mean since you've flown up here you must have thought this through as you do everything else."

"Not really. I say we shoot from the hip. Let's do this, brother. Let's do this." He led the way up the trail and into a deep cold so bitter I wondered if it would actually stop the year from changing over. Within less than an hour walking up the trails behind the last city street, we came upon what Terra had once told me about. It was indeed an old mining warehouse, and even in the pitch of frozen night I could tell how blackened the building was. Marion said it looked like a mountain-sized piece of broken charcoal as we both looked at each other wondering what to do next, or how to do it next, whatever it was.

It was a place like no other that I had ever seen and was quite certain that Marion hadn't ever seen such a place either. Its entrance had the terrifying appearance of what I had seen in so many historical photos of Nazi concentration camps. That overwhelming feeling of entering something completely dreadful, completely damning, completely designed to ruin, destroy, and murder the whole of all human spirit.

The warehouse looked like an ancient place of horrors. Blackened with the charcoals from Hell's finest furnaces, the face of the building looked like a tortured shadowy face of the Brobdingnag, or what could be Lucifer himself. We were both too exhausted from the hike to debate whether to enter, both of us giving each other the silent agreed upon nod that only brothers understood. Not entering wasn't even an option. I could see that he needed to know what was going on inside as much as I *had* to know, even though Marion hadn't experienced anything Terra-related. I sensed that he could feel what I had been feeling the past months: that the world had indeed died.

We could hear an assortment of sounds coming from within the building, could see bizarre and dimly lit areas of the building's insides as if the building itself was brewing something below.

But it wasn't the outside of the building that was so awful. Even the trudge up the trails in mid-winter and the sudden shock of the building's ominous overtones and what was certain doomed foreshadowing, that wasn't by far what was most awful.

And I should have known before we entered.

I should have known what was in store with all that I'd seen from the moment Terra was stretched over my bed. She used her body to seduce men into frenzied passions they could never live out, never quench, never even scratch that endless itch, that endless chasing of the dragon of immorality, those months ago just before I'd seen The Hooded Darkness lumber its vile evil over Stan Smitts' snowy lawn.

I should have guessed that behind the walls of that Auschwitz Welcome were the insides of a belly of the beast that had killed our world, that had raped to death small-town America and turned her out as a prison bitch who had once been an elite executive in an America that once housed such strength.

And I should have told Marion what I should have expected.

It was all for naught as we gave each other once again that brotherly agreed-upon nod; it was time to enter and face whatever it was we were to face.

We knew there were many untold variants of deviancy going on when we found Terra's mountain den, but what blasted us first with a fierce knock on reality was an impossibly long hallway that was far longer and far wider than what the building could ever contain. A hallway made of broken parabolas that looked like massive concrete tear drops that had been poured by hand centuries ago. It was an allusion that was designed to trick all allusions for allusion's sake.

Chants that sounded like howls echoed and bounced around the hallway walls, ceilings, the very floors, as Marion and I continued our way deeper into the charcoaled pit. We came upon a spiraled stairwell that had to be at least a thousand steps down into an abyss. All we could do was proceed with caution as the chanting howls grew louder and louder, with more rhythm, a rhythm that grew into a thumping and a shredding bass effect laced with stretched violin strokes in a distance too far to recognize.

As we finally stepped on the last step of the stairwell, what then opened before us was a banquet hall the size of a Walmart warehouse. A concrete block lay at the back, equally wide and probably five feet high. There, Terra Drake stood center stage with Dr. Pinault right by her side, both dressed as wooden puppets, with the puppet clothing fitted so tightly onto them, it looked like they wore paint. They stood over the child slave from the auction who lay before them on a Sacrificial Altar. Both Terra and Pinault held large bowie knives across the child's body.

I couldn't tell who or what was chanting or howling, as it was only the two demon women on the concrete stage about to shred to pieces the child slave. No one else filled the entire scene of gothic mayhem, as if the intended demon audience decided to stay in Hell for the night.

No Burkenstock.

No black couple arguing from the fair and church.

No salon witches.

No Mr. Partner In Crime.

No giant pigs.

No possessed preacher and his masseuse lover, Terrence.

Only Terra and Pinault, painted as seductive puppets, occupied the concrete block stage with the sole purpose of butchering the child slave.

Before I could study our surroundings even further and deeper for what surely housed more layers, Marion didn't hesitate to pull his gun from his ankle holster, aim it directly at the women on the horror stage, and shout, "Don't you fucking move."

The command filled the walls with a booming shock

wave.

They didn't drop their Bowies but stood straight up in their painted costumes, which highlighted every perfected demonic curve that Satan himself had sketched. Suddenly, before Marion could continue, before anything was spoken from the concrete stage in rebuttal or protest, from the ceiling shot spectacular light beams that burst out in such splendor and color it looked like the ceiling itself had exploded in a rush of violent stained glass panels, each a squared hundred feet, shattering in unison, and from the floor in an equal explosion arose Adrian Cain dressed in his fly mask, cape, and hood. He blasted across the floor toward us like a gigantic praying mantis striking to kill us where we stood. Marion still with gun in hand, pointing it straight on, and me with my own body and mind frozen in just as much awe as terror, we heard Cain scream, *"Get thee fucking Hence from this House of Thieves, you limping flesh of your aimless God."*

That was it.

Had no idea how long we'd been out, as I awakened and found myself in the local Odella hospital, where I'm sure I saw Marion with me in the same room. Whatever had happened, whatever blast we had sustained from Cain, I had somehow ended up in a hospital bed. Still alive. Still with purpose. I couldn't tell if I had any injuries, other than the complete black out that had clearly taken both Marion and I after Cain leapt into us, nor could I tell what had happened to Marion, if anything, as I thought he looked sound asleep in utter peace in his hospital bed. What I did know was that I could no longer have my brother part of what I knew was something between only Terra and me, and that I had to finish it on my own. I left the hospital without a peep to anyone, not even to Marion, back to the Odella hotel where

I'd plan another assault on her Snow Crest City house of horrors.

***

It wasn't the last time Steve saw Terra.

Far from it.

But it was the last time he'd see Marion.

A few months after New Year's when he and Marion had been blown from the evil spew of Adrian Cain, Steven Paul staggered into the elevator of the historic Odella Hotel after a long day and night of drinking in the lounge. Scruffy, smelly, and unshaven, his cotton shirt a dirty rag, his slacks piss-stained, he fought to stay standing and clung to the handrail as if it were the final lifeline he'd ever grasp, ever hope to grasp.

The mirrored walls reflected his ruined image as it grew smaller and smaller, endlessly into oblivion, forever locked in a shattered and hopelessly infinite world where his mind began to fill with all the images of what his life could have been, what he could have accomplished, riddled with a complete inability to erase the million memories of his awful mistakes.

The long, terrible months he'd endured under Terra's lethal thumb, and the endless drink he'd consumed during the months since, had taken its toll on his body, now saturated and destroyed by the drink he could not stop pouring down his depleted esophagus. He had taken in no nutrition other than the empty calories of wine and whiskey. He'd lost all muscle mass; his stomach was bloated and stretched where all core strength had been lost. His gumline was bleeding, his teeth caked with tarter and gore. Fingernails filthy and long and torn at the ends. His eyes bloodshot and filmy. But more than that, his confidence was shattered, his emotions nothing more than acid spit.

His last day of suffering started out much the same as the others. Exhausted. Shaking. Needing shot after shot to attempt a shave and shower, but failing, ignoring his teeth because they were too goddamn painful to brush. Instead of tending to his hygiene, he drained the mini-bar in his room before the lounge opened for lunch and more liquor.

He remembered the lunch crowd stream in, some drinkers, some talkers, some just for the food, in which he had no interest. Nothing killed a buzz faster than real nutrition. From his barstool, he'd told his woeful tale, talked about Terra and the things that went down, actually drew a small crowd of the curious...but mostly disbelievers. Still, he soldiered on, telling them how it all started when he found Terra in his bedroom after he'd seen his neighbor, Stan Smitts, whose body was utterly failing him, Covid he thought at first before he saw the dark hooded figure lumbering about Stan's yard, something more evil at play than the dreaded virus. Yes, that evil was Terra; Terra had destroyed him, and only God knew how many others had fallen victim to her charms. How the murders went down. All of the gore.

He spoke of Misty the hostess of demons and her demon children Brother Garrett had yawped on about in his church office filled with judgment and pity. The dreadful scene Garrett had seen in the kitchen while trying to give aid to a beloved member of his congregation, where perhaps Terra stood in panties and tank top and filth, of all things. He spoke of the fair that awful day, the elfish freak Burkenstock, parking attendant and philosopher; Mister Partner in Crime and his one-ton pig, Harmony, the grandest spectacle of all;

of Terrance the master masseuse and his torture chair; the dream of the pigs, and the even far more awful auction of the slave girl in chains; of priests turned to warlocks on a church stage while massive flies roared on before Terra entered as the mock Christ bleeding at every pore.

Rounds were bought, drinks were drank. He was Mr. Storyteller, as Terra had been during those endless months that led him to Dr. Pinault and the Ballroom A Voodoo Horror Show, the strange details of his MRI and the blown-to-fuck moments from Cain Himself in Terra's Snow Castle.

With every tale gone by, the clock ticked away the hours and minutes of the rest of his life, vodka shots going down two fingers at a time. At one point those around him gave him pause, for their faces took on the very features of Dr Pinault's audience, their eyes and mouths gaping in absolute horror. But not of his stories. No no, for every ruined fool there were stories galore. It was his complete annihilated state, as he must've gone completely insane, and though he knew how bizarre his tales sounded, how utterly impossible they seemed, he rambled on in his present drunken state, confessing to the wrongdoings of his past, how he'd blamed his endless mistakes and insane choices on the ever-present insatiable drink that he used to push ever onward the destruction of his life, the loss of his Anna and nearly everyone and everything he'd ever held dear.

Of course, he blamed Terra; she was the demon who'd dropped this evil upon him with all the horrors she'd assaulted him with, she and her co-conspirator, Adrian Cain, The Hooded Darkness Himself. As proof to his listeners, he went back over and over again the Black Sacrament rambling on and on about the Church of Flies where Terra crucified herself as the savior of mankind from soberness and common sense.

It was after this tirade that his listeners diminished and moved on to other things they deemed more important than the end of small-town America, leaving him alone to drink and grovel in his own misery and tell his bar napkin how he fought back, how he and his brother had stalked Terra to her mountain lair just in time to witness her and Dr. Pinault place the slave girl on a concrete altar to be sacrificed, but he and Marion were blown out of Terra's unholy castle with a wrath of fury from Adrian Cain, and how, to that day, he didn't know, and agonized over, the fate of the slave child.

The past few months had been absolute absence of sanity. Small-town America had landed in an ever-sinking quicksand pit where God refused to lend a helping hand. And worse, no amount of liquid courage could coax him to climb that mountain again, to Snow Crest City, to confront his demon Terra Drake.

Steven Paul was officially done with all of it.

The elevator walls creaked and squeaked and barely made it up, floor-by-floor, as if pulled and pushed by something other than a pulley system. Bent over as he was, he noticed the floor of the elevator was covered with dank, rustic carpet that hadn't been replaced since the day the hotel had been built. His instinct was to let go of the handrail and fall to the carpet, curl up in a ball, and let oblivion welcomingly overwhelm him, but the elevator jerked to a stop, the doors began their slow and groaning spread to reveal an elderly couple waiting to board.

The twilight's last gleaming? Was that the song now playing in his head?

Janet and Bill Covington, who were also staying at the Odella Hotel, were about to find out just *how* done Steve truly was when they stepped into the elevator with him, still wearing their masks, for fuck sake. Steve thought he would vomit all over them, but he gritted his teeth as he gripped the handrail in a feeble attempt, at best, to hang on to some crass form of the universe's lunatic fringe.

Steve was sure he'd seen the Covingtons in the bar, locked in a discussion far more lurid than his own, that they'd even looked over their shoulders to witness the show: Steven Paul's Last Rant.

But he wasn't sure.

The elevator doors closed.

Steve was locked inside with the couple who then took off their masks. And stranger still, the elevator, once perpetually a struggle to move up and down, suddenly flowed into a smooth ride. Effortless. Silent. As if it were floating upward, the absence of any pully system.

As drenched in alcohol as Steve was, he was still able to see into the elevator's mirrored walls a shift in time. A shift in everything *known* by time. He felt the Covingtons and himself become cradled in some Stephen Hawking black hole moment where the universe's boundless colors and streams of infinite mathematical equations all rushed in and around the elevator as its floor titled with the physical shift.

Steve braced himself the best his drunken stupor could muster while Mr. Covington grew taller and wider, Mrs. Covington younger and younger, both morphing and transitioning into Adrian Cain and Terra Drake.

Laughing at him.

Steve knew as real as the transition in time and space had taken place, it was his final moment to show any last morsel of dying defiance that remained in his destroyed spirit, every last whisper of hope, his brain erupting into a massive migraine as Terra spoke.

"Well, well, well. Look at you now, Stevie. Nothing but less than a shell of what you'd ever been. Nothing but a soft mass of alcohol-soaked flesh and mushy bone, inebriated clear down to the marrow.

"Fuck you," Steve whispered.

Terra belted out one of her awful cackles, but it seemed to ring more true and more insane inside the time-trapped elevator. Cain smiled to show each and every one of his blocked teeth.

"Really, Steve?" Terra cooed. "One more *fuck you* for the road, is that it? You've probably missed me but I've left you for dead since I had no further need of you."

"It's not just a fuck you. I curse you. The both of you who've done nothing but destroy everything around you—"

"We've destroyed nothing, Stevie Boy," Terra purred. "Nothing at all. Heard all your rants inside the lounge. Your sad and pitiful goings on about witches and warlocks and piggy pig-pig dreams. Ha! Maybe none of it happened, Steve. Maybe it was your own sopped mind that made you see such things so you could hide behind the lies of all you've become. Of course you couldn't have seen that truth over the months since we met. Your noodle was far too wet."

"It happened. You fuck. Everything you touched turned my town into your own demon fest. Or maybe it was his." Steve looked to Cain.

Terra scoffed. "Maybe. But maybe there was no fair of villains and freaks, of slave auctions or giant pigs with shredded flesh. Maybe there were no moments in your room, us together listening to Sinatra and Rob Zombie. Maybe meeting the man wearing all white in the coffee shop was nothing more than your pathetic hope that someone could walk in and save you."

"Fuck if it was all in my head. I saw you knock Stan out of his chair to die on the floor."

"Hmmm. I think that was Stan's own addiction putting him in the grave. Have you considered that?"

"No. You're wrong," Steve managed as the elevator swept upward, faster and faster, as if time and space no longer had meaning. Steve looked directly into Cain's black eye sockets where there were no eyes that he could see. "Who the fuck are you anyway, if not her royal pimp?"

"I am the Darkness that follows all of sin and depravity. That one cancerous growth you can never shake. You embraced your weakness around my darkness and drove away your Anna and everyone else who ever meant a thing to you since you spilled from the womb. Anna's leaving you was proof of that. She couldn't bear to stand by and watch you destroy yourself, that's how much she loved you, until she couldn't anymore. That's what you threw away, for us." Cain leaned into the faltering Steven Paul. "And we're all you have left, forever."

"I don't believe any of what you say. What about the turning, Terra? What about that?"

Terra took a few steps to where she was directly in Steve's space, drilling her lavender eyes into his helpless dying pupils. "You think you've not turned? Or do you think that the little troll Burkenstock told you the truth, that there is a way you can win? There's no truth to it, Stevie. You can never win against me. What was it that Pilot asked Christ just after he had been whipped and scourged? 'What is truth?' None of it matters. Nothing matters when you are left here, alone, ruined from the inside out, giving one last moment to justify your rotten excuse for even existing."

With that, Terra raised her taloned hand to strike Steve down, but held back as he fell to his knees in front of her. Fell to her feet much as Steve saw the child slave fall before her on that fly-infested day of false worship.

He could take no more. His body shut down. His heart had no more effort left to pump a single drop of tainted and poisoned blood through his shriveled veins. The migraine in his brain exploded. With one final swipe of her hand, she struck him down, as she had pummeled Stan to his own death. Steve collapsed to the rustic carpet in this elevator bound for oblivion. As his brain shut down, his other organs followed suit; his bladder spilled, and his last conscious vision was of the elevator doors opening, the couple lumbering out, arm in arm, and the doors then closing him in perpetual darkness.

***

The world Steven Paul fell into after collapsing dead on the elevator floor was one where all pain and suffering had instantly come to an end, as if an overwhelming and enveloping shower of healing had been turned on, a force of cleansing and pureness, a force of such goodness and love that he felt as if he'd never known any suffering. That the meaning of suffering itself was unknown. A shower of such bathing relief and comfort that Steve fully understood that his brother, Marion, would be okay. An understanding that had the depth of healing that only this world, whatever it was, could produce.

All was so much more than well.

He walked into a room of angelic hosts, a room where silver velvet seats adorned golden floors paved and designed with such intricacy Steve not just *knew*, but *understood* such detail had to have come from something no human could produce. The room was shaped as a dome with paintings of colorful god-like murals weaved in and out of the dome's ceiling as if sewn in by a master seamstress of magical threads. He felt an instant invitation to continue walking forward from the room's entrance that appeared out of nowhere at the moment of his death.

His previous life.

Just as magical, and just as suddenly out of the next nowhere, Steve saw the stranger in white from the coffee shop so long ago, the stranger who knew so much more than Steve ever could imagine, but now could understand with perfect clarity, a few feet in front of another door that led to another domed room. The stranger signaled for Steve to keep moving forward, to keep exploring, when even more suddenly, as if yet a new shift in the space-time continuum just riveted across the entire celestial plain, in the next domed room he saw Anna standing next to a brass podium with quarter-sized diamonds that ran up and down the podium's astonishing beauty and design. His Anna. His love. His long-lost kindred spirit who had never entirely left him but had been watching over him during the entire ordeal on the earth below.

Or the earth above.

Steve had no idea how or when she'd arrived here, only that his beloved Anna was standing there before him, signaling him with her endless encouragement and love she had always shown him, even during the most troubled of times, until she could take no more of his drinking. Anna signaled him to come forward. To come to her. To be with her as if needing him to be with her, for them to be together endlessly. Her arm waved in a lovely forward direction of pure tenderness and guidance. Steve looked upon her with such love and honor he felt his ethereal heart would burst inside his chest, so great were the feelings of purity.

As he moved forward toward her, he felt he was hovering, each step just a touch off the ground, as if walking on a cotton floor with gravity near absent. He approached Anna, his arms outstretched to embrace her fully and completely.

Just as he felt Anna's tender touch, in the harmony of two souls restored in spiritual benevolence, a sudden and jarring force pulled him away from her, farther and farther away as if being shoved down a strange hole that began shifting into an entirely different realm from the room where he'd almost reunited with Anna.

She was gone. The glory of seeing her again was gone. Every hope he'd suddenly hoped for their eternity together was gone.

But Steve was far from gone.

Far from dead again.

He blinked over and over in hopes of seeing some reason in this sudden reversal until a new realm opened up into a cave-like prison, walls of smoked mirrors where endless celestial didn't exist, but only the wretched image of his soul reflecting all around him, smaller and smaller into eternity. Yet in this awful new room of grotesqueness, his trapped soul felt such a depth of loneliness that he began weeping. The distant reality and endless presence of what he'd done wrong his entire life, as a selfish destructive alcoholic who's spun out of control prevailed in his mind, endless and reoccurring thoughts of his Anna, lost. His ruined relationships with family and friends played in an endless loop, the jobs he couldn't hold and the countless shit decisions and sacrifices he'd made for the sake of drinking and drugging. These things that had caused his downfall became constant nagging and ferocious memories and reminders of all he'd done wrong, rolling over and over in his mind, constantly, torturously, and interspersed with insights into all he could have done right, all the things that could have made the difference had he only defeated the drink. This would be his eternity, seeing himself, his battered spirit grotesquely cracked and sickly aged, in his kaleidoscopic prison with only a vicious, endless hangover and his regrets to accompany him.

Out of the corner of his eye, then moving into his full vision and appearing endlessly alongside him in those gruesome mirrors, stood a woman, as clearly as if she'd walked out of that family portrait he'd seen that awful night so long ago. She wore an overly accentuated conservative dress that covered her entire chest to her neck, chokingly tight, hair pinned up in a bun, prim and proper, but for the thickly applied lipstick smeared all over her face. Though her complexion was grotesque, cracked and sickly aged, her deadly lavender eyes convinced him, without a doubt, that he knew her all too well. His ethereal being sunk into a depression his addiction on earth had never produced, as he knew she was Terra...

Winking at him.

ABOUT THE AUTHOR

Dean Patrick was born and raised in Houston, Texas. Educated at The University of Houston with Masters Degrees in Professional Writing and Literature, he works as a writer for a Houston-based orthopedic center and for software technology companies in the Salt Lake City area. He lives in Morgan, Utah, on a small ranch with his wife, Lisa. To this day, he considers his sobriety his greatest victory.

Dean Patrick

Enjoy more novels and short stories from

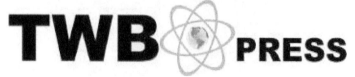

www.twbpress.com

Science Fiction, Supernatural, Horror, Thrillers, and more

Made in the USA
Middletown, DE
18 April 2023